THE NEW DESTROYER:
DEAD RECKONING

THE NEW DESTROYER:
DEAD RECKONING

Warren Murphy and James Mullaney

TOR®

A TOM DOHERTY ASSOCIATES BOOK
NEW YORK

THE NEW DESTROYER: DEAD RECKONING

Copyright © 2008 by Warren Murphy

A Tor Book
Published by Tom Doherty Associates, LLC
175 Fifth Avenue
New York, NY 10010

www.tor.com

Tor® is a registered trademark of Tom Doherty Associates, LLC.

ISBN-13: 978-0-7653-5761-8
ISBN-10: 0-7653-5761-5

First Edition: April 2008

Printed in the United States of America

0 9 8 7 6 5 4 3 2 1

For a whole bunch of aunts and uncles: John, Eileen, Mary and Ann, as well as Betty, Dick and Sue.

For www.warrenmurphy.com, where one of us can be reached; and for www.jamesmullaney.com, where the other one can.

For www.destroyerclub.com, official home of the Destroyer on the Web (now in Sinanju-O-Vision). . . .

—J. M.

And especially for Patricia Chute Sapir and Devin Sapir . . . good traveling companions on our long and winding road.

—W. M.

THE NEW DESTROYER:
DEAD RECKONING

PROLOGUE

The little sewing shop where toiled Abdullah the tailor was on the edge of the bustling bazaar in the city of Khwajah, two camel marches north of Baghdad.

It was to this shop on a Saturday afternoon late in May, just a few years shy of the end of the nineteenth century, that a handsome young Turkish soldier came.

Many natives who lived in the conquered territories of Iraq would spit on the ground wherever the foreigners walked although fear and prudence made certain that they did so long after the soldiers had passed.

The Turks, it was true, were hated by nearly everyone in Khwajah but Abdullah the tailor did not hate them. The soldiers had always been polite to him. He had rarely had a problem with payment and when he did he merely shrugged it off as Allah's will and went about his business.

"Be nice," Abdullah hissed to his daughter when this particular soldier came into the shop.

He had already cautioned her the night before.

"The Ottoman Empire of these Turks is dying," Abdullah

had told his daughter over supper. "They are fighting too much with Russia. Arabia will not belong to them forever. And so it is true that these soldiers will not be here forever. We will marry you off to one before they are sent off to some other stupid war."

The Turk was handsome and tall with strong arms and eyes of a strange green that Abdullah had never before seen.

Abdullah's daughter giggled and played with the stacks of silk and every once in a while she glanced at the soldier as he searched through bolts of cloth.

Abdullah wished she would not giggle so much for it was not attractive in one so old. The girl was no longer young, having seen her eighteenth winter a few months before. Of course Abdullah still insisted that she was only fifteen but she could only be fifteen for so long. As her hips swelled, her teeth grew long and heavy bits of her began to sag, it was getting more difficult to get people to believe the lie.

And so his daughter must be married soon and why not to this handsome foreigner who was poking around his shop?

The soldier made his selections and Abdullah took his measurements, assuring the young man that the garment would be most elegant, especially on so handsome a Turk. And when the matter of payment was brought up, Abdullah waved it away with the back of one hand and offered a different proposal.

"Sir, my daughter is young and comely, and will work hard to please you. It would honor me if a good Turkish soldier such as yourself would take her as your bride."

Abdullah clutched folded hands to his chest and smiled hopefully at the young Turkish soldier. Behind him, his daughter bit her lip with her big, crooked teeth and batted her eyelashes at her would-be husband.

The Turkish soldier looked from the little old man to the beaming girl who stood at her father's side. When the soldier began to laugh, the girl shrank away.

"Forgive me, sir, but I would not have your daughter as a servant, much less wed one as ugly as she."

Abdullah was shocked. He had looked at his daughter all his life with a father's eyes. To him she was the most beautiful maiden in the Middle East.

"I—I do not understand," Abdullah said.

"That is because you are an Arab dog," said the soldier to the man whose land he had invaded. "It is not your fault, old one. Not being a Turk, you are stupid by your nature, just as your daughters are ugly by Allah's design. Only a foreign fool would be dumb enough to marry a homely mongrel girl and only a homely mongrel girl would be desperate enough to marry a foreign dullard. You see now how Allah provides even for the lowliest of his creations? Although you may find it difficult to find even a foreign devil stupid enough to marry one as homely as this child of yours." Laughing aloud, the handsome young Turkish soldier left the tailor's shop.

Abdullah's daughter was inconsolable. A widower, he had no wife who would know the right things to say to comfort a heartbroken child. The young girl cried for three days, and on the fourth day when she fell silent and Abdullah thought all might be well again, he entered his daughter's chambers only to discover that she had cut open her wrists and bled to death during the night.

"I will have my revenge on that Turk and all like him," Abdullah said to his three grown sons after the funeral of his beautiful only daughter.

"Do not, father," his eldest warned.

"The Turks rule our country, slaughter at will, and take what they want," said the middle son. "This soldier could have done worse to our sister, father."

After his older sons had left him, Abdullah's youngest son had pulled his father aside. "My brothers are timid men, father," he had whispered. "They fear for their positions in the community, for their fortunes and their lives. That is why they offer you such counsel. But I tell you there is a way to avenge yourself for your daughter, my sister." Abdullah's youngest son was a trader and on a trip to the east had come into possession of an ancient parchment torn from a book that was lost to time. The words were a spell which, when spoken during the proper ritual, would summon an avenging spirit from the shadow realm.

Abdullah was no fool. He knew that he was living in a new age when exploration and science had begun to disprove the superstitions of old. But just because something was old did not mean it was wrong and he had faith that some of the old magics and teachings were true. As a good son, his youngest had sold him the parchment for only three gold pieces.

"But be warned, father, that jinns are powerful spirits, and must be bound to an object so that they might be summoned and controlled. It will follow your commands but be careful what you wish for, for it is in their nature to deceive."

And learning the common item his father planned to use as anchor to the spirit in this realm, and offering a final warning to take care, the youngest son left his father.

Abdullah brought the parchment back to his tailor shop. Bolting doors and windows, he traced the sacred circle on the floor, lit the lamps and candles, put out the object to which the spirit was to be bound on this plane, and offered the incantations as written on the ancient paper.

When the last word was uttered, a great wind rose up from the east, and a howl like the tortured chorus of all the world's dead assaulted Abdullah's ears. Once when he was a boy Abdullah and his father had been caught in a sandstorm. This sound was like the roar in his memory only worse, and when the boarded windows burst open Abdullah expected to be consumed by a flooding sea of sand, but instead the candles flickered out, the oil lamps were extinguished, and the room where he had conducted his ritual was consumed by a silence and a darkness made all the more thick and terrifying by the clamor that had preceded it.

With shaking hands, Abdullah relit one of the extinguished lamps. He nearly dropped it, spilling oil and flame to the floor, when he saw the figure standing calmly within the sacred summoning circle.

"It has been many ages since one has dared summon us," the figure in the circle said. "Only I remain, alone I heed the call to this world of mortals."

Abdullah was stunned by the ordinariness of the spirit. In appearance, he was a man. Fat of face, with skin of a strange yellow and eyes the shape of almonds. He was clothed in the garments of the wealthiest sultans, and wore rings of priceless gems on his thick fingers. Even his voice was ordinary; clipped and precise, but with a nasal quality.

"Speak, Arab, that I would know why I am here."

Abdullah's mouth was dry. It took him a moment to find his tongue. "Perfect health," he said. "For myself and my sons, and their sons. I would have perfect health for my family and all of my bloodline."

If the request was too great for the spirit, his expression did not show it. He merely smiled and nodded as if he had heard the same entreaty many times before.

"There is something else you desire."

The spirit had read Abdullah's face. Perfect health was only so that he might live to see his second wish come true.

"I want the foreigners out of this land," Abdullah the tailor said. "I want the foreigners fighting each other. I want them killing one another. I want them dead, spirit. Can you do this thing?"

The spirit pondered Abdullah's request, nodding as he considered the words. "Trickier," he said. And he smiled.

There was a strange shimmering of air that seemed to envelop the spirit. Before Abdullah's eyes, the visage of the spirit changed. The fat face and colorful robes melted away. The face became what appeared to be an animated skull, the robes turned the color of night. Long fingers of bone extended from billowing black sleeves, and when the spirit held out its arms, Abdullah backed away in fear.

"Fear not, old one," the spirit intoned. "I have changed

only in appearance for I have become what you want me to be. No more, no less. What you ask for shall be."

And Abdullah was alone.

The old man searched around the shop but the spirit had fled. No matter. He had gotten all he wished for.

For several days, Abdullah searched for the soldier who had insulted his daughter and driven her to suicide. He scoured the dusty streets of Khwajah, and at last he found the Turk in the bazaar at the stall of the crazy merchant Dunzyad. The young soldier and his fellows were searching through a pile of foreign fruits and abusing the merchant at his counter.

The soldier barely felt the punch on his shoulder even though Abdullah delivered it with all his might.

"Filthy Turkish dog," Abdullah snarled.

It took the soldier a moment to recognize the tailor, which made Abdullah the more furious. Momentarily, a spark lit in the young soldier's eyes and he shook his head.

"It is the one I told you about," he laughed to the Turkish soldiers in his company. "The old garment sewer with the homely daughter. I already told you, old man, that I would marry a camel before I wed your ugly child."

The Turks laughed raucously.

While the foreign devils laughed, Abdullah slipped a dagger from his tunic. Unfortunately he had not asked the spirit to return to him the quickness of youth, and the Turk spied the blade before it could slip into his belly.

With one hand, the soldier snagged Abdullah's wrist, staying the blade an inch from his gut. The other hand grabbed the old garment maker by the throat.

"Your pride has been wounded, old man," the soldier whispered, his eyes dark with warning. He squeezed Abdullah's wrist and the knife dropped to the dust. "Leave now, and be happy that you suffer no deeper wounds."

The Turk shoved Abdullah to the ground. When the soldiers turned to go, Abdullah pounced on the knife and lunged at the young Turk's back.

And then there were a few very loud pops and Abdullah

felt slaps to his chest. And then he saw the smoking rifles which had been slung over the shoulders of the Turkish soldiers and were now in their hands. And he felt the warm blood of his life soaking his loose tunic and he was falling in a heap to the dirt of the street.

The soldiers tossed a few coins to the merchant at the nearer counter to pay for disposal of the body, and without a glance at the dying old man the Turks melted into the dense crowd of shoppers and were gone.

On the ground, Abdullah gasped.

"Leave, flee," he hissed. "I will shed this temporary pain like a snake sheds skin and when it is gone I will be on your heel once more, Turkish dog."

And the pain did ease a little. It was replaced by a cold numbness that seemed to seep up from the core of his being, despite the warm blood that continued to gurgle from nearly a dozen gaping wounds. And, unlike other living creatures who meet with puzzlement those last moments before the inevitable end, Abdullah realized that he was dying.

Abdullah then called out a single word to the spirit who had betrayed him and that word was, "Why?"

The spirit came to him then, in the dirt and blood and sweat of the crowded bazaar. Though others could not see it, Abdullah could. The face was ghastly, white flesh pulled tight over bone, eyes sunk deep in blackened sockets, and a smile that frightened the fluttering heart of the dying tailor.

Although this vision looked nothing like it first had in the back room of his little shop and had grown even more horrifying in appearance since last he had seen it, Abdullah knew in his dying heart that this was the spirit he had summoned to avenge himself upon the hateful Turk.

"I was to have perfect health," Abdullah said.

"And so you have and so too shall your descendants for I keep my word. But perfect health, foolish tailor, meant only that sickness could not touch you. It did not mean that death could not claim you. And so I shall."

"You tricked me," Abdullah gasped.

"No, I gave you what you asked for even if it is not what you wanted. And your other request I will grant as well, although not as you desired. The foreigners will leave as you requested and they will be replaced by others and then they will leave and still more will come. And they will murder one another and you and those like you will murder them and each other and it will be quite glorious."

"I do not understand," said Abdullah.

"Of course you do not. How could you, a mere sewer of garments, understand what you have summoned? I tell you that I am what you will me to be. You have wished for death, so death is what I will deliver. The spirit you have raised, foolish one, is the spirit of death. And death delights me."

And with those delighted words ringing in old Abdullah's ears, the spirit vanished to work mischief on the world.

And the man who had summoned him silently begged forgiveness of his ancestors and from his descendants for the horror he had unleashed upon civilization.

And in the dust of the Khwajah bazaar, near the fruit stand of crazed Dunzyad, the insignificant little tailor Abdullah Mohammed surrendered his last breath of life.

He had never had a cold. Not so much as a sniffle in his forty-four years of life.

When he was little, a virulent strain of measles had attacked the village. Many had died, most of them children. He had watched the bodies paraded past his window, mourners shrieking, dressed in black. In his parents' house he was healthy and happy and wondered why he could not go outside to play.

He had never had a childhood experience with the flu virus, which was probably just as well. There was no Sudafed, TheraFlu, NyQuil or the thousand other palliatives that were available in every corner drug store in the West. The only thing in the village to relieve influenza symptoms was aspirin and even that was not available most of the time. When one got sick in his small village in northern Iraq, one either toughed it out or died. But, thank Allah, flu was not a problem for Mustafa Mohammed and the rest of his family. They simply never got sick.

As a boy he had once stepped into a nest of cobras and

been bitten a dozen times. The other adults were certain he would die but his father knew better. Mustafa sloughed off the deadly venom as if the poisonous snakes had injected him with water. The fang marks had taken a little while to heal. Mustafa remembered that they had itched a little.

Measles, mumps, chicken pox. Mustafa had never had any of them, nor had his siblings or father or any of his father's blood relatives as far back as anyone could recall.

One time there was some funny bug in the water. It was so small that you could not see it with your eyes but it had made everyone in town go from both ends for weeks. All their playmates were ill so Mustafa and his siblings played alone until the Red Cross came and fixed the problem by pouring something in the well.

The real test came after the end of the first Gulf War when the glorious leader of the great Republic of Iraq flooded Mustafa's small village with nerve gas.

Half the village population died overnight. The rest crawled through the poisoned dust, longing for death.

When the television crew from *Frontline* came to do a film documentary on the village a decade after the gassing, they found victims blinded, subject to spasms, crippled. They were shocked to find that the effects of the gas had leached into DNA and was being passed down to children born long after the attack. The crew filmed infants with missing limbs or limbs growing where limbs should not grow. The saddest were the children born with only brain stems who were living lives in permanent vegetative states. The television crew filmed everything they could find and then bundled up their cameras and film and left forever. They never asked about the boarded-up house at the edge of the square, the building that had housed three generations of a family that could not fall ill.

After the nerve gas attack, news of the family that was impervious to the toxin reached Baghdad. When further research revealed that no member of the family had ever fallen ill and that all members of this one unique family had lived in perfect health until extreme old age, trucks came to the village to cart away Mustafa and his relatives.

The family with the miraculous inability to suffer sickness even with chemical bombs raining down on their roof was brought to a special facility outside the capital and turned over to the great leader's finest medical minds.

One of the first things the great leader's brilliant doctors had done was chop off Mustafa's father's hand with a big knife. Afterward, they sat around smoking cigarettes to see if it would grow back. They waited two hours.

As Mustafa's father screamed and wept, one of the scientists finally spoke into a tape recorder that by Western standards had gone out-of-date with the eight-track, but which was state of the art in the great leader's Iraq.

"Limbs amputated do not regenerate."

The scientists decided that perhaps they had gone too far with a full amputation. Deciding to apply rigorous scientific discipline, they used hammers to give Mustafa's father a compound fracture in his forearm. They studied the broken bones protruding through the skin to see if they would mend before their eyes. But not only did the shattered bones fail to mend, the whining old patient threw a bone fragment into his bloodstream and died in a matter of minutes.

"Subject appears dead from complications resulting from second procedure. Observation continues."

Perhaps the miracle of this family's alleged perfect health was only manifested when the body was pushed to its limits. The patriarch, poor old dead Hunsien, could not be pushed any further. Teams of doctors watched the body in shifts but when the stink grew too strong, it was determined that the first test subject had failed them.

"First subject's moribund state persists after thirty-six hours. Moving on to second subject."

Mustafa's mother had been fed feet-first into a vat of acid. Quickly dipped, in and out, like french fries in a decadent American fast food establishment.

Mustafa and his aunts, uncles, brothers and sisters heard

his mother's screams from the little cages where they were being warehoused like lab animals.

Mustafa's older relatives tried to explain that it was only those of Mustafa's bloodline who possessed the inability to become ill, not those who married into the family. But the doctors were efficient and would not be told how to be scientists by a bunch of weeping peasants in dog cages.

So away family members went to Allah, stabbed, bludgeoned, shot, drowned, strangled. When there were only ten men left the doctors finally moved on to nerve and viral agents and all manner of toxins.

The scientists had not believed the stories about this family were true, especially as the pile of corpses in the mass grave outside of town grew. But the great leader had charged them to learn what protected these people so that he might obtain the secret of perfect health for himself. And so they moved from bullets and blades down to things that could only be viewed under the lens of a microscope.

At last, after weeks of testing, these men of science discovered that the stories were true.

Men who had been sealed in glass tanks flooded with anthrax were as healthy coming out as they had been going in.

Sarin did not kill these strange men from the north. One died when he was exposed to mustard gas, but that was only because the doctors had gone to lunch and left him in the locked booth too long and he died of dehydration. Another asphyxiated in a sealed tank filled with smallpox when they forgot to flip the little switch that fed him oxygen.

And so they went through the entire family, with little accidents that would here and there claim another life because while science was perfect scientists were not, until only two were left, Mustafa and his older brother Achmed.

"They will murder us too, Mustafa," Achmed whispered at night to his brother from his dog cage.

The doors of all the other cages were open now. The room where they were warehoused seemed empty. All of their relatives, from elderly Uncle Karim all the way down to little two-year-old Samir, were dead.

"They will not take our lives," Mustafa insisted.

"Of course they will," Achmed said. "They have slaughtered us one by one, Mustafa. They are not going to spare us. We are not special."

"I am." And Mustafa giggled.

Achmed was used to such behavior from his brother. Mustafa had always been an idiot with no sense of the world around him. The great leader had poisoned their town and murdered their family members one by one, yet Mustafa still bowed reverently whenever the bloodthirsty maniac's name was mentioned. And even though Allah seemed to have abandoned them all at the moment when they needed Him most, Mustafa insisted on reading from the family Koran daily, his fat lips moving as he carefully sounded out the big words.

He was reading the Koran now. Achmed had read from the same holy book as a child. The book had belonged to great-great-grandfather Abdullah. The goat leather cover was reddish brown and frayed at the edges. The pages were gilded with raised Arabic writing decorating cover and spine. A single rip in the corner of the front cover had been stitched closed with Chinese silk by grandmother Habbab.

Mustafa turned a page, careful not to wrinkle the ancient yellow parchment.

"Mustafa," Achmed began slowly, for when one had something important to say to his brother it was important to speak slowly so that he understood it all. "We have none of us wanted to tell you this because we were sensitive to your feelings. But since we are both going to die, it is time you learned something important. You are stupid, Mustafa. You are not as bad as those poor souls born with bad brains who must be cared for all their lives. Unlike them, you can function in the world, Mustafa. You have worked, and you can read and speak well enough. But when it comes to thinking, you are lost. Yes, you are stupid, Mustafa. And even dumber than I thought if you think we are special and will somehow be spared the certain, terrible deaths these people in the white coats have planned for us."

"I did not say *we* would be spared, Achmed, I said that *I* would be spared. I do not know your fate, only mine."

Achmed shook his head in pity. "How do you know?"

Mustafa pushed his Koran aside and crept to the edge of his cage. Looking around to make certain no one was eavesdropping, he pressed his blubbery lips between the bars. "Because, brother—" Mustafa's voice slipped to a barely audible whisper—"the Prophet came to me last night while you slept and told me that I was destined for greatness."

For Achmed it was not even worth arguing with Mustafa. He said nothing the rest of the night and did not say goodbye to his brother when the scientists collected them both for more experiments the next morning.

More poisons were tested on them in the ensuing months. At one point Achmed was told that thanks to his family, a new virus had been developed. Rather than use Achmed's immunity to illness to heal, the scientists had used it to develop something that would kill on contact. This supervirus was undetectable, unkillable, and could be concentrated in small, lethal doses. A single smuggled dose could be hidden easily on an individual and remain dormant until activated. Once the supervirus was active, it could obliterate an entire city in a matter of hours. Best of all, the West had no idea the substance even existed.

Achmed and Mustafa were allowed out of their cages. They were not free to leave the complex but they could move about inside it. The two brothers were put to work as janitors. Mustafa accepted his broom with joy.

"Why are you always singing?" Achmed asked his brother as they swept the laboratory where the supervirus had been perfected. "Stop your singing, crazy one."

"I cannot help but sing," Mustafa said, "for the Prophet has told me that my time will soon be here."

"End this now," Achmed snapped, so loudly some of the scientists glanced at the dirty middle-aged man with the broom. Achmed lowered his voice. "You are out of your mind. The Prophet has not come to see you, fool."

"Yes, Achmed, he has. And I can prove it."

"Then do so, fool."

A gleeful smile on his face, Mustafa used his broom handle to point across the room.

"He is here now."

A man had just entered the lab. Achmed had not seen him at the complex before. He was tall, well over six feet, and walked rigidly as if his spine were an iron rod. He was thin, skinnier than any man Achmed had ever seen. His skin was as pale as bleached bone and his thinness lent him the aspect of an ambulatory skeleton. He wore a long black lab coat over a deep black suit. It was the only lab coat of that color Achmed had seen in all the time he had been held in captivity in the secret laboratory. So gaunt was his face that to look upon it was like looking at a living skull. Thinning white hair brushed his collar.

A pair of fat black rats scurried around the man's feet. Rats were frequently used in testing when the supply of human beings ran low. Occasionally they were known to escape from their cages, as these must have. The rats, their fur mottled and their tails long and pink, were fat from feasting on the flesh of the dead. Achmed had never seen rodents so brazen as these. The other scientists recoiled at the animals and shouted for the researchers to catch them but if their presence bothered the skeletal man his face did not show concern. The rats played around the hems of his robes.

The cadaver-like man conferred with the scientists, and seemed to be a source of great wisdom for the eager attention they gave him. When he glanced over at the two Mohammed brothers and smiled, Achmed felt something cold and strangely familiar wrap around his thudding heart.

Achmed tripped over his own broom handle in his haste to leave the lab. Later, Mustafa asked his brother why he had seemed so frightened to see the Prophet.

"Because I know this thing even if I have never before laid eyes upon it. If it speaks to you again, ignore it, Mustafa. Run away from it as fast as you can."

"I cannot ignore the words of the Prophet."

"That is not the Prophet, Mustafa. Stay away from it."

But for the first time in his life, Mustafa could not listen to his brother's advice. Achmed was usually clever but this time he was mistaken. When his brother described what this being looked like to him, Mustafa laughed.

"A skeleton? Now who is feeble-minded?" Mustafa said. "He has a face of unsurpassed beauty. A perfect Arab face. His skin is not white, but healthy brown. And you say he has no beard but his beard is thick and black. You must have been looking at someone else, brother."

But Achmed knew he had seen the true face of the being that was not the Prophet and that his foolish brother was only seeing that which he wanted to see.

Eventually the weapons programs were put on hold. The Americans were holding one of their fool elections again and Iraq's great leader wanted to remain quiet during this time. Despite Achmed's warning, Mustafa continued to speak with the Prophet. Achmed heard them some nights whispering, saw the figure draped in black at his brother's bedside. The loose rats of the weapons complex danced at the hem of his robes.

Achmed asked for and was granted quarters on the other side of the complex, as far away from his brother as possible. Achmed was not present in Mustafa's dirty little room on that fateful night when the Prophet came to visit his chosen and most faithful disciple.

"You have to act fast," the Prophet said. He had entered Mustafa's quarters without opening the door. One moment he was not there, the next he was standing before his loyal follower. "They're shutting down the . . . oh, get up off your knees, for heaven's sake."

"Forgive me, Prophet," said Mustafa, and he scampered obediently to his feet.

"Old mustache-puss is getting cold feet. He's shutting down the whole shooting match for a year or two. All those beautiful dead bodies are being put at risk because he's scared the Americans are going to elect someone who might get the nerve to finally drop a blockbuster on his palace."

Mustafa had never seen the Prophet agitated. For an instant, the beatific visage seemed to phase out, replaced by a ghastly white skull. It looked much like what Achmed had described all those months ago. But as soon as he saw the image, it was gone. A trick of the light.

"What must I do, Holy One?"

When the Prophet laid out his instructions, Mustafa did not know what to make of them.

"Why must I do this, Blessed Greatness?" Mustafa asked.

"Because mine is the name of death and death delights me." When he saw the confusion on Mustafa's face, the man in black shook his head and sighed, his breath like a thousand rotting souls. "Because Allah is great and I'm telling you to do it. Is that what you want to hear? And take that with you." A slender finger aimed at Mustafa's bed.

Mustafa dutifully gathered up the object that the Prophet had pointed to and hustled out into the hallway.

It was night and no one but the ghosts of Mustafa's relatives was left in the complex. The Prophet knew all the codes that Mustafa needed to punch into the special keypads to get into the most secret rooms.

The lab that housed the supervirus was being dismantled. Decals of skulls on walls and doors warned of the danger. In a sealed plastic room at the rear of the laboratory, Mustafa found a large fish tank. The rectangular tank sat in the middle of the cement floor. It had two short metal and two long Plexiglas sides. Special tubes and wires ran from one metal side to monitor and regulate temperature and other environmental factors. The lid was sealed with a gummy substance, like moist rubber.

The man in black accompanied Mustafa into the special sealed room.

"Open it up," the man in black commanded.

"It is not safe, Prophet. Only my family cannot be harmed by the substance in this tank. They have told me that it was created using something from our bodies. My brother Achmed and I are the only ones it cannot kill. All other men on earth will die if they come in contact with it, even though it is so small it cannot be seen."

"Hello, genius," the man in black said. "Who do you think you're talking to? Hurry up and open it."

Reluctantly, Mustafa did as the Prophet instructed. He slit the seal with a knife and lifted the lid. There was a hiss and a release of yellowish steam. Mustafa held his breath and watched the Prophet's face.

Once it was perfected, the scientists had tested the supervirus on many guinea pigs. Mustafa had seen the terrible results and knew what to expect. He was delighted to see none of them appear on the Prophet's face. The man in black was completely unharmed.

The next command was puzzling.

"Take that and sink it."

Mustafa picked up the object he had carried with him from his cell. Holding it in both hands, he plunged it deep into the substance in the tank. It was a liquid, but not really wet. It was cold, but not freezing. Mustafa held the item beneath the yellow mist for several minutes, and only when the man in black told him that it was long enough did he remove it. It was damp when it came out of the tank, but the wetness evaporated seconds after exposure to air. There was no evidence that it had ever been inside the damp tank.

Mustafa replaced the lid and left the lab. The Prophet guided him through empty corridors. There were many flights of stairs. Mustafa had not realized he was so far underground. At each door was a keypad and every code was known to the man in black. Eventually the last door swung open and for the first time in nearly a decade Mustafa was breathing free air. And he was alone.

A voice on the breeze carried faintly to his ears.

"You have pleased me, Mustafa Mohammed. This thing you do for me today will end in a great, terrible act of destruction. Flee this place now, that you may bring glory unto us. And be sure to keep it dry. That is most important of all. Dry, Mustafa. It must never get wet."

And the voice was gone as well.

Mustafa jumped when he heard squeaking at his ankles. A pair of fat black rats raced from the stairwell and disappeared into the desert night. Mustafa's heart thudded.

The offer of freedom after a decade of captivity was a temptation almost too great to resist. Mustafa was about to flee into the desert when a guilty thought struck him. Propping the door open with a cinder block, he raced back down into the complex. Mustafa's brother was sound asleep. Mustafa had to drag sleepy Achmed from his bed.

"He has freed us," Mustafa whispered.

"What are you going on about?" Achmed asked groggily.

"Look, brother."

Shaking his head in anger, Achmed glanced down the corridor. His mouth dropped open when he saw that a door that was always sealed was hanging open wide. Shoving feet into boots and grabbing up a few clothes, he ran with his brother up into the free air.

In the dark of the desert night, towers and walls rose behind them. The laboratory complex had been constructed deep beneath one of the great leader's palaces.

"Praise Allah but who has given us our freedom, brother?" Achmed asked. "One of the scientists?"

When Achmed saw the stupid knowing grin on his brother's face, he understood the truth.

"He is not the Prophet, Mustafa," Achmed insisted. "He is something from our family's past. I know this now. I felt it when I first saw him and I later remembered a story passed down from grandfather Abdullah's time."

But Mustafa would not hear it. "We are free because of him, and I now have a mission, praise his name."

Since he could see there would be no persuading Mustafa

otherwise, and knowing that he did not want to get anywhere near the creature that was absolutely not the Prophet, Achmed parted ways with his brother.

With unaccustomed acumen, Mustafa assumed he was no longer safe in Iraq, so he stole across the border into Iran where the next few years were a blur.

There was only one thing he carried with him from his past. Mustafa had with him the item soaked in supervirus solution when he travelled to Saudi Arabia, where he fell in with the al-Khobar terrorist organization. It was clutched to his chest in England, where he spent a year acclimating to the decadence of the hated West. He carried it with him on the plane to Canada and brought it with him when he sneaked on foot across the border into the United States. It was with him on the seat during flight training where he learned how to fly a plane into a building. And it was under his pillow when he hit the snooze bar on his alarm clock one too many times and failed to catch his flight at Logan International Airport in Boston on September 11, 2001.

Mustafa Mohammed fled back to England, was extradited back to the U.S., dubbed the "twentieth hijacker" by the media, was tried for the attempted terrorist act of flying a plane full of innocents into the White House, and locked away in a tiny cell in a federal prison for the rest of his natural days.

And there he rotted for five long years.

It was not the life of a man who knew that he was destined for greatness. Why had the Prophet chosen him if his intention was to forsake him? Why had Allah given the gift of perfect health if not to use it to glorify His name? Why of all his relatives was he one of only two to be spared death? Surely there was a purpose to it all. Yet, Mustafa realized, his brother Achmed had been right about one thing. Mustafa was not very bright. If there was an answer to the riddle of his life, he could not see it.

Every day for five miserable years he prayed for guidance. And in the early months of his sixth year of confinement in the United States, he could take it no longer. Mustafa raised his hands to the cold, dank ceiling of his cell and cried out in a loud voice. "Why have you abandoned me, Prophet?"

He jumped when a voice behind him answered.

"Don't get on my case. You have any idea when my last vacation was?"

When he wheeled to the source of the words, Mustafa could scarcely contain his joy.

Although the cell door was still locked tight and had not opened, a figure stood in the small cell with Mustafa Mohammed. Gone was the black business suit and black lab coat he had worn back in Iraq. In its place were flowing black robes as dark as a starless midnight. Slender fingers extended from billowing sleeves. The face that seemed to float in air above the nothingness of the robes was as benign as ever, with no hint of the skull-like features Mustafa's brother had described. Long thinning hair brushed a bundle of black cloth attached to the back of the tall man's robes. Mustafa realized that the extra cloth was a hood.

"Prophet, it truly is you!" Mustafa cried with joy.

"You want to keep your voice down already?" the figure said. "Do you still have it with you?"

There was one thing that he had been allowed to take with him into federal prison. The one item that had made the long trek with him from the hell of the subterranean Iraqi lab through his travels in the West to his failure to exalt the name of Allah by flying a commercial jetliner into the home of the hated infidel president.

Mustafa retrieved his ancient family Koran from the shelf above his metal bunk. This was the item he had submerged in the tank in the laboratory back home.

Mustafa had obeyed the Prophet's order to keep the book dry. He had been around the scientists long enough to know what would happen if the book were ever to get wet.

"They didn't take it from you," the creature in black said, nodding with pleasure. "Excellent."

"They examined it, but found nothing wrong," Mustafa

said. "They were not even allowed to touch it without wearing gloves. I don't think the cloth gloves would have helped them before, but now, Prophet, I am not sure if it is even dangerous any longer."

At this, the man in black laughed. "No, Mustafa, the gloves wouldn't have done them any good. Not if this baby had gotten wet. And I assure you, it's as wonderfully poisonous as ever. I can feel death upon it. It is time for you to use the book, Mustafa, to bring glory upon us."

Mustafa felt his chest swell with pride. "Very well, Prophet. When will you release me from the infidel prison?"

"Who do I look like, Alan Dershowitz? This isn't Iraq, you know. This place is crawling with guards. Get out on your own. Then take out a city for me." The man in the black robes tapped a long finger to his chin and considered. "The big one's bound to hit the West Coast any day now, so no sense wasting it there. Death doesn't double-dip. You should go east. New York or Washington. Boston is pretty uppity. There wouldn't be too many tears if Beantown gave up the ghost. Tell you what, why don't you surprise me?"

The man who was not the Prophet did not fade away, he was simply gone. As if a switch had been flicked.

Mustafa was alone once more.

On the floor where the Prophet had stood was a puzzled gray mouse and a few cockroaches that had come out of hiding in the prison walls. They scattered from the light.

Mustafa held in his hand an object capable of inflicting greater human suffering than an atomic bomb, an object he had hidden in plain sight of the Americans all this time, yet to use it as the Prophet wished he had to get out of prison.

Mustafa taxed his brain but as usual it did not pull its weight. It was no use. Mustafa needed another brain to think for him. Luckily the soft Western justice system had a tried and true method of getting guilty men like Mustafa out of prison so that they could commit fresh acts of evil too horrible to describe. Mustafa decided to take a cue from something the Prophet himself had said, something that would not even have been possible in the nation of his birth if not for the intervention of the hated United States. Mustafa went to the door and shoved his blubbery lips between the bars of his cage, as he had that night years before in his dog cage prison back in Iraq when he told his brother that he had been blessed with a visit from the Prophet.

"I want to speak with my lawyer!" shouted Mustafa Mohammed, 9/11's infamous twentieth hijacker.

2

His name was Remo and the courtroom had not
changed. It was the same ugly, depressing chamber he remembered from that day more than thirty years ago when
the state of New Jersey decided that it was in the best interest of the people that an innocent man be executed.

The walls were still the same ghastly green he remembered, more appropriate to the exterior of a strip-mall car
wash than to the interior of a court of law. At some point in
the past the hard benches had been stripped and revarnished,
but that was decades ago as well, so the state of disrepair
Remo found them in was about the same as he recalled. On
the bench where Remo sat at the back of the room, a car thief
artist had invested a few pre-trial moments in carving a
penknife engraving of a naked woman in the solid oak. The
same fluorescent fixtures hung from the water damaged ceiling, although Remo imagined that the buzzing bulbs had
been changed since he last sat and waited to hear the words
of the black-robed judge.

The judge. Now that was different. The judge was not the

same one Remo had faced as a defendant, back when he was young and naive enough to trust that he would find justice in a system that seemed determined to railroad an innocent man. The judge in that kangaroo trial had been a tired, bloated lifetime civil servant more interested in protecting his job than meting out justice. This new judge, who had just entered the room from a door behind the bench, was a tired, bloated lifetime civil servant as well but was a good two inches shorter than the last one.

"All rise!"

The courtroom obeyed the order of the burly bailiff. Feet shuffled as men and women clambered to their feet. Remo stood with the packed crowd, keeping a special eye on the individual who was seated at the defense table.

Another change, a different defendant. Where once Remo had sat was a woman of about fifty. Her hair was cut in the pageboy style of the boy on the paint can, but on her it was as cute as a silk ribbon on a mudslide. Her rough skin was decorated with eczema blotches, her thick neck was like an inflated inner tube of doughy flesh, and her body had the same blockish shape and squared corners as a mailbox.

During his trial, Remo had been nervous, but this woman seemed unconcerned with her circumstances, and as the audience took once more to benches and chairs, she leaned in to the younger of her two lawyers and laughed.

Remo found it strange that someone could laugh with their life in the balance.

In Constance Arnold's case, it was life as she had known it, the comfort of an occupation that would be forever lost to her if the proceedings this day went against her.

Arnold was a lawyer who had been found guilty the previous year of passing information from her terrorist clients to operatives in the international al-Khobar terrorist organization. Whereas aid to the British in the Revolution, to the South in the Civil War or to the Nazis in World War II would have brought a severe penalty, usually involving the perpetrator swinging from the end of a rope, Constance Arnold's sentence for treason had been nine months in a federal health-spa penitentiary and suspension of her law license. She was in court this day to have the license restored and the record of the conviction expunged.

In front of the court, the ruddy-faced judge made a show of shuffling through some papers for a few minutes. The name plate on the bench identified him as Judge Harmon Gates.

Remo recalled that there had been no paper shuffling during his trial. The court had no windows so Remo's judge had merely stared at the wall for most of the proceedings.

Although Remo had not known it at the time, the outcome of his own trial had been determined long before a dead drug pusher was found beaten to a pulp in an alley with the badge of Newark beat cop Remo Williams clutched in his dead hand.

Almost before the bloodstains had dried, Remo had been arrested, tried and executed. Luckily for Remo, the electric chair had been rigged to not work. He had awakened from death in an ivy-covered building on Long Island Sound, and from there had embarked on a new life and a new mission.

The building was Folcroft Sanitarium, cover to CURE, America's most secret crime-fighting agency. Trained there to the peak of human perfection, Remo was to become the agency's one-man enforcement arm. For years he had toiled away in secret, eliminating the enemies of America at home and abroad. And now his covert life had seemingly come full cycle. Remo Williams, that innocent man who had been framed in order to fight for truth, justice and the American way, now found himself back in the courtroom where it had all begun, observing the hearing of a woman who had betrayed everything for which Remo, CURE and America stood.

At the defendant's table, Constance Arnold listened to a few whispered words from the younger of her two lawyers and laughed again. Smiling, she shook her head and her bangs bobbed appreciatively. A broad grin on her face, she turned her attention to Judge Gates.

The judge had finished shuffling his papers. "Get up here, both of you," Gates growled from the bench.

Lawyers from both sides approached the bench. Remo noted that unlike his trial, the jury box was empty for Constance Arnold's hearing.

Constance remained seated, a smug smile on her toad-like face, as she drummed her fingers on the desk before her.

The room was full but there were not many reporters present. A few men and women scratched notes on lined paper. No cameras whirred since the judge had banned all video equipment.

This phase of the Arnold affair had drawn little interest. Indeed, the press had seemed to go out of its way to look elsewhere during her trial the previous year. Remo's trial had been similarly ignored by the media. Back then there had been a few second stringers from some of the smaller New Jersey and New York papers.

Remo could focus his hearing better than others could focus their vision and had he chosen to, he could have picked up every sound coming from the front of the room, including the whistling noise of the judge breathing through knots of wiry white nose hair. But Remo found little of interest in what lawyers had to say and that went double for judges.

As lawyers and judge yammered softly, the crowd waited expectantly, the handful of reporters scribbled furiously, and Constance Arnold smiled knowingly, while Remo examined his fingernails and recalled the phone conversation with Upstairs the previous afternoon.

"You want me to whack a lawyer and it's not even my birthday?" Remo had asked. "How much will I owe you?"

"This is a serious matter," Remo's employer had insisted, his voice the audio equivalent of a bag of squeezed lemons. "Constance Arnold was attorney to several high profile terrorist clients, including the so-called Deaf Mullah as well as Mustafa Mohammed, the 9/11 hijacker."

"Yeah," Remo said agreeably. "But she's a lawyer. Everybody gets a lawyer, right? The Constitution. Blah, blah, blah. Why's she on the list?"

"Because she is the worst of the lot. She would visit her clients in prison along with an interpreter and then allow the interpreter and client to carry on separate conversations to send out orders to terrorist groups. It was only by luck that Arnold was apprehended."

"Wait a minute . . . Arnold. I remember her now, 'cause she had the same name as the talking pig on TV. Same face too. Wasn't she convicted?"

The voice on the other end of the line grew so sour Remo swore he felt the phone receiver pucker in his hand.

"She could have been sentenced to twenty-four years and even that would have been too lenient. Instead she got nine months. Judicial insanity. Even so, she served her time and I would be willing to turn a blind eye on her past crimes if not for this hearing. She sees the same judge who passed sentence on her and I think she might just get her right to practice law restored. If that happens, she'll be right back passing messages between terrorists and getting Americans killed. We can't let that happen."

"Enough," Remo said. "You had me at 'kill the lawyer.' "

"Do not take this lightly," said Harold Smith, Remo's employer. "These are perilous times."

"They're always perilous, Smitty."

"Not like now," Smith said. "Distance and oceans no longer protect us from our enemies. We have a difficult enough time defending ourselves from forces without. Treason from within needs to be punished."

"Okay. I'll zap her in her house."

"No." Smith's voice was rock steady. "This needs to be more public than that. The press will no doubt be present for her hearing tomorrow. A sudden apparent heart attack after the ruling might send a message. Our enemies are superstitious in a great many ways. If even one of them believes that some supernatural force somehow intervened and struck this woman down, that might be one less attack we will have to deal with down the road."

"I'm the hand of God. Gotcha," Remo said.

He was surprised when Smith told him that the courthouse was the same one in which he had been tried. Smith was obsessed with secrecy and generally steered Remo away from anything that would have him intersect with his old life.

Remo glanced up as Judge Gates issued his ruling, which caused a minor uproar at the front of the courtroom.

"Your honor, you can't do this," the federal prosecutor, a young man in a neat suit, was pleading.

"Don't tell me what I can and can't do, Mr. Simmons."

"But your honor . . ."

"Get out of here, counsel," the judge snarled, waving the federal prosecutor away with an imperious flick of his gavel. "Ms. Arnold?" The woman at the defendant's table rose, and the judge nodded in her direction.

"This court apologizes for any hardships you have endured over the past year. In this nation's fanatical persecution of alleged terrorist suspects, the rights of innocents have been trampled repeatedly, and I'm afraid you have fallen under the stormtrooper's boot as well.

"But not in this court. No, ma'am. The court has taken into account all of the good work you have done over the years for the wrongly imprisoned, the destitute, and for groups and individuals that might not otherwise have gotten a fair shake. Suffice it to say that ours is an imperfect system, and sometimes good people are punished wrongly. The court finds that this was the case with you. Consider yours a clean slate, Ms. Arnold, with my apologies for what America has become."

The minor uproar that followed the last bang of Judge Gates's gavel was all the cover Remo needed. Supporters of Constance Arnold cheered, critics howled outrage, and Remo slipped to the edge of the aisle and waited for America's latest celebrity traitor to pass within arm's length.

Just a touch of the fingertips would be enough. An innocent touch, just a tiny tap, and that would be it for Ms. Arnold. Remo had seen a few cameras in the hallway outside the courtroom. If he timed it just right, the unnatural rhythms he would establish in her heart would reach a crescendo right around the time she was stepping in front of the cameras. Constance Arnold would drop dead at her moment of greatest triumph, Upstairs would be happy, and Remo would be back in his car by noon and heading for a cheapo movie matinee.

It was all going to work out swimmingly for Remo Williams, exactly as it had not worked out for him in this same courtroom thirty years before.

Constance Arnold pushed past the little swinging gate that separated trial participants from the public. Her lumpy, blotchy face beamed victory as she swept toward Remo. Several print reporters peppered her with questions as she walked. The perfect cover. In the confused jumble of moving limbs, no one would see a single hand snake out.

Eight feet, five feet, three feet.

As she walked past, Remo reached out. And then Constance Arnold glanced back over her shoulder and winked broadly toward the judge's bench.

Remo's hand froze.

Away from the madness, Judge Gates allowed a flashing smile amid his sagging jowls before he gathered up a few manila folders and hustled out a rear door.

Just like that, Constance Arnold was given a reprieve. The crowd passed, the lawyer at its center like a thick, bumpy log being whisked downstream.

When Remo exited the courtroom a moment later, the woman was already standing in front of a dozen news cameras.

"Of course I feel vindicated," she said, her voice a drawling whine. "This system railroads those who dare speak truth to authority. I would not toe their line, and was punished for the crime of helping the helpless."

The few television reporters present were only too eager to record every word.

Remo decided to allow Constance Arnold a few more moments in the sun. Finding the edge of the crowd, he slipped out the door and into the bright day.

No one gave him a second glance. He was of average height, on the thin side, with dark hair and high cheekbones. His only distinguishing features were dark eyes that were like peering into the deepest reaches of space, and a pair of abnormally thick wrists. He wore a blue T-shirt and matching chinos and appeared oblivious to the cold as he passed through the gleaming glass courthouse doors.

It was a crisp January afternoon, and the winter sky was cotton white blended with the faintest tinge of pale blue. Remo skipped down the steps to the broad sidewalk.

Across the street an old man sat on a park bench, a flock of cooing pigeons bobbing around his feet.

Although not discernible on a conscious level, the way the wizened figure sat somehow intimidated strangers from joining him on the broad bench. As Remo approached, one lawyer on a lunch break attempted to take up the free space for a quick bite to eat. Before his rear end had touched the bench, the attorney's McDonald's bag was flying in one direction and his briefcase was sailing off in the other.

"What the hell did you do that for?" the lawyer screamed at the elderly Asian in the blue-trimmed gold kimono.

"I?" the tiny figure asked, his voice a squeaking singsong. "What is it that I, an old man in failing health, have done but sit out in the cold and await my son, who went into that ugly building on business but who has doubtless been placed in manacles and tossed in a deep dungeon?"

"That was my lunch," the lawyer snarled.

"Your arteries may thank me later. Even if you do not."

"Who the hell do you think you are?" the lawyer said.

"He thinks he is the center of the universe," said a cold voice behind the red-faced lawyer, "and most days the universe and I are happy with that arrangement. Now vanish."

When the attorney spun to the voice he found himself staring into eyes that were at once cold and hostile. They were eyes more frightening than those of any of the guilty men he had fought to keep on the streets. They were a killer's eyes. The lawyer blanched.

"I was, um . . . that is, he . . ."

"That's some silver tongue, Clarence Darrow," Remo said. "Now go lick a hydrant and sue the dogs for pissing on it."

The lawyer, who had been more than happy to verbally abuse an old man, was suddenly even more happy to turn his attention to other pursuits. Whispering a soft prayer under his breath, he trotted off on stubby legs to scoop up some documents that had spilled from his tossed briefcase.

Chiun, Master of the House of Sinanju and Remo's teacher in the most deadly and ancient of all the martial arts, returned his attention to the pigeons at his feet. A hamburger bun that he had plucked from the attorney's lunch bag appeared in his fingertips, and he pulled away tiny bits of bread and tossed them to the delighted birds.

The old Korean's fingers were long and tapered to sharpened fingernails. His skin was the hue of walnut, as thin as ancient parchment and threaded throughout with delicate blue veins. Above shell-like ears, tufts of white hair tinged with yellow caught the soft winter breeze.

Remo flopped down on the bench next to his teacher and watched the main entrance of the courthouse.

"Well?" the Master of Sinanju asked as he tossed a bread crumb to a brown pigeon with white speckles.

Remo eyed the courthouse sadly and sighed. "You can't go home again, Little Father."

"I ask a question and you answer with a riddle," Chiun said. "Should I assume by your non-answer, Remo, that you failed to get it?"

"Get what?" Remo asked.

"Playing dumb and being dumb are two different things. Stick with your strength. You know very well what."

Remo sighed. Yes, he knew. But he had been hoping that Chiun had forgotten.

"She wasn't in there, Little Father. I told you, this is the real deal. She wouldn't be caught dead in a real court these days. I think she's in California."

"I know that," Chiun said. "But she came from this province and so should be known to the magistrates here."

"I think she's from New York, not New Jersey."

Chiun arched a thin eyebrow. "There is a difference?" he asked. "No matter, for those two squalid provinces are neighbors, and the magistrate class doubtless commingle. Did you ask any of them if they knew her?"

"I only saw one judge, Little Father, and I think he's up to something."

The doors to the courthouse suddenly burst open and Constance Arnold appeared in all her two-hundred-and-thirty-pound glory. Reporters dogged her down the broad steps.

"My aged eyes are obviously failing me, Remo, for it appears as if the behemoth Smith sent you here to dispatch still breathes."

"A technicality," Remo said. "My gut tells me there's more here than meets the eye."

"This is America," Chiun sniffed in reply. "If anything, there is far less than meets the eye. What one sees is what one gets, and all of it is lacking. What I would give for a little palace intrigue, but no. You people do everything out in public. Hang your hearts on your sleeves and toss your brains out the window." His pointed chin decorated with a tiny wisp of beard aimed in the direction of Constance Arnold. "In any civilized nation, at any other time in history, for the treason she committed that woman's neck would have met an executioner's ax."

"Take a gander at that bull neck of hers, Little Father. A squad of ax-men working tag team couldn't hack through it by Labor Day. And it doesn't matter, 'cause by the end of the day she'll be dog meat anyway. I just want to check out a hunch first."

"May the gods of all heavens above spare this poor aged soul the hunches of Remo Williams," Chiun said. "And since you refuse to get a simple gift for your father in spirit, you may go chasing after this wild moose on your own." Brushing bread crumbs from his hands, the old man marched away. Pigeons scattered in fear from his sandalled feet.

Remo let his teacher go. Chiun always found his way home, usually courtesy of a taxicab driver who immediately thereafter left the profession in terror. Remo meanwhile had fatter fish to fry. Across the street, Constance Arnold had battled her way through her adoring throng and was collapsing into the backseat of a taxi. Twirling his keychain around one finger and whistling all the way, Remo hustled for his own parked car.

The dingy apartment was a decorator's homage to radical chic. Framed posters of Che, Mao and Jane Fonda hung from red walls. Throw pillows were embroidered with yellow hammers and sickles. The living room rug was a smaller replica of the famous Oval Office carpet, but here the seal of the United States was encircled in red and bisected by a slash in the international code for "no." On shelves were Russian stacking dolls of old Soviet leaders as well as Stalin and Trotsky salt and pepper shakers with a cute little ceramic ice-ax in the back of Trotsky's head.

Constance Arnold sat on the couch in a simple flannel nightgown that Barnum and Bailey could have found a use for. She was talking on the phone.

"Well, dear, I've spoken to the prison and they have no record of anyone visiting you, especially in your cell. Are you certain it wasn't a guard playing a nasty trick? No? What? Slow down, dear, slow down." Constance jotted a few notes on a yellow legal pad. It felt good to be writing notes for someone other than herself again.

She had talked to a few of her more high profile terrorist clients in the seven hours since her court appearance. Most of the men had grievances about their treatment. Several had peed on their own prayer rugs and were now blaming the soldiers who were guarding them, two were wondering if they would be released in time for the Hajj and one was irate because he suspected one of his guards might be Jewish. And then there was Mustafa Mohammed, the poor boy who had been imprisoned not for the crime of flying a plane into the White House, but merely for *wanting* to do so. "If merely the desire to destroy federal buildings is a crime, we should all be in prison," Constance had unpersuasively argued to Mustafa's jury three years before.

Mustafa's guilty verdict was an outrage, a miscarriage of justice on a par with Constance's own imprisonment. She promised him yet again to do everything in her power to get him out of jail and back into one-way flight school, but he no longer seemed interested in flying into the White House. She had not expected him to be so agitated. After such an exhausting day she had only expected to touch base with him.

"Yes, I have it all written down," she assured him once he was through dictating. "Don't worry, Mustafa, dear, I think we have a good shot of getting you out on appeal. Well, within the year. No, not sooner. I'll get—No, Mustafa, I can't. Maybe Tuesday. I'll call you tomorrow."

She hung up the phone with a heavy sigh, paused a moment to collect herself, then lifted the receiver and placed a call to a number her client had just given her.

"Hello, dear, this is Constance Arnold. Thank you, I'm very happy about it as well. Yes, that's right. I was just talking to Mustafa. No, he didn't want to call you himself, dear. He's afraid they might overhear. Anyway, do you know anything about some big killer weapon or something? He's claiming he smuggled it into prison somehow. Heaven knows how, but he seems quite certain, and he says now's the time to use it. Well, he told me to mention it to you, dear, so I thought you knew. No, I don't know what he could be talking about, but I'll know more on Tuesday. Right, I'll be seeing him then. Yes, dear. I see. Well, good night."

As if hanging up the phone were a cue, a voice called from down the long hallway next to the kitchen.

"Are you coming to bed, Connie?"

Constance had lifted the phone once more. She pressed it tight to her ample bosom. "In a moment, dear," she called back. Humming a John Lennon tune, she placed a few more calls before finally pushing the phone and notebook to one side. She lumbered up the hall.

Judge Harmon Gates was sprawled naked on Constance's sagging mattress, with only a thin sheet covering his body.

The judge patted the edge of the bed and grinned lasciviously as Constance came into the room.

"It's about time," the judge said. "A man can be just so patient, Connie, darling." He began lifting the sheet when a voice cut in from across the room.

"Hold that nauseating thought."

The sheet fluttered from the judge's shocked fingers. Constance and Judge Gates spun to the strange voice. They were shocked to see that a thin young man had somehow melted up out of the shadows next to Constance's highboy.

"Who the hell are you?" Constance demanded.

"I'm the Spirit of America," Remo said. "I'm every man who froze to death at Valley Forge or was gunned down at Iwo Jima. I fought and bled and died so that heifers like the two of you could make a mockery out of the criminal justice system."

"Well, Spirit of America," Constance spit the words sarcastically, "this is breaking and entering." As she spoke, she inched toward her night table.

"No, this is justice," Remo said. "Real justice. Not what happened in that court today."

Judge Gates had propped himself up indignantly on a pile of pillows. "Do you know who I am?" he spluttered.

"If I say yes, do you promise to keep that sheet on?"

"I am a federal judge, young man, and you would be wise to march out that door and not look back."

While Judge Gates distracted the intruder, Constance continued to move slowly toward the nightstand.

" 'I'd really have preferred not to see any of this," Remo said. "But still, the Spirit of America is proud of itself. I saw that chummy little look you two swapped in court today. So wipe the little darling's slate clean, right? What's a little treason between radicals? By the way, not that the law matters to either of you, but there are ordinances against bestiality."

Judge Gates was helpless beneath his sheet. A New Jersey judge without a weapon was like a Caribbean beach without sand, but apparently Judge Gates had forgotten to bring a howitzer with him on this evening's booty call. Luckily Constance Arnold, rabidly in favor of gun control but only for the lower orders, had them covered.

She lunged for her nightstand and ripped open the drawer. Wheeling, she aimed a 9mm Heckler and Koch pistol at Remo's chest and squeezed the trigger.

"Hah!" she howled in triumph.

The crack was like a peal of thunder in the small bedroom. Constance was so certain that she would not miss she was already lowering the gun before she realized that not only was the thin young man not lying dead in a pool of blood on her bedroom floor, but that her aim had been off. Way off. Somehow in the flash of an instant after she pulled the trigger but before the bullet exited the gun, the barrel had been redirected. In fact, now that the room was coming back into focus, Constance realized that her entire massive body had been redirected as well.

The smoking barrel now faced the bed. A small hole surrounded by a halo of black powder burns decorated the forehead of Judge Harmon Gates. His honor's glassy eyes were shocked and his mouth hung open in death. A goodly chunk of one of the most mediocre judicial minds of his generation was splattered over pillow and headboard.

Constance felt warm breath on the back of her neck.

"I just want you to know, from the Spirit of America, that this is personal as much as it is business, sweetheart."

Constance felt her arm suddenly stiffen. The crazy young man who could move faster than a fired bullet had pinched her elbow between two fingers. To her horror, the gun in her hand rose slowly up to her own chin.

Constance strained with all her might to lower the gun, strained until beads of sweat oozed across her greasy forehead, but it was no use. She felt the hollow tip of the barrel press deep into the flab folds under her chin. Her broad nose sniffed the acrid scent of gunpowder wafting from the barrel.

"But—" she began.

Then she heard a far off click that might have come from the apartment next door, so soft was it. Then came a burst of light brighter than the light of a thousand exploding suns, and then a darkness so great it was beyond all human understanding, and then she was a plus-size corpse in a grimy flannel nightgown pitching onto the bed with her dead boyfriend. The frame could not take the strain of their combined weight and the bed collapsed to the floor.

Remo averted his eyes from the mass of jiggling flesh just in case the sheet fell or the nightie rose.

As a courtesy to the coroner who might have eaten a late supper, Remo snapped off the bedroom lights.

"The Spirit of America is greatly pleased," Remo announced to the darkened room. Dusting his hands, he slipped into the hall and was gone.

3

Dr. Harold W. Smith, director of the supersecret agency known only as CURE, was not pleased.

Those who met Smith for the first time suspected that displeasure might be Smith's natural state but that was only because they did not know him well. Those who knew Smith for any length of time knew beyond any shadow of doubt that this was the case.

Smith's expression rarely changed, and with his pinched facial cast and ashen complexion, he had the appearance of one who had just smelled a foul odor.

The office in which he sat reflected the personality of the solemn man who had occupied it for over four decades.

A door to a private bathroom, closed in deference to old-fashioned good taste, stood beside a row of old wooden file cabinets. A threadbare carpet over wooden floors and a leather sofa near the main office door had seen better days. Since it was winter, a porkpie hat and gray woolen overcoat hung on a rack across the Spartan office.

Smith's normal work attire in winter and summer was a

three-piece gray suit, crisp white shirt and striped Dartmouth tie, knotted tightly to his Adam's apple. His rimless glasses were as clear as the gray eyes behind them.

The lone window in the room at Smith's back was large and looked out over a sprawling lawn that dipped sharply down to the shore of Long Island Sound. Special one-way glass prevented anyone outside from seeing in.

The room and its occupant were throwbacks to another age. The only modern addition was the broad onyx desk behind which Smith sat. Beneath its gleaming surface, canted so that it would be visible only to Smith, the unblinking eye of a computer monitor stared up from the depths. A capacitor keyboard was hidden at desk's edge and only became visible at Smith's touch. The keyboard remained dark as did the expression of Harold W. Smith.

Harold Smith was not a man who laughed. Life was far too serious a thing to waste time laughing. He could not recall the last time he had smiled, but on those rare occasions he did so, the smile was always followed by a pang of guilt. Smiling was frivolous, and Harold Smith did not have the luxury others had to engage in frivolity.

But even though displeasure was Smith's natural state, those levels could increase or decrease depending on circumstances. At the moment, he was near the highest level of displeasure he could achieve.

Smith read the short news story from New Jersey. A small picture accompanied the article. In it, a very much alive Constance Arnold had no difficulty smiling.

Smith frowned at Constance Arnold's grinning face as he picked up the blue phone at his elbow. He dialed a Connecticut number from memory. The phone rang for several minutes and Smith was ready to give up when it was suddenly answered. A familiar thin voice came on the line.

"You have reached a wrong number," announced the voice. "Bother me no further." The phone clicked dead.

Smith quickly redialed. This time it took a good five minutes for the phone to be answered.

"I will not tell you again," said the same singsong voice, this time laced with menace, and before Smith could say a word the phone hung up again. On the third attempt, Smith blurted out the words the instant the ringing stopped. "Master Chiun, it's Smith," the CURE director said. "Is Remo there?"

Smith swore he heard a resigned sigh during the brief pause that followed. Then the voice was back, and Smith once more could not get a word in edgewise.

"Greetings Emperor Smith, most wise and benevolent of rulers, guardian of the precious Constitution, defender of the Eagle Throne. Most blessed are we happy few who hear his lilting voice, for it is nothing less than light in a world grown otherwise dark and desolate, the fullness of his sweet words nourishment for hungry souls brought out of darkness and into the warming rays of his awesome munificence."

"Er, yes, thank you, Master Chiun," said Smith.

"The Emperor must not thank his humble servants," the Master of Sinanju said. "Instead, we thank him for deigning to speak with us, especially on a vulgar instrument that is clearly beneath him, for it has obviously been designed specifically to disturb tranquil souls who were attempting to meditate in the few minuscule moments of peace they are able to find in the waning days of a life fraught with the perils one faces when one so loyally serves the crown, as has your servant."

Smith was not certain how to respond, so he apologized again.

"Irrelevant," Chiun dismissed. "Speak."

"Chiun, is Remo at home?"

"No, he is not." There was a bitter undertone to the words. "I have not seen my son since he abandoned me to the wolves this morning and I was forced to hire a taxi to bring me home."

"You were with him in New Jersey this morning? Do you know why he failed to carry out his assignment?"

"Remo is now a full Master of Sinanju, Emperor Smith,

and Masters of Sinanju do not fail. On rare occasions we have postponed success but never do we fail. And pleased am I that I could straighten out this little misunderstanding and put your regal mind at ease. Hail Smith the Informed!" A dial tone buzzed in Smith's ear. He replaced the blue receiver, the frown lines at his mouth growing deeper. The lines became limitless black crevices in the weak light cast from the banker's lamp at the edge of his desk.

It was unlike Remo to fail in an assignment, especially one so simple. For despite what Chiun had said, the fact that Constance Arnold had walked through the courthouse doors and back into her old life meant Remo had failed.

There were men and women, in uniform and out, who daily put their lives at risk for the freedoms of those back home. Constance Arnold had done her best to aid the enemies of freedom. To have her sentence tossed out and her right to practice law returned to her was an outrage. And to add insult to insanity according to newspaper accounts, Judge Harmon Gates had actually offered the woman an apology.

Remo obviously did not find this as offensive as Smith or he never would have let the woman live.

Having spent his youth in service to his country, in the OSS during World War II and in the Cold War-era CIA, Smith was no stranger to the dangers of espionage. The judge's insulting apology cut as deeply into Smith's patrician soul as Constance Arnold's perfidy.

Checking his computer, Smith noted that Gates had been appointed to the bench almost thirty years before by former President Samuel Albert. Smith was not surprised.

Smith swivelled around in his chair to face the window at his back. Early evening was dark and cold this time of year and Long Island Sound would be churning black and capped with white waves. But the single splotch of light from his desk lamp reflected against the pane, obliterating Smith's view of the sound. Staring at the blackness that rimmed the light, Harold W. Smith leaned back in his chair and waited for CURE's enforcement arm to call.

Remo left Constance Arnold's Newark apartment building by the rear alley entrance. The shriek of approaching sirens sounded in the distance.

It could be that a neighbor had heard the gunshots and the authorities had already been called or maybe the police were simply responding to one of the billion other crimes which nightly plagued America's streets. Either way, Remo would be gone if or when the cops arrived.

A minute later he was back behind the wheel of his car and driving the streets of his youth.

Remo's childhood had been spent with the nuns of St. Theresa's Orphanage. The orphanage had long burned down and the adjacent grammar school had closed years before, abandoned to vandals who had smashed its windows until the diocese finally boarded them up. Remo drove past the building where he had spent eight regular school years and one miserably hot session of summer school.

In the parking lot play yard, ghosts of his youth danced among the dirty snow and brittle winter weeds.

The car seemed to know where to go better than Remo himself, so he allowed it to take him wherever it led. Main streets fed to back roads, the busy evening traffic fell away to a few lonely cars, and soon Remo was alone and pulling to the curb before a pair of familiar gates.

Rusted scrollwork on a wrought iron arch read WILD-WOOD CEMETERY. Beyond gates and fence, cold headstones rose dark in uniform rows from the rolling landscape.

Remo shut off his engine and stepped out into the cold.

The wind had picked up. Strong gusts tousled his short hair as he walked to the gate.

The cemetery was closed and locked for the night. Remo grabbed a cross bar and swung up and over the fence. He landed without a sound on the main gravel drive.

Smith had cautioned him never to visit the vestiges of his
old life. Beat cop Remo Williams was dead, buried in a
simple grave that Remo was never to see. Despite Smith's
warnings, Remo had come to this place a few times in the
past. Besides, if Smith hadn't vapor locked at the idea of
Remo sitting in the actual courtroom where he had been sentenced to die, he sure as hell couldn't complain about Remo
visiting the empty cemetery where his alleged body had al-
legedly been buried.

The headstone was no more impressive than the last time
he had seen it. A cheap little granite number, carved with
his name and a simple cross. No glitz, no flash, no Remo.

For a moment he wondered who *was* buried beneath his
feet. Smith had mentioned in passing years before that it
was merely some indigent CURE had found on the street.

Did the man have a name? A family? People who loved
him and wondered where he was, even after all these years?

Remo did not keep track of how long he stared at his own
grave. Only when the weak light of a new day peeked over
the horizon did he realize he had stood vigil all night.

He had not realized it at the time, but the visit to the
courtroom had troubled him. Not that it should have. That
rigged decision years ago had set him on the path for which
he was destined. As a matter of truth and law it had been a
travesty, but for Remo there had been some cosmic justice
at play, even if the world would never know it.

He turned his back on the trip down memory lane. The
past was gone. It was time to look forward. As he headed
back to his car, the grave next to his caught his eye.

A few sunny days had melted most of the thin snow cover,
exposing clumps of knotted weeds, and this grave was in
worse shape than Remo's own, for at least the muddy ground
around Remo's headstone was not choked with growth. In
fact, Remo could not even see the marker through the brush.

Feeling sorry for the occupant of the neighboring grave,
Remo went over and pulled up a few clumps of weeds.

He had not been able to see a headstone because there

wasn't one. There was no stone marker of any kind. A stick not even in the shape of a cross had been pounded in at some point when the mud was soft. A faded name was drawn down the length of the stick in crooked Magic Marker. "Craig McAvoy."

Remo thought the name rang a bell.

He had grown up in Newark so it was possible this was someone Remo had encountered in his old life. It was not someone from the orphanage. To forget a fellow orphan would be like forgetting the name of one's sibling. Maybe McAvoy was someone Remo had worked with on the Newark police force. Or maybe he was one of the hundreds of lowlifes Remo had arrested before CURE and a new life had come calling.

Whoever McAvoy was, he seemed to be having a crummier afterlife than Remo's, and rather than boost Remo's mood it made him feel even worse. At least Remo was alive and kicking after his death. This poor guy did not even have family to buy a headstone or pull a weed.

Remo cleaned the grave up as best he could and straightened Craig McAvoy's marker. When he had done all he could do, he stood back up.

"Sleep tight, buddy," Remo said to the sad little grave.

Turning his back on the dead, Remo headed out onto the path back to the main entrance to Wildwood Cemetery.

She hated war because in wars people died and they were rarely the right people.

She hated the tools of war. Hated them so much that sometimes she and her friends in the Tuesday Peace Brigade sneaked onto military bases and damaged multimillion-dollar equipment in order to demonstrate her disapproval.

She hated most of all the men who fought wars. One time she had been arrested for damaging a dozen U.S. Army aircraft, and at her sentencing she got up in court and yelled that the real criminals were the butchers in uniform that the United States sent around the world to fight its imperialistic campaigns against the brown and yellow man. She had been given a fine and probation, and the next week she was arrested with a pair of wire cutters and a bagful of wrenches on an aircraft carrier at Norfolk, Virginia.

The only good wars were the kinds against poverty or hunger. Sometimes she and her friends baked bread and sold it in the backs of churches to raise money for those, the only just wars. But the wars with the guns and bullets and the bombs and the planes were always bad.

America had no right to attack Afghanistan after 9/11. She had protested that atrocity all the way to Washington. It was up to the U.S. to understand the poverty and helplessness that had motivated those poor hijackers to murder three thousand American citizens in cold blood. After all, violence invariably led to more violence. What violence had the U.S. visited on the poor Arab man to make the mass murderers of September 11 do what they did?

The invasion of Iraq was a criminal act far worse than snipping a few wires on military planes or throwing wrenches into navy helicopter engines. Just because Iraq had broken every term of the 1991 cease-fire, and just because some people thought it was too risky to leave a madman in power in a post-9/11 world was no excuse. Turn the other cheek, and if that one gets burned off by chemicals or radiation, well, turn right around and offer the other.

Not that she was naive. She knew that the United States wasn't the only evil in the world. Britain and Australia were no great shakes. And everyone knew the Israelis were to blame for the apartheid situation in Palestine. Former President Sammy Albert had even written a book about it.

The Palestinians wanted peace, the Iraqis wanted peace, the North Koreans wanted peace, the Iranians wanted peace. It was America and its lackey so-called democracies that were the greatest pothole on the road to real world peace.

"What about Pol Pot?" her son once asked after learning about Cambodia's killing fields. A bright boy, he learned about Cambodia on his own. School focused entirely on America's failure in southeast Asia and never hinted that men with yellow faces had been involved in horrifying atrocities. "Would it have been just to stop him from slaughtering all those people?"

She was baking cupcakes for the Sandinistas at the time and looked up from her container of Betty Crocker frosting.

"War is never the answer," she insisted. And for the moment that had been enough for her little boy.

"What about Cuba?" her son had asked another time, older now and in junior high school, but still asking questions. "Castro has murdered political enemies for years. It's a dinky little country right off of Florida, Ma. We've already got a base there even. We could give the Cubans freedom in a week I bet. Would that be just?"

She looked up from the posters she was painting for her Palestinian Peace Now! group, her nose smeared with red glitter paint representing the blood of innocent Arabs.

"War is never the answer," she said sternly.

As he grew older, her son had grown more skeptical of her worldview. Finally one day after high school graduation he had come to her with a final question.

"What about Hitler, Ma? Was it okay to fight Hitler?"

"War is never the answer, Craig," Sally McAvoy had told her son one last time. "Adolf Hitler was a man just like any of us, driven to do the things he did because of militaristic pressure placed on him by Western democracies led by the United States. We are to blame for creating Hitler."

"Bullshit, Ma," Craig McAvoy had said. "Hitler was a bastard maniac, Pol Pot was too, and so was every other guy I've asked you about since I was little. The best thing the U.S. ever did was bomb the shit out of Germany and nuke the hell out of Japan and the worst thing we ever did was bail out of Vietnam. I love America. We're not perfect, but we're as close as anyone else has ever come. And to show my gratitude for all this nation has done for me and everyone else in this world—you included, Ma, even if you don't realize it—I've made a decision. I've enlisted in the Army. I leave for boot camp next week."

Sally refused to see her son off. She was at a protest against a U.S. espionage facility that trained spies from South America and told her ex-husband to go without her.

She had not attended Craig's graduation ceremony from basic training. When he was shipped to Germany, unlike other military moms, she never sent a single CARE package overseas. When her son sent letters home, she threw them in the fire unopened.

After 9/11, when Craig was sent to fight in the mountains of Afghanistan, she had apologized to her fellow Tuesday Peace Brigade members for raising a little bloodthirsty tool of capitalist oppression.

"He gets it from his father's side," Sally McAvoy had insisted. "They're the ones who worship that flag with the red stripes that represent the blood of the native Americans whose land we stole, and fifty stars, one for every million African slaves that this corrupt nation dragged here in shackles. I tried to teach him to beat his sword into a plowshare."

When word reached her that her son had been killed by a roadside bomb, Sally McAvoy slammed her front door in the faces of the soldiers who informed her of her son's death, then called a press conference for 6:30 sharp.

"I demand an audience with the president so that I can question him about the morality of sending our children off to spill their blood for the oil fields of Afghanistan."

None of the press in attendance bothered to inform Mrs. McAvoy that the fields of Afghanistan grew poppies and that the nation had about as much oil as the average Western teenager's forehead. It was clear in that first press conference that Sally McAvoy was not terribly bright and seemed a bit on the crazy side but her heart was in the right place, and besides, no one had the right to question the motivation, intelligence or sanity of a grieving mother. Especially one who hated the White House and who would say anything to get on television.

Her story was picked up by the national press. Thanks to the drumbeat of the press corps, Sally got her meeting with the president. The leader of the free world had offered his condolences on the loss of her son and expressed appreciation on behalf of himself and the nation. When he attempted to give her a consoling hug, Sally McAvoy jumped on him and tried to bite his face.

"Liar! No blood for oil! Peace in our time!"

She had been dragged off the president and barred from the White House. But Sally McAvoy was not about to give up the bully pulpit God had given her. For Sally was devout in her faith and knew beyond all doubt that her burgeoning celebrity was a boon from the Almighty Himself. The death of her son was the miracle she had waited for all her life. At least the kid had been good for something.

Sally began camping out in a muddy ditch at the side of the road outside the president's sprawling Texas ranch.

Her antics quickly elevated her from the status of media darling to secular saint. The fawning press could not put her on television enough. "Camp Craig," as her temporary home in the ditch came to be known, grew into a tent village for news media and anti-war activists.

"I only want to speak to the president," Sally insisted in all of her interviews. She invariably failed to mention the fact that she had physically assaulted him in a private meeting once already and in most cases the reporters left the fact of the earlier meeting out of their stories.

"What would you say to him if you had the chance?"

"The Bible tells us that it is acceptable to pray for the death of tyrants." Her coarse face was hangdog, her eyes vacant. "I would tell him that I was praying for him." She became the darling of tinpot dictators looking to score domestic points by thumbing noses at the United States. Sally was flown around the world to meet with despots that she had heretofore been able only to worship from afar.

"Forgive us our sins," she apologized on behalf of the country she hated on a visit to Venezuela. "As you know, the United States is the ultimate evil in the world," she said at a rally in Havana. "It does not act in the name of all of its citizens. It is up to individuals like me to preach the true American word."

"Reaching out to friends in poor countries, perhaps by means of a redistribution tax on wealthy Western nations, would be a good start to righting the injustices we have committed against you," she said during a whirlwind tour of a dozen African dictatorships which had basically reinvented poverty and starvation only after the European colonialists left.

But as with many manufactured celebrities, the star that flared white-hot quickly burned itself out. When a hurricane leveled a major American city, the press corps relocated to its ruins, abandoning Camp Craig. Two years had passed, yet Sally McAvoy continued to sit in her Texas ditch and, like the apostles watching the skies after the Ascension, continued to await the return of a camera crew from *48 Hours*.

When she heard the sound of a vehicle pulling to the shoulder of the road near the collapsing tents of her once thriving gypsy village, Sally peered up from her ditch like a hopeful gopher. But it was not the press returning.

It was an old yellow school bus that had been salvaged from the ruins of New Orleans and given new life in the anti-war movement. It had been repainted powder blue with murals on its sides depicting smiley faces, happy daisies and black hands shaking white hands. White doves surrounded the words "Tuesday Peace Brigade," which were painted in bright primary colors.

Men and women climbed down from the rickety old vehicle. Some carried lawn chairs and blankets. As Sally sank dejected back into the dust, the representatives of the Tuesday Peace Brigade joined her in her ditch.

The meetings took place every month and never varied. After some polite hellos, the membership would sit around eating hash brownies and plotting the overthrow of the U.S. But this day something was different.

"I've got some amazing news!" Loretta Sanders-Parker said, face flushed with excitement.

Sally was disappointed. It was Loretta's turn to bake the brownies this month and her hands were empty.

"You left your Tupperware on the bus," Sally said.

"Never mind that," Loretta said. "You know Kerri Marcil

from Midnight Justice? Her husband's trial for trying to blow up the Vietnam War Memorial is coming up and she was talking to her lawyer last night."

"Who cares?" Sally said. "I hope you brought the brownies."

"Forget that and just listen. Anyway, the lawyer said that Mustafa Mohammed, that young Arab freedom fighter who was supposed to blow up the White House, has smuggled some sort of super-duper weapon into prison with him."

"How is that possible?" asked a skeptical woman in a flannel shirt, boots and dirty sweatpants. "They would have searched every orifice for wires and stuff. No way anyone sneaks a big-time weapon into prison. Not after he's been given the Abu Ghraib once over."

Loretta Sanders-Parker pitched her voice low. "Oh no? Mustafa's lawyer was Constance Arnold, just like Kerri Marcil's husband. Kerri tried to call her this morning. Guess who was murdered by the fascist oppressors last night?"

Sally McAvoy's eyes widened. "The brownshirts murdered Constance Arnold?"

"Yes," Loretta said. "Well, they're saying that she shot some man and then killed herself, but the fact there's no evidence proves it. I smell a government conspiracy."

The others could not argue with the inescapable logic of Loretta Sanders-Parker.

"Mustafa has a weapon," Sally whispered, awed.

"Yep," Loretta said, big jaw firmly set. "And we're going to go get it."

"In prison? How?"

"Easy," Loretta said. "You. You're the only one of us who could get in there. Demand to see him. Say his human rights are being violated. God knows they must be. Get in there, find out what he's got and get it from him before the government does. You know what a blabbermouth Kerri Marcil is. They'll Abscam it out of her in ten seconds, assuming they haven't got it already. We need it for us."

"But we're against wars," Sally said. "We sneak onto army bases to destroy weapons, remember?"

"God, you really are thick," Loretta said. "We're going to turn the weapon against the weapon makers. The huge Rally for a Free Kabul is the day after tomorrow. We're all going to be there anyway. We can unveil it there. Show the fascists in charge we're not going to take it anymore."

"I think we should use it on West Point," said Steve Sanders-Parker, a man so sensitive he had joined his wife's maiden name with his own. Loretta had suggested that they flip a coin to see whose name would be first. Steve had insisted that coins were misogynistic because they were stamped with the faces of men. Loretta had said they could use a Susan B. Anthony dollar. Steve allowed that this clever solution that had not occurred to him proved women were superior to men in every way and argued that it was proof her name should be first. Sometimes he thought if he tried real hard he could menstruate. He wore panty liners in his BVDs just in case.

"Great idea, Steve," Loretta said. "Hit the little fascists-in-training."

"Oh! Oh!" cried a man with a big belly and bushy beard. "How about Walter Reed Hospital? The soldiers there are just recuperating from injuries sustained in the illegal oil harvest anyway. Great symbolism."

"A hospital?" Loretta said. "I'm not sure about that. I agree with you, but will the average boob tuber get it? No, we've got a million army bases around the country and around the world. Any one of them would be good."

"Take out Guantanamo and our brother Cubans would toss rose petals in our path and anoint our feet with oil," a woman with stringy black hair, an overbite, thick glasses and unblinking eyes suggested. The only boy she had ever kissed was a picture of Jesus.

"Put that on the definitely maybe pile," Loretta said. "But it all hinges on you, Sally. You're our ticket into that prison. You with us?"

Sally glanced around the ruins of Camp Craig. Although she had tried for a long time to deny it, even she could now see that its glory days had passed. Many of the tents had blown away. Those that remained were torn and had thrown stakes. Rope and vinyl flapped in the wind.

Craning her neck to see up out of her ditch, Sally looked beyond the small gathering of anti-war zealots. The Secret Service had forced her so far away from the main ranch proper that the buildings were not even visible. Unable to camp out at the main gate, she was stuck way out on the far left fringe. God had given her temporary fame but then had cruelly taken it from her. There was no way she could get it back the same way she had before. She had no more children to sacrifice to Him and she was too old to make any more.

But He worked in mysterious ways. Maybe this weapon that could be turned for good was His way of saying I'm sorry.

Sally McAvoy climbed up from the mud, a determined expression on her plain face. "Thy will be done."

"You bet your ass," Loretta Sanders-Parker said, leaping to her feet. "Oh, right. You mean . . . Yeah, of course, Him too, obviously. Let's go."

5

Smith's reliable old station wagon passed through the main gates of Folcroft Sanitarium at precisely 7:25 a.m.

His reserved space was waiting for him. He pulled his car in next to that of his assistant.

These days Mark Howard arrived earlier and stayed later than Smith. The young man had surrendered his life to CURE without a clue what he was getting into. How could he? Even though it was not Smith who had brought Howard into the agency, the CURE director still felt the usual twinge of guilt in his belly for the life that would forever be denied his assistant. That little daily ritual over, he gathered up his battered briefcase and, pulling his overcoat collar tight against the wind, hurried inside the sedate brick building.

The executive wing of the building was virtually deserted. Down the hall, Mark Howard's door was closed to prying eyes. On his way to his own office, Smith passed a janitor who was polishing the hallways but the man did not look up as Smith passed. Most Folcroft staff had grown used to ignoring and being ignored by their taciturn employer.

The outer room of Smith's office suite was empty. His secretary was not scheduled to arrive until eight.

Scarcely taking time to hang his hat and overcoat on the rack beside the door, Smith hustled over to his desk where his first act was to try Remo once more. This time when he called the Connecticut condominium Remo shared with the Master of Sinanju, Smith got only a busy signal.

Frowning, he hung up the phone and booted his computer. After reading the preamble to the Constitution, a daily ritual for over four decades, Smith threw himself into the work of another day as head of CURE.

Some time around eight, his matronly secretary brought in a tray with coffee, toast and yogurt from the cafeteria. Smith scarcely acknowledged her polite "good morning." He ate while he worked.

An hour later there came another knock on the door and Smith's assistant of the past seven years entered the office.

Mark Howard was in his late thirties, of average height and build. He wore a dark blue business suit, white shirt and black tie. At first, Smith had regarded him as insufferably young, but now his light brown hair was beginning to gray and the youthful bounce was disappearing from his step. *This job is aging him before his time,* Smith thought with a tinge of sadness. Smith knew that Howard kept a child's drawing of Superman on his desk. He wondered how long it would be before that was gone too, along with Mark Howard's youth.

"Morning, Dr. Smith," Howard said. "You decent?"

"Come in, Mark." Smith waved to a chair. "I didn't realize it was nine o'clock already."

Smith pushed aside the tray Mrs. Mikulka, his secretary, had brought him, surprised to see that it was empty. He had been so engrossed in his computer screen he had not realized he had finished breakfast while he worked.

"Did you ever get Remo?" Howard asked as he took his regular hard wooden seat across the desk from Smith.

"I tried him again this morning with no luck."

"Well, there might be some more bad news on the Constance Arnold front. You know how I've been keeping track of her phone conversations? I spent the morning going through all the ones she made yesterday after the ruling. Most of them were to Colonel Sanders, Domino's and Mr. Lee's Chinese Takeout. No fast food joint is going out of business with her in the neighborhood. A bunch of calls were to clients. Most were nothing—demands for more toilet paper, prison porn, stuff like that. But she made one call to Mustafa."

A flicker of distaste crossed the CURE director's face. "That's not a surprise. I guess she's his attorney again."

"Yeah, but get a load of this."

Howard produced a clean white sheet of paper from his briefcase and slid it across the gleaming black desk.

Smith scanned the transcript Mark had made of the phone conversation between Constance Arnold and Mustafa Mohammed, then looked up, puzzled. "Are you certain of this, Mark?"

"Tracked the phone numbers and heard them talk with my own ears. I can forward you the data. He says he's got a secret weapon."

Smith shook his head. "No." He was scanning the transcript a second time. "Just impossible," he said. "He must be bluffing. Possibly hoping that his conversation is being monitored so that he will be moved to another facility. There was that attempt to free him eight months ago. Perhaps this is part of some elaborate scheme by fellow terrorists to break him out."

"I considered that too, Dr. Smith, but you've got to hear his voice. The guy's not kidding. And she must have bought it, at least a little. She mentioned it to about a dozen other radical clients of hers. So much for attorney-client privilege. In case you didn't know it, she's not a very good lawyer."

"Do any other agencies have this information?"

"I don't think so. Who'd bug her but us? Eavesdropping on terrorists who want to murder Americans is the biggest sin there is these days. Way worse than, say, being a crooked congressman who stuffs ninety grand in his freezer and then successfully runs for reelection."

"Mark," Smith admonished.

Howard sighed. "Yeah, I know. Sorry."

The younger man had grown bitter over the shackles that were lately being placed on law enforcement. Smith did not blame him, for indignation was the privilege of the very young. But with age came, if not wisdom, at least sensible resignation. Smith had been gently reminding his assistant that there was an ebb and flow to such matters. Besides, the new limitations did not affect CURE.

Smith passed the paper back to his assistant. "I'll make sure that prison officials conduct a thorough search of Mustafa Mohammed's cell. But I'm certain they've done so many times in the past. If he had some weapon, it surely would have been discovered by now."

"You're the boss, boss," Howard said, slipping the paper back into his briefcase. "I'm still going to forward you the audio. I want you to hear this joker when he says it. He had me sold."

Their meeting was over and Mark had just gotten out of his seat when the blue contact phone at Smith's elbow jangled to life.

"Thank you, Mark," Smith said by way of dismissal. "That will be all."

Smith waited for the young man to close the office door behind him before lifting the receiver.

"You never let it go to five rings," Remo's voice said. "Did I catch you in the shower?"

"You failed to complete your assignment."

"I don't know what papers you're reading, Smitty, but they're about twelve hours behind the breaking news."

"Are you saying that you . . . er . . . removed Constance Arnold?"

"Removed is such an ugly word. I prefer greased. And if no one knows about it still, maybe you should put in an anonymous call to the cops. Those bodies are going to be tough enough to haul out of there fresh. I'd hate to be the poor slob who has to schlep them to the morgue once the raccoons have started nesting in them."

"Those?" Smith asked. "You were supposed only to eliminate her. Publicly, I might add."

"And if ifs and buts were candy and nuts we'd all have a merry Christmas, Smitty. Relax, she's history. And so is that judge who thought treason was less bad than jaywalking."

"I don't understand," Smith said. "Remo, please say you did not eliminate Judge Gates as well."

"Don't worry, Smitty," Remo said. "It was a twofer. I tossed in Judge Fatso no charge."

Smith took a deep breath to calm himself.

Outside his window, Long Island Sound sparkled in the winter sunlight. A few intrepid sailboats battled wind and cold, tiny white sails dipping and rising on the waves.

"Remo," Smith said evenly, "I risked sending you into the very courthouse where you were tried because there was a specific purpose that I felt warranted the risk. I did not agree with Judge Gates but there are many judges I do not agree with these days, and being a fool is not a capital offense in this country. Now, if there is a good reason you eliminated him as well, please tell me. And I would appreciate it if you did not preface your explanation with suggestions that I should relax or not worry."

Remo, who was about to do just that, said simply, "How about they were knocking Birkenstocks?"

A notch formed at Smith's brow. "Are you saying that the two of them were having an affair?"

"They were having something. You know Catherine the Great? Whatever she was having with her horse, that's what these two were having. I'll be soaking my eyes in bleach the rest of the week."

Remo gave a rapid rundown of the previous night's events at the Newark apartment of Constance Arnold. As he spoke, the computer on Smith's desk came to life and the CURE director saw the transcript from Mark Howard of Mustafa Mohammed's boast about his secret weapon. He read it quickly, then realized Remo had stopped speaking.

He was getting old, Smith thought. Once he could handle a half-dozen problems at once, juggling them all at the same time, but lately it seemed that he could only concentrate on one issue at a time.

Constance Arnold was the issue right now and he realized that Remo was correct. Discovering Constance Arnold dead in bed with the judge who gave her little more than a slap on the wrist for her treachery, lovers apparently involved in a murder-suicide, would be a thing even the national media could not ignore. And those enemies of America who believed in divine intervention would perhaps think some otherworldly force had punished the two of them for their actions.

"Very well," Smith said.

Remo grunted. "That's all I get for thinking on my feet? Guess I shouldn't expect more. Hey, one more thing while I've got you, Smitty. I need you to check out the name of a stiff for me. A guy by the name of Craig McAvoy."

Smith did not need to consult his computers. His lips thinned to a tight frown. "You have been to Wildwood Cemetery," he accused.

"It's been a crap day so don't get on my case, okay, Smitty? You obviously know who the guy is."

Smith removed his glasses and pinched the bridge of his nose. "Craig McAvoy was an army private killed in action in Afghanistan. He was the son of Sally McAvoy, the antiwar activist."

He heard Remo snap his fingers.

"I knew I should know that name. It's been bugging me all morning. You didn't tell me he was buried near me."

Smith replaced his glasses. "That is because he is not.

That is not your grave, Remo, and since you obviously know that you are not interred there and are indeed one of only a small handful of people who know that to be the case, I fail to see why you would have any emotional attachment to it."

"You fail to see why people have emotional attachments to puppies, Smitty. So what's up with the grave they put that poor kid in? I'm not exactly buried in the fanciest plot in town but he doesn't even have a headstone. What's a celebrity like him doing in the cheap seats with me?"

Smith could not understand why Remo persisted in laying claim to a grave and body that were not his own.

"Apparently that was the last plot available in that part of Wildwood. I admit I was worried when I learned that the McAvoy boy had been put in the plot next to yours. His name was not well known when he was buried, of course. It was only his mother's activities after his death that made her son a posthumous celebrity of sorts. But my concerns were unfounded. In all of the coverage of Sally McAvoy there was only one story from a right-leaning magazine concerning her son's grave. Everything else was about Mrs. McAvoy."

"Yeah, I've seen her on her grandstand. I figured with all her boo-hoo blather that her kid's grave would be in better shape."

"It is not my concern, nor yours, Remo. I've cautioned you before about returning to that grave. There is nothing for you there and each trip risks compromising CURE security. Please don't go there again."

"Okay, okay," Remo said. "Anything else?"

Smith's eyes wandered back to his computer screen and the report on Mustafa's phone calls from prison.

"One thing, Remo. Do you remember Mustafa Mohammed?"

"Should I? One Mohammed's just like another one," Remo said. "The world's filled with them." He paused. "Wait, he's the one that al-Khobar tried to break out of prison?"

"Yes," Smith said. "He's in Berkwood Prison. One of Constance Arnold's clients."

"Right, right."

"Mark intercepted some phone calls and this Mustafa is talking about having a powerful new weapon to attack the U.S."

"Probably hummus with extra garlic," Remo said.

"Perhaps, but I'm not so sure. You might think about paying him a visit at Berkwood Prison."

It was hard for Remo to hide his disgust. "Whatever you say, Smitty. Are we finished?"

"For now," Smith said, and their conversation over, the CURE director reached back and hung up the blue phone.

For several minutes he stared out at the boats on the sound. One sail drew his unconscious attention, and he tracked it with a lazy eye as it battled the bitter gale.

"Hmm," Smith said.

Turning his back on the winter scene, Smith's knees settled back in the well under his desk. Arthritic hands sought desk's edge, and the amber bursts of an alphanumeric keyboard flashed as sure fingers struck keys.

A name appeared on Smith's monitor: **John Whiteman**.

A brief biography appeared next to a very old high school yearbook photograph. Smith scanned the scant details of the sadly unremarkable life and, looking one last time at the photograph, with a single keystroke once more consigned the data to a dusty corner of CURE's mainframe computers.

6

Mustafa Mohammed paced his tiny cell in Berkwood Federal Penitentiary and for the hundredth time that morning strained to hear the sound of footsteps closing in on the locked steel door.

His palms were sweating, his mouth dry as desert dust. He had not felt so anxious in confinement since those terrible days beneath Iraq's shifting sands when he'd watched his entire family taken away and murdered one by one.

But their deaths had not been in vain. He knew now that they were martyrs to a greater cause; they were the sacrifice required so he might fulfill his great destiny.

Unfortunately, he had awakened that morning to bad news on several fronts.

His first thought upon opening his eyes was disappointment that he was still in prison and could not immediately fulfill the wishes of the Prophet. An infidel city must be destroyed but how to get out and obey that great command?

Mustafa was not a great thinker and he had pondered this

conundrum up until breakfast, when he heard even worse news.

"I'm tellin' you, she's dead," a serial killer who had murdered seventy-two women whispered to Mustafa in the chow line. The serial killer was carrying his usual breakfast tray of ice cream, pretzels and Mello Yello, the only items that could be served him thanks to a lawsuit that claimed balanced meals were a violation of his civil rights.

"I spoke with her yesterday," Mustafa said.

"And she's dead today," said the serial killer. "Found her in her apartment. Shot herself. She was your lawyer, wasn't she? Tough break."

Mustafa would have to find another lawyer, and then break him in. And who knew if a new one would be as receptive to Mustafa's ideology as Constance Arnold had been? He placed a desperate call to a former attorney general of the United States whose life was now dedicated to defending America's enemies but had been told there were a hundred al-Khobar terrorists in line ahead of him.

As if that was not bad enough, after breakfast he had gotten the worst news of all. The inmate in the cell next door—a sniper who had murdered innocents at gas stations and fast food restaurants all around the Washington, D.C., area—claimed that he had overheard some guards talking just a few minutes before. Apparently they had been given a tip to thoroughly strip Mustafa's cell. Every item was to be removed and searched. Under a microscope if necessary.

The forces of evil were allying against him.

His Koran sat in the middle of his unmade bed. The book that had been passed down from the time of his great-grandfather Abdullah was open, although Mustafa had not read a single word in it this day.

Three steps, turn, then back to the rear wall where the commode sat four inches from his bunk, then turn again.

Mustafa did not like to admit it but his brother Achmed was right. He was not terribly bright and he was certainly not a planner. But without someone else to guide him, his brain was being forced to improvise.

Wiping one wet palm on his trousers, he continued to pace the cell. He nearly jumped out of his skin when the bell shrieked. The sound echoed throughout the prison.

The protracted howl of the buzzer that followed the bell indicated that the main door at the end of Mustafa's maximum security hall had been opened.

"Here they come," hissed the sniper in the cell next door. "Hope it's warm in there, 'cause from what I hear they're gonna be stripping you down to your bare butt."

Another short buzz was followed by a metallic click and the steel door to Mustafa's cell swung open. Two burly, armed prison guards were framed in the door.

"Let's go," one commanded. "Out."

The second guard grabbed the first by the wrist.

"Oh, geez, Harry, get a load of that," the second guard said, blood draining from his face. He aimed a truncheon at the Koran on the bed. "He's got the book open. Damn. We're going to get blamed for breaking the binding. I don't want to get hauled in front of the damned review board again."

At once both guards noticed what the twentieth hijacker was holding in his shaking hand.

"Sweet Jesus," whispered the guard named Harry.

Mustafa had torn a page out of his own Koran. He was holding the yellowed parchment over his cell toilet.

They were going to get blamed. If there was one thing these terrorists knew better than blowing up innocents it was how to play the American justice system. Mustafa had defiled his own Koran and was now going to blame it on his guards. There would be hearings, disciplinary action, screaming lawyers and reporters, and maybe firings. The prison would be tied in knots for months over this. And through it all Mustafa Mohammed would be laughing at the weak Western system that became so panicked over the rights of the guilty.

But at this moment Mustafa was not laughing. Before they

could order him to stop what he was doing, the Iraqi opened his hand and let the parchment flutter from his fingers.

The Koran page caught the edge of the porcelain bowl, and for a moment the guards held their breath. They dared not move, lest movement stir the air in the cell and cause the parchment to fall in.

If it didn't hit the water, maybe it would not be so bad. Maybe some Scotch tape could save their jobs. But if the charge of flushing a piece of Mustafa's Koran stuck, they were both as good as unemployed.

And then the page unstuck, pitched forward, and fell into the toilet without so much as a tiny plunk.

Above the commode, Mustafa noted little marks in one corner where he had been holding the page. His hand had been soaking wet with sweat and the spots where he had perspired into the paper had turned deep blue. He could plainly see the whorls of his fingerprints on the ancient parchment.

Two heavy thuds at his back distracted him from the mesmerizing fingerprint stains. He turned to find the two guards dead in his doorway.

Both men had grabbed at their throats in the instant before death. Their skin was bubbling red, like a poison ivy rash. Arms and legs twitched a spastic dance.

Another thud in the cell next door. Mustafa grabbed his Koran and tiptoed over the dead guards.

His sniper neighbor had been sitting on the toilet when Mustafa sank the parchment. The man was now lying on the floor, prison-issued pants still around his ankles. The killer's legs, in death spasms, kicked wildly at the wall of the cell.

As if Allah himself had reached down to strangle life from the infidels with a single grasping hand, Mustafa soon found that men all around the prison had died where they stood. Uniformed bodies were strewn across corridors. Inmates who would never rise again lay on bunks.

Mustafa could not believe that so much killing strength

to see their deceased loved ones, the family members wept and hugged one another as they waited for news from inside.

Remo and Chiun passed the group in respectful silence. They had crossed through the gates and were heading for the main building when an angry voice yelled from behind them.

"What the hell do you think you're doing?"

When Remo glanced back he saw a middle-aged man in a hazardous materials suit chasing after them. The man had just removed his hood. His graying hair was slicked with sweat and his face was flushed and covered with perspiration. A tag labelled Centers for Disease Control and Prevention was clipped to the collar of his yellow suit. The tag bobbed as he ran.

"We'll just be a sec," Remo called. "I forgot my copy of *The Cat in the Hat Does Crack* in my conjugal trailer."

Leaping in front of them, the man threw out his arms. "No one goes inside. Now get out of here, both of you."

"Remo, obviously this costumed fool who thinks he can give an order to the Master of Sinanju is demented," Chiun said. "Give him a candy bar and send him on his way."

"Who are you two?" the CDC agent demanded. "How did you get in here?"

Remo showed his Homeland Security ID. "Terrorist act on U.S. soil. My little plastic card outranks your little plastic card." He started for the door, but the CDC man bounced and stumbled back in front of him.

"Not this time," the man said. "You go in there, you don't come back out. This place is locked down. We have no idea what was let loose in there. Could be viral, chemical, anything. The only thing we know is it's not radiological, since the place tested negative for radiation. But even that I'm not sure of. The blistering is consistent with radiation burns. Right now we don't know what we've got, and if you go in there and then try to leave you'll be shot."

Remo rolled his eyes and sighed. "Look, what do we do? We have to get inside."

The CDC man waved at a van, as big as a Winnebago, parked nearby. "Two hazmat suits!" he called.

As men hustled to scare up another two suits for Remo and Chiun, the Master of Sinanju tugged at the back of Remo's T-shirt. "A candy bar would have been quicker," he mumbled.

Remo pitched his voice low so that only his teacher could hear. "They're only doing their jobs, Little Father. Let's be grateful we've got guys like them on our side."

Chiun stuffed his hands deep inside the voluminous sleeves of his kimono. "I am on my side. Occasionally yours, when you are not too annoying, which is however most of the time. These ones may have entirely to themselves whatever side it is they are on."

While they waited, Remo took in the scene around them.

Three layers of fencing had been ruptured. The front gates were damaged, and one of them hung from thick hinges. An overturned tractor lay in a gully outside the gate. There had been a breakout at Berkwood. But with all the feet that had kicked up the crime scene since that morning, there was no telling how many prisoners had escaped.

Remo sensed no danger emanating from the prison. When he questioned the CDC man he learned that instant death had claimed the guards in the towers. The dead on the catwalks were not far from where Remo stood. If there was still a risk, all of the men this close by would be dead as well. Still, he was not entirely certain what they were dealing with, and for safety's sake as much as to keep peace, Remo put on the suit he was handed. It was difficult finding a hazmat suit that would fit the Master of Sinanju's diminutive frame. The smallest suit and a few strategically tied belts later, Remo and Chiun entered Berkwood Federal Penitentiary.

The doors and gates were all open wide. There was no longer any point in locking them. The residents of Berkwood were no longer a flight risk.

The first bodies they encountered were civilians, visitors to the prison who had gotten no further than the check-in area. Amid the early dead was a man in black, a Roman collar identifying him as the prison chaplain. Guards in gray uniforms lay sealed behind Plexiglas barriers like exhibits in some morbid museum.

Remo understood now why the CDC man had mentioned radiation burns. The skin of the dead was red and blistered. Yellow matter oozed from eyes and congealed on faces. The eyes themselves were open wide and drained of color. The extremities had split like cooked sausage and blood had hardened black in the gashes.

"Ever see anything like this before, Little Father?"

Despite the helmets, the elderly Korean's voice was crystal clear in Remo's ears.

"I have not," Chiun replied.

Remo had come to expect that in his long life Chiun had met and defeated every obstacle possible. But an invisible cloud that could kill in so brutal a fashion and then dissipate, seemingly without a trace, was new even to the senior Master of Sinanju. With this troubling thought ever in mind, the two men walked deeper into the prison.

Bodies at desks watched with milky white eyes as Remo and Chiun passed by. Every now and then they encountered other federal agents in suits like their own, FBI as well as Disease Control. Blood, saliva and skin samples were being harvested from the dead and locked inside misting containers marked on all sides with biohazard warnings.

In his hazmat suit, Remo felt like an alien observer. The entire prison had a weird, otherworldly quality to it.

"Just because we are here, don't think that I am not still upset with you," Chiun said as they passed the warden's suite of offices. Remo could see two female secretaries and several men in suits lying dead at desks.

"And why wouldn't you be?" Remo said. "Doesn't today end in a Y?"

"It is only one little request," Chiun pressed, as if his pupil had not spoken. "One would think that after being given everything, your heart would rejoice to be given a chance to show gratitude to your father in spirit."

"Are you on this again? Chiun, this isn't the time."

"Of course not. It is never the time for me. Tell me, Remo, when will it finally be my time? Will it be the day after the dirt is shoveled over me? Is that the day when you will finally grant an old dying man's request?"

"You're not dying."

"If one can die from the shame of having an ingrate for a son, I am dying."

More doors. A sign advertising the laundry room was ahead. Dead convicts were piled in the doorway.

"I told you, she wasn't in that courthouse in Jersey, no one there would have known her anyway, and I don't have a clue how to track her down."

"A good son would find a way. A good son would move heaven and earth to get the one meager little gift his father has ever requested. But, lamentably, the foundling house was out of good sons the day I went shopping for one and so I wound up with ungrateful you."

"What the hell is so goddamned important to you about getting Judge Ruth's autograph?"

Chiun had recently discovered the *Judge Ruth* courtroom reality show on daytime television. Judge Ruth was a bitter, angry old woman who belittled and browbeat those dregs of society foolish enough to enter her televised courtroom. Remo could see why Chiun was enamored of her. The two of them were so alike, the first time Remo saw the program he wondered if some hoodoo shaman had accidentally body-switched the Master of Sinanju with the TV jurist.

"Is it not enough that it is important to me?" Chiun asked. "Why must I constantly be forced to justify myself to you? Never mind. Forget that I even asked. Why should your untroubled mind be burdened with the agony of making me happy? I only hope that I do not die tomorrow. At my age every day brings me closer to the Void, and I would hate to think that I marred our last day together by hanging the millstone that is my happiness around your carefree neck." The old Korean offered a pathetic little nursing home cough.

Remo sighed. "Maybe they send out autographs in the mail. I'll see what Smitty can do."

"Tell him not to be too pushy. She does not like pushy people."

"She doesn't like any people," Remo grumbled. He picked his way across the field of corpses that filled the hall in front of the laundry room.

The laundry room seemed to have been hit harder than the rest of the prison. The flesh of the men near the washers looked as if it had been flayed off. In the adjacent showers, the carnage was worse. The exposed flesh of the men who had been showering at the time of the attack had turned a gelatinous purple. Skin hung from bodies in gruesome sheets.

Remo asked directions from a passing FBI agent, and he and Chiun were soon inside the cell of Mustafa Mohammed.

The first thing Remo noticed was the lack of a body. The other maximum security inmates in this section of the prison, all dead, were still locked inside their cells. He asked the FBI men who were searching the cell where Mustafa's body was.

"We haven't located it yet," an agent said. "We're doing a search of the prison, but we're almost through and he hasn't turned up. There was an escape this morning, so it's looking more and more like he's on the outside now. Agents are going through video surveillance footage right now."

"How soon until you know?" Remo asked.

"We've got men checking the security videotapes. Results could be any minute," said the FBI man. "But we'll have the head count in half an hour, tops. Positive IDs will take longer. Some of these bodies are a real mess." He seemed relieved to have someone new to bounce thoughts off of. "This is a real baffler. It looks like maybe al-Khobar broke into the prison with some kind of agent, maybe to spring Mustafa. But then why does it look like someone punched their way out the front gate?"

"Beats me," Remo said. "I'm Homeland Security. We're still too busy trying to get the hang of this whole bloated bureaucracy thing. Right now our focus is getting big-screen plasma TVs in all our regional offices and smoke detectors in old folks' houses that cost ten times more than the ones you can pick up at Home Depot."

"Um, yeah," the FBI agent said slowly. "Well, don't touch anything." He returned to his examination of the small cell.

There was not much to examine. Mustafa Mohammed had only one personal item, a prayer rug that was rolled up under the bed. On the bunk's covers sat a plastic bag which contained a piece of wet parchment. There were blue marks in the shape of fingerprints in one corner.

"What's this?" Remo asked of the parchment.

"We found it in the toilet," the agent said. "We think it's a page of the Koran, but we're not sure. That writing looks Arabic. We'll get a language expert to check."

"Chiun?" Remo said.

The Master of Sinanju came forward and glanced down at the sheet inside the plastic bag. "It is from the Koran," he said, nodding. " 'When ye encounter unbelievers, strike off their heads until ye have made a great slaughter among them, and bind them in bonds; and either give free demission afterward or exact a ransom.' "

"Ah, yes," Remo said. "The religion of peace and love. I think we've found our Christmas card for next year."

"You can read this?" the FBI agent said. "Is there anything there that might give a clue what they're up to?"

Chiun cast a bored eye across the page. "Murder, extortion, lopping off of heads. Their god could do it all if he wished but he is apparently too busy so they must kill for him." The old man looked up and shrugged. "The usual."

The FBI agent grunted in frustration. "Well, it's all we've found out of the ordinary here." He tried to scratch an itch, but the bulky suit made it impossible. "Damn."

Remo had seen all he needed. "Let's get out of here and let these guys work, Little Father," he said quietly.

The two Masters of Sinanju stepped from Mustafa Mohammed's cell, leaving the frustrated FBI agents to ponder the greatest locked door mystery in the annals of American crime.

7

Sally McAvoy played the guitar and the Tuesday
Peace Brigade held hands, smoked pot and sang all the way
from Texas to Colorado. They stopped to pick up a hitchhiker in the Oklahoma panhandle who, after hearing
"Michael Row the Boat Ashore" and "Kumbaya" a dozen
times in forty miles, threatened to put out his eardrums with
his own penknife if they did not abandon him on the side of
the road. When Steve Sanders-Parker attempted to wash the
man's feet as he left the bus, the hitchhiker punched his
face.

Steve was gingerly pressing a can of cold wheat juice to
his black eye when the Tuesday Peace Brigade climbed
down to a side parking lot at Berkwood Federal Penitentiary.

Loretta Sanders-Parker marched up to the first authority
figure she could find, a local police officer who had been
kicked to the curb when the feds arrived.

"We demand to see our poor mistreated Muslim brother,"
Loretta demanded. "We demand to see Mustafa." She raised

her fist and encouraged the other Peace Brigade members to join in. "We demand to see Mustafa! We demand to see Mustafa! We demand to see Mustafa!" the little crowd cried.

Loretta wheeled in triumph to the policeman.

The cop was unmoved by the impromptu chant. "No one gets in," he said.

"We are on a humanitarian mission," Loretta said. "The Lord commanded us to visit the imprisoned. Besides, we know how innocent Muslim prisoners are mistreated by this country. I can put in a call and have Amnesty International knocking down your nude pyramid just like that." She snapped her fingers.

"What's going on over there?"

Sally McAvoy had left her guitar and her stash on the bus and found her way to the front of the group. She was squinting with bloodshot eyes at the men in funny suits who could just be glimpsed through the prison gates.

"You know who this is?" Loretta demanded of the policeman. Grabbing Sally by the shoulders, she shoved her toward the cop like a shield. "This is peace activist Sally McAvoy, buddy boy. She is to be our representative to go in the prison and make sure you don't have poor Mr. Mohammed up on a box in a hood with dogs barking at his privates."

"Listen, lady," the cop said, "I don't know what you cuckoo clocks think you're doing here but if you want to visit anyone who was in there, you can do it at the morgue."

"I don't understand," Loretta said.

"They're all dead," the cop said. "Something killed everybody in that place. If you and Amnesty got a problem with that, take it up with the feds. They came marching in here and kicked all of us to the sidelines hours ago."

The police officer wandered away from the peace group.

"Mustafa is dead?" Loretta said, crestfallen.

"The government must have found out about that secret weapon he had and killed everyone to get it," a potbellied woman said.

"We drove all the way up here for nothing?" Steve Sanders-Parker said, disappointed.

Beside Steve and Loretta, Sally McAvoy was still looking toward the distant gates. A strange expression had settled on her drooping face, like a dog who has just seen the bag of Beefy Snaks being taken out of the kitchen cupboard. When she saw cameras filming weeping women and children, Sally's eyes grew wide with delight.

"What is it?" Loretta asked.

But Sally was no longer there. America's most famous anti-war activist was running at a sprint toward the main prison entrance. One shouted word drifted back as she ran toward the sobbing little crowd near the gate.

"Reporters!" yelled a delighted Sally McAvoy.

Remo called Smith from a bank of pay phones outside the prison walls.

"Report," the CURE director said by way of greeting. Smith's voice was anxious.

"It's bad, Smitty. Whatever he's got killed a couple hundred people. FBI doesn't know it was him yet. They think the attack might have come from outside but I don't think so."

There was some sort of commotion across the parking lot.

The crowd that had gathered were all friends and relatives of the dead people who had worked in the prison and their numbers had swelled since Remo and Chiun's arrival at Berkwood. Widows still wept, children still clutched mothers in confusion, but now there were others with the crowd and these new arrivals seemed unsympathetic to the mourners. The men and women in grubby clothes had shown up while Remo was inside. With an eye toward the news cameras, they were yelling themselves hoarse shouting at the bereaved.

"They got what they deserve. Jesus hates torturers!"

"I hope you sons of Judas enjoy your PlayStations! They were bought with blood money!"

"Hey, hey! Ho, ho! Prisoner abuse has got to go!"

As the Tuesday Peace Brigade picked up the chant, the press stood back and filmed the confrontation. Crucifixes and fingers were waved in the faces of the crying widows and orphans. Much of the media attention was focused on a plain, middle-aged woman in a saggy sweatshirt.

Remo tried to ignore the protestors and hunched into the phone.

"What is that din?" Smith asked.

"Apparently God doesn't close a prison without opening a nuthouse," Remo said. "Mustafa wasn't in his cell. Looks like he tried to flush part of his Koran for some reason."

"And he's not among the dead in the prison?"

"No. They've done a head count, and there's only one prisoner missing and no one can find him. I'm assuming once they get to the videotape they're going to find him busting down the front door. You want me to let them know he's on the loose?"

"Leave it to me," Smith said. "I will inform the proper authorities that they are searching for Mustafa Mohammed." He hesitated. "I should have sent you earlier."

"Smitty, get over it. Coulda, woulda, shoulda just doesn't cut it. Not in our business."

Despite the shouting nearby, Remo could hear the drum of Smith's fingers on his keyboard as he issued surreptitious orders that would filter down to federal, state and local authorities. As Smith sent out photos and a description of Mustafa, Remo glanced around for the Master of Sinanju.

Chiun had shed his biohazard suit and was standing beyond the fringe of shouting protestors. The old Korean seemed uninterested in the Tuesday Peace Brigade. His back to the protestors, he was studying the ground.

"It is most troubling," the CURE director's lemony voice

said, drawing Remo back to the phone. "Why was Mustafa the only one to escape when everyone else died?"

"Maybe he got the Olympic gold for holding breath. Or maybe al-Khobar baked him a cake with a hazardous material suit in it."

A final few taps, and Smith stopped drumming his keyboard. "Be serious," he said. "There would be no conceivable way anything could be smuggled in to him."

"Are you kidding? I am serious. Prison is a country club these days, Smitty. Convicts riot if they don't get filet mignon three meals a day or if devil worship isn't recognized on equal footing with Christianity. The guy probably claimed a diving bell would help him commune with the Great Gazoo."

"Maybe, Remo, but not in this case. Mustafa Mohammed was more carefully watched than any other prisoner in federal custody. In fact, it was by watching her meetings with him that federal authorities were able to apprehend Constance Arnold. He would certainly not have a biohazard suit or any other extraordinary equipment in prison. Anything out of the ordinary would be discovered so we must assume the likeliest alternate theory."

"Bigfoot?" Remo asked.

"Mustafa is immune to the effects of whatever it is he used to kill the prison population," Smith droned.

"I like my theory better. Anyway, whatever he did here, Smitty, this place is one giant morgue. We'd better hope that whatever this weapon is it's only a one-time deal."

"Don't assume. After all, whatever it is, it seems he smuggled it in with him to prison and held it there for years undetected. Until proved otherwise, we must figure it can be used again. I have sent his picture to every police agency in the region. The manhunt is now for him alone. Hopefully the authorities will apprehend him before he does more damage, this time on a larger scale."

"It's pretty bad here already, Smitty," Remo warned.

"Which is why he must be caught quickly. Join the search.

And keep in regular contact. We will monitor interagency chatter from here. The instant we learn he has been spotted, I'll let you know."

"Got it," Remo said.

He hung up the phone and wandered over to the Master of Sinanju. Chiun had left the parking area and was standing at the mouth of the main drive. The old Asian was dragging his foot through a patch of damp sand near a granite curb when Remo sauntered up beside him.

"What have you got?" Remo asked.

"What time did this barbarism take place?" Chiun asked.

"I heard a fed say around ten."

"There," Chiun said, pointing to a half-frozen tire tread in the sandy gutter. "Your Arab is heading east."

Judging by the condition of the tread, Remo could tell that Chiun was correct about the time.

"Yeah, but how do you know this isn't somebody else and that Mustafa didn't walk?"

Chiun folded his arms. "Tell Smith the car was blue," he said firmly. "With a dent in the right door. And that one of the front wheels is losing air. And tell him that when he wishes to thank me the inscription should read, 'To His Awesome Magnificence, Chiun, who does all the work. With undying admiration, Judge Ruth.'"

8

Mustafa Mohammed's stolen blue car with the
dented right door had gotten a flat tire five miles from Berkwood Federal Penitentiary. After rolling the vehicle into a
ravine, he went back to the road, stuck out his thumb and
was picked up by a young couple with a pair of adorable
little children, all of whose throats he would gladly have slit
under different circumstances. However, he was under orders of the Prophet to destroy a major East Coast American
city, so right now the greater will of Allah would be served
by forbearance. And besides, the children didn't look like
Jews so he settled into the backseat next to ten-year-old
Timmy Wilcox and eight-year-old Rebecca Wilcox and endured the compassion of the infidel.

"So your car broke down, you say?" said Grant Wilcox,
smiling behind the wheel of the family's speeding minivan.
"Is it still under warranty?" He glanced in the mirror at the
Wilcox family's new friend.

In the back, Mustafa held his Koran tight to his chest as if
it were a sickly infant.

There had not been many cars in the northern Iraq village of his youth and though he had seen an astonishing number of them after emigrating to the West, he had never owned one himself. The word "warranty" was alien to him.

"Yes?" Mustafa said slowly.

"Good thing," Grant said. "We had the transmission go in the Ford, but we were lucky it was still under warranty. Still a pain in the ass though."

"Language," warned Lynda Wilcox. Grant's wife was in the front passenger seat. As was the Wilcox family custom, Lynda was paying more attention to the highway ahead than was her husband so that she could catalogue every potential risk he took with their lives, from driving too fast on snow to driving too slow in falling rock zones, and so she was first to see the flashing lights of the police checkpoint.

"Geez, it must be a drunk stop," Grant complained.

"Good thing they didn't stop you New Year's Eve," Lynda said in a stage whisper loud enough for the children and the escaped terrorist in the backseat to hear.

"Knock it off, Lynda," Grant grumbled.

Hitchhiker in the backseat forgotten, Grant pulled obediently over to the side of the road.

Timmy craned his neck to see what was happening while Rebecca continued to play with a Raggedy Ann doll that had been a recent Christmas present from her grandmother.

State police were searching each vehicle one by one. More officers, these with German shepherds on leashes, were poking around the woods at the side of the road. Grant exhaled loudly and checked his watch impatiently a dozen times as the cops slowly waved vehicles through the blockade.

"This is taking forever," he grunted after five minutes.

Lynda and the children were watching the canine officers as they disappeared into deeper woods.

"What's going on, Dad?" Timmy asked. He had put down his handheld Nintendo to watch the dogs.

"Probably a missing doughnut," Grant said.

"Grant," Lynda warned.

"Well, I mean c'mon, Lynda. You know this is nothing. Some divorced dad probably snatched his own kid from his crack ho wife and now all of Colorado is on lockdown."

"Don't trivialize kidnapping, Grant," Lynda said.

"Here we go," Grant said, exhaling loudly.

As the Wilcox parents descended into bickering, Mustafa Mohammed watched the state police through the minivan's tinted windows and felt his stomach go squishy.

The book in his hands held more destructive power than a nuclear bomb. Mustafa knew that now. But the supervirus could only be released in contact with water. He had overheard the scientists in Iraq many times, and they had been very clear about that.

There was snow beside the road. If he had to, he would try to get out of the van unseen and stuff a piece of parchment in the snow. Only one page, because the book was to be saved for the destruction of New York or Washington. Besides, the utter ruin of Berkwood Federal Penitentiary made clear that one page was more than sufficient.

But would the supervirus that currently lay dormant in the parchment be released by snow? He was not sure. Was snow the same as liquid water? None of the Iraqi weapons scientists had ever talked about snow.

Up ahead, another car was waved through the barricades. The minivan edged forward a single car length. Here and there, people were removed from cars and taken inside a big state police van parked at the shoulder of the road.

The police moved forward in pairs, stopping at each car in turn until they were finally tapping on Grant Wilcox's window. Grant powered down the window.

"What's going on here?" Grant demanded.

"Honey," warned Lynda Wilcox.

The police ignored the husband and wife. Their attention was drawn to a figure in the backseat.

Mustafa held his breath while the two state troopers whispered to one another.

The younger of the two shook his head and said, "But what about. . . ." And then he whispered something into the ear of the other state police officer.

When he glanced at Mustafa, sweating nervously and clutching his family Koran to his chest, the twentieth hijacker was afraid that he had been found out.

Outside the minivan, the older officer shook his head firmly at his subordinate. "Racial profiling," he said. "We can only do every fourth . . . them's the rules . . . which means—" He pointed to each passenger in turn. "—one, two, three . . . that one."

Eight-year-old Rebecca Wilcox was hauled out of the backseat and dragged off to be strip searched.

Her parents jumped out of the vehicle and began arguing furiously with the state troopers and Mustafa sank deeper into the backseat and allowed himself to exhale. He had not realized he had been holding his breath so long.

Truly the Prophet was guiding his sacred mission.

Mr. and Mrs. Wilcox were allowed to go to the van where their daughter had been taken. The police moved away from the minivan and Mustafa released another sigh of relief.

Mustafa watched as Grant and Lynda climbed up into the police van where their daughter was undergoing a full cavity search. Mustafa could see a policewoman tearing the head off Rebecca's Raggedy Ann doll as the girl stood crying.

The distant door was slamming shut when all at once the Wilcox minivan was rocked gently on its shocks as a big green blur rocketed past.

Mustafa was startled at the green car's abrupt appearance. It had come up from behind, racing along a highway where all other cars were stopped. The vehicle flew in the breakdown lane alongside the row of parked cars and squealed to a stop a few hundred yards away, up near the police cars with their flashing lights. Wary troopers hustled over to the car even as the doors popped open and two men sprang out.

The younger of the two was white and of average build. Mustafa would not have given him a second look if not for the man who had gotten out of the passenger seat.

When Mustafa saw the wizened Asian in the orange kimono, he blinked hard as if trying to awaken from a dream. But when he opened his eyes once more and the two figures had not vanished, Mustafa Mohammed knew that this was no dream.

An old Asian and a thin young white.

In recent years, stories had begun to circulate in the underground community where dwelled the scavengers who picked the dead flesh of human misery. Mustafa had first heard it just before he was extradited back to the United States from England to stand trial.

Rumor had it that a terrifying force had been unleashed on al-Khobar. Terrorists around the world were being systematically hunted down and eradicated. A few men had been left alive to issue warnings to those that remained and these survivors told tales of a pair of assassins who lurked in the deepest shadows and who could kill in a whisper.

"One is a young white, an American," Mustafa's brother Achmed had told him. "The other is very old and is thought to be either Japanese or Korean."

"This story of the two killers," said Mustafa, "sounds, brother, like something you have made up to scare me."

Achmed shrugged and nodded at the Koran that his younger brother still carried with him. "You still have kept that old family book after all these years? Why have you not replaced it?"

"The Prophet would be angry were I to lose it."

Achmed shook his head. "I have told you that thing that appeared to us is not the Prophet, Mustafa. Why does he want you to keep that book? What is so special about our family Koran?"

But Mustafa would not reveal to his brother the great secret of his most treasured possession. "It is his will," he said vaguely. "Tell me about these two men, Achmed. You say the Prophet of my visions is false, but I say these two killers from the West could not possibly exist."

"Believe what you want about your Prophet, my foolish brother, but trust my word about these two men. If you hear they are nearby, Mustafa, run. For if you see them it will already be too late."

Mustafa had never directly encountered the assassins, although they had briefly entered his orbit. His one brush with the two killers had come nearly a year before. The would-be hijacker had been meeting with his lawyer, Constance Arnold.

Arnold's Arab interpreter had been arrested the previous week for trying to blow up a building in Chicago and so she and Mustafa had been forced to converse in English, a decision which would ultimately be the undoing of the overconfident defense lawyer.

"You are not doing enough to get me out," Mustafa had whined that long-ago afternoon.

"My way is the long way, dear," Constance said. "Appeals take forever and who knows if you'll get the right judge? But there are others working for your release." She winked broadly, and Mustafa understood what she meant.

"How soon?" he whispered.

"Not as soon as I hoped, I'm afraid. Our mutual friends sent a task force to liberate you but it was dismantled in the desert down near the Mexican border."

"What do you mean dismantled?" Mustafa asked, confused. "They have been sent to different prisons?"

"No, dear," Constance Arnold had said. "Dismantled. As in arms and legs ripped from bodies and stacked like cordwood. The tools of Big Oil in Washington have been working a serious number on the proud Muslim man these past couple of years."

Mustafa, dim as he was, understood. The men who had come to liberate him had met the force about which his

brother had warned him. For long months afterward,
Mustafa had waited in fear, expecting them to show up in
his cell.

They never did. But the Prophet had and Mustafa finally
had his mission, and now out of the blue here were the
American assassins looking for him, and Mustafa was no
longer afraid of them. Oh, there was a slight tingle of something almost resembling fear. But overwhelmingly Mustafa
felt pride. Here was the best the West had to offer, and they
had been sent after insignificant little Mustafa Mohammed
from the northern Iraq village of Khwajah.

Mustafa had been selected to carry out a great deed, so it
only stood to reason that the hated West would send the
greatest devil force they possessed to thwart the glorious
plans of the Prophet's chosen herald.

At the police cordon, Remo and Chiun got back into
Remo's car and sped away. At the same time, the back of
the police van opened and Lynda and Grant Wilcox stepped
down with their sobbing daughter.

The Wilcoxes settled their inconsolable little blond-haired,
freckle-faced girl in the backseat next to Mustafa Mohammed. Rebecca's Raggedy Ann doll was spilling stuffing
from its torn-open neck. She clutched the head to her belly as
she bawled.

If only the doll could bleed. If only Mustafa could slash a
million such necks, a hundred million.

Soon. A city to the east. His destiny awaited.

The barricade opened and allowed two more cars to pass.
The minivan inched forward slowly.

And as he settled back in the seat next to the sobbing
little girl, a broad smile stretched the dark face of Mustafa
Mohammed.

9

Alawi Sulayam was trimming the back toenails of a high-strung little Pekingese when the pager on his belt buzzed.

He ignored the first page. Mrs. Rochester's dog was a nipper. One time last fall when the Pekingese was in for grooming, Alawi had made the mistake of taking his eyes off it for just a moment and the little bugger had snapped his finger. He still had the white scars where the stitches had gone. And so he let the pager buzz without a glance.

It had stopped buzzing a minute later when Dr. Bennet stuck her head in the door. "Al, did you pick up those treats for the waiting room?"

Alawi did not look up from the dog.

"No, I am sorry, Dr. Bennet. I was going to pick them up on the way home tonight and bring them in tomorrow."

"You'd better do it at lunch. The canisters are almost empty. And you're taking a long time on the Pekingese, aren't you? We're backed up here today. Let's get going."

The door swung shut.

Alawi was annoyed with himself. He had noticed that the courtesy dog treats on the waiting room counters were running low two days ago and he had planned to stop by the market after work last night. But yesterday had been a crazy day at Bennet Veterinary, Grooming & Kennels in Cincinnati, and the dog bones had slipped his mind. Now part of his lunch hour was going to be wasted in line at the supermarket.

Alawi was finishing up the last toenail when the door opened once again. The new clinic assistant stepped hesitantly into the room.

She was a young high school girl, barely over sixteen. She only worked at the vet clinic a few afternoons a week and every other Saturday. The girl always seemed uncomfortable around Alawi, especially when they were alone in close quarters. At first he had tried to relieve her tension by smiling, but she somehow sensed the insincerity of his convivial attempts and so he had stopped.

"Dr. Bennet told me to get Mr. Muffin," the girl said. She wore a blue smock that hung over her hips. Today she was wearing jeans, but sometimes she wore skirts that shamelessly exposed the flesh of her legs.

Alawi held the dog tight as he unwrapped the leash that had held it in place. True to form, the Pekingese squirmed in his arms, twisting desperately, its nasty little bat teeth bared.

As he was handing the nuisance dog off to the shameless little American slut, his pager buzzed once more. Alawi checked his beeper. When he saw the caller's number, he almost could not hear the voice of the young girl who was with him in the small room over the loud ringing.

"You okay, Al?"

The dog was twisting in her arms. She was looking at him as if he had been stricken ill. Alawi realized the blood was pounding in his ears and the loud ringing was a noise only he could hear for it was sounding inside his head.

Alawi was tempted to snap the neck of the furry little rat.

He contemplated raping and killing the young American whore with her painted face and silken hair. Instead he pushed his way past both of them.

"Don't forget the dog treats," Dr. Bennet said when she passed him in the hallway.

Alawi did not acknowledge his employer. Without a word to customers or fellow employees, he marched out into the waiting area. Although it was two hours before his scheduled lunch, Alawi shoved his way outside and hurried to his parked Ford Taurus. Once safely locked inside, he checked his new cell phone for his latest text messages.

The order was not what he had expected. An Iranian agent, he had been sent to America for a specific purpose but now that mission had been overridden. The man he had been sent to free from prison had apparently freed himself in a most spectacular fashion. Mustafa Mohammed was still the focus of his mission but now for an entirely different reason.

When Alawi read the brief commands, the Iranian's hands trembled. Not in fear, for Alawi Sulayam was not a man who feared. The trembling was anticipation from a man of action finally let off his leash.

Although his heart screamed for him to race, he drove under the posted speed limit and obeyed all traffic lights and signs on the way to his one-bedroom apartment.

"Home early today, Mr. Sahl," the elderly Jew who owned the building commented when Alawi passed the row of lobby mailboxes. The tag on Alawi's mailbox read "Al Sahl."

Alawi Sulayam grunted something unintelligible to the nosy Zionist pig and hurried upstairs. In his apartment he made only one phone call. The number was not written down anywhere but Alawi knew it well since he had repeated it in his head a hundred times every day for the past seven months.

"Paco's Pizza. Today's special is our meat lover's calzone," the voice that answered the ringing phone said in accented English.

"*Sharmuta manyak*," hissed Alawi.

As he hung up the phone he heard a sharp intake of breath. There were no other calls.

The Paco's Pizza employee was Alawi's contact. That man would call the next, and he would call the next and so on.

From Paco's Pizza in Delaware, a call went to the dorm room of a journalism student at Columbus University in New York City. The words "sharmuta manyak" were relayed, and the student quickly paged a produce manager at a grocery store in upstate New York. The produce manager called a car wash attendee, who phoned an off duty cabdriver.

Meanwhile, in his Cincinnati apartment, Alawi Sulayam carried a butcher knife in from the kitchen to his bedroom. He yanked off the bedcovers and began carving at the mattress. Once the stuffing was torn away, Alawi pulled out several packages that were wrapped in plastic and taped tightly. He cut away the tape and peeled off the plastic.

The telephone page at the kennel had come from his masters in the Middle East. After months toiling among the despised Americans, he was finally free to do what he did best.

Carefully, meticulously, Alawi Sulayam, leader of the Elite Incursion Martyrdom Brigade 2, began to lay out the guns, explosives and ammunition that he and his team of killers would need in the glorious campaign to retrieve some mysterious and mighty weapon from Mustafa Mohammed.

In his cramped Folcroft office, Mark Howard monitored the spike in activity among terror suspects in North America.

Both he and Dr. Smith had feared that the unknown weapon of Mustafa Mohammed, which the deaths at Berkwood Federal Penitentiary revealed was now much more than myth, would be like a drop of blood in shark-infested waters. But the response was coming even faster than he had expected.

The government, not knowing what it was dealing with, had every agency on the highest alert since 9/11. There was even chatter about shutting down all civilian air travel throughout the United States. But so far news of the real danger had not yet leaked out to the general public and all the interested agencies still believed that the attack on Berkwood Prison had come from the outside.

A small Colorado paper had been first to break the news of Mustafa's escape. The story had spread first onto the Internet, and then into broadcast and print. The nation's most notorious terrorist was on the loose, sprung from prison in a daring daylight raid by a team of terrorist allies possessed with an as yet unidentified biological weapon.

Everyone was looking for a group of terrorists. But Mark Howard knew the danger was not from a group, it was from one man—a lone man who had somehow kept hidden in his federal prison cell a weapon of awesome destructive power.

But the groups were massing. Mustafa had been alone this morning but in the afternoon, once the news reached TV, all bets would be off. And Mark Howard feared that Mustafa Mohammed might have actually begun to assemble his "Terror Squad," which was what the major news outlets were calling Mohammed's phantom group.

Already, the FBI had lost track of two dozen potential terrorists that they had under surveilance. Men who had been under observation were slipping down the rabbit hole all over the country. Was it one group or many? Mark didn't know yet, but whatever it was, it was all happening so fast, and was so perfectly timed, that he was sure they were all after a single goal: Mustafa's weapon.

Back in his office, Smith was going through photographs of Mustafa's cell, taken during inspections over the course of several months. The CURE director hoped that the photos would give up the weapon. But Mark Howard was discounting no scenario. It was possible the weapon had been hidden in Mustafa's body, by injection or even surgery. Perhaps Mustafa himself was the weapon. Off-duty guards were suspects. Maybe they had smuggled something in to Mustafa. Even the dead guards at Berkwood Penitentiary were not above suspicion. Until there were concrete facts, nearly anything was possible.

As his employer searched for clues in the details of Mustafa's incarceration, Mark continued to monitor the increased activity among terror cells at home. He was sifting through the personal data collected on a missing terror suspect in Wichita when his desk phone buzzed.

It was the outside line, Folcroft Sanitarium business. Mark continued to work as he scooped up the phone and jammed it between ear and shoulder.

"Assistant Director Howard," Mark said.

"Hello, Mark," said a familiar female voice.

Mark stopped typing. "Hi, Ma. Everything okay?"

"We're all fine," his mother assured him. "I hate to call you at work, but no one seems to be able to reach you at home these days. I've left messages on your machine but maybe you didn't get them."

"I got them, Ma. I've just been swamped at work."

Mark switched the phone to his other ear and returned to his keyboard. The CURE mainframes had just rerouted a fresh report out of Denver. He nearly cheered when he saw that the FBI had picked up two heavily armed terrorists.

"We're getting a little worried about you," Mark's mother said. "You didn't come home for Christmas again this year." Her tone was one of concern, not rebuke.

"You don't have to remind me, Ma," Mark said as he scanned the details of the report. "I'm the one who wasn't there, remember?"

Apparently the Denver terrorists had been in the U.S. on expired visas. Like many of the others who had that morning slipped through the net, they had been left at large in the hope that they would eventually lead to bigger fish. The al-Khobar gang who had tried to break Mohammed out of prison a year earlier had also entered the country through its leaky borders. Were there more of them around? Were they behind this successful escape? All questions. No answers. At least not yet.

"Are you happy, Mark?"

Mark pulled his eyes from the FBI report. "What, Ma?"

"I'm worried about you. You're just so busy at that . . . well, I won't call it a nuthouse again. But I think you were happier when you worked for the government."

His mother had danced around the subject of Mark's happiness for the past several years, ever since Mark left his job with the CIA to join CURE. Of course, she knew as much about his work with Central Intelligence as she did about his current employment. Back then she thought it was the Department of Labor, now it was Folcroft Sanitarium, a convalescent and retirement facility which Mark's sister, after a short visit two years before, had described as giving off "a creepy Bates Motel vibe."

How could Mark tell his mother that his happiness was irrelevant and that it was the work that mattered? After all, Dr. Smith was not happy and he had been at the job for more than forty years. But Smith, whom Mark's sister had described as a metal file cabinet without the warmth, wouldn't have been exactly the happiest soul in Christendom, even outside of Folcroft. Mark doubted Smith would have been happy if he were foreman at a candy cane kitten factory. For Smith it was all about the work, and the director of CURE was content to know that his work made a difference.

But despite Smith's efforts to mold his subordinate in his image, Mark Howard was not Smith.

Yes, the work was grueling. Any hope of a life outside of Folcroft was gone. Dr. Smith had issued him a suicide pill not long after Mark joined the secret agency and now his life was his job and if the day ever came that the job ended, so too would Mark Howard's life.

So the $100,000 question was could a man whose life

was his work, who had grown older than his years from stress and toil, who carried a poison pill in his pocket, and who participated in the execution of individuals for the greater good be truly happy? The answer for Mark Howard was simple.

"Yeah, Ma," he said. "I'm happy. I'm doing work that matters here. I'm making people's lives easier. Maybe not mine, but it makes me feel good knowing that I'm making a positive impact. So knock off worrying, will you?"

They continued to talk for a few minutes longer. Mostly it was Mark's mother who did the talking which was fine with Mark. He continued working, offering an occasional yes or no, and when he hung up the phone a few minutes later, his mother felt better and Mark had a lead for Remo to follow.

The Denver FBI had questioned the two men in custody and like most captured terrorist suspects they had cracked in two minutes flat. They had already surrendered several names. On his computer monitor, Mark's cursor blinked untiringly over the first letter of one name in particular. Achmed Mohammed.

According to the FBI report, the suspects in custody insisted that he was the brother of the twentieth hijacker.

A quick check of CURE's database confirmed that Mustafa Mohammed had a brother Achmed who had disappeared after the 2005 London bus and railway bombings. His whereabouts were currently listed as unknown.

Apparently many of the al-Khobar terrorists who had gone on high alert since Mustafa Mohammed's escape were gathering at a hideout in Security, Colorado, outside Colorado Springs. The terrorists who had devised an attack on 9/11, the same number as America's emergency telephone prefix, had likely delighted in the irony of creating a haven for themselves in an American city named Security.

"Let's test how secure you are," Mark said.

Dr. Smith would have to be informed. Mark wished that his mother could see the sincere smile on his face as he reached for the phone.

10

The four-story brick apartment building sat in a quiet neighborhood just outside downtown Security, Colorado.

"Why did you park so far away?" the Master of Sinanju asked, hazel eyes narrowing to suspicious vellum slits as he and his pupil walked along the tree-lined sidewalk.

"We'll be more inconspicuous this way," Remo explained. "These mooks are probably already on high alert. And they're probably so stupid they'll be sitting with their fingers on the triggers waiting for SWAT cars to park right outside their door. They won't pay attention to two unarmed guys strolling up the street."

"Obviously, you know much more about stupid than I do. Anyway, you think that it is wiser to walk out in plain view where all can see us, Remo, even though we have spent the past several years eliminating these cretins at Smith's command, to the point where many know us even when they have never before seen us? This is what you think? Because I want, Remo, to be certain that is what you think."

"Trust me," said Remo.

In Korean, the Master of Sinanju muttered an appeal to his ancestors to deliver him from insanity.

From the sidewalk as they neared the building, Remo spotted the dark eyes of an Arab Kilroy peering over the roof ledge. The black barrel of a gun poked up beside him.

It was true that the terrorist was watching the street but he was also keeping an eye on pedestrians, and when he spotted Remo and Chiun sauntering up the sidewalk, he let loose a stream of furious Arabic.

"Is this part of the plan, Remo?" Chiun asked when the terrorist on the roof opened fire.

Orange bursts blasted from the roof. Chunks of cement chipped from the sidewalk around Remo's feet.

"Okay, so they're even a little more trigger happy than I thought," Remo admitted as he slid around a stream of machine gun fire.

"Arabs are always trigger happy," Chiun said, kimono whirling to avoid whizzing bullets. "Their infants are given guns in the cradle." Beside him a tree trunk burst white chunks of pulp. Frightened birds took flight.

"Hey," Remo called up toward the roof. "Knock it off. I'm observing my holy month of Ring-a-Ding."

In reply, a bullet cracked the sidewalk, flipping a deadly three-inch-long shard of cement toward Remo's abdomen. Before the shard could puncture soft flesh, Remo's hand shot out. With a single fluid motion, he flicked the cement missile at the tip, slapped it into his palm and, with a little bounce, snapped it from his fingertips.

The triangular cement shard rocketed like a cannon-launched arrowhead up to the roofline. The terrorist's head snapped back and the gunfire abruptly stopped. The man sank to the roof, a chunk of cement buried between his eyes.

"Safe bet they know we're here now," Remo sighed.

They took but a single step toward the building when a noise of breaking glass sounded above their heads. A small, dark object dropped from a second-story window. It missed Remo and Chiun, bounced off the curb and rolled under a parked car. The ensuing explosion lifted the car in the air, flipping it over onto its roof. Shrapnel shards attacked buildings and parked cars across the street. Remo ducked to avoid the flaming hood. In the vacuum of unreal silence following the blast there rose the whoops of car alarms as far as a block away.

"See?" Remo said. "My plan was solid. If that had been our car, we'd be really inconvenienced right now."

Another grenade whistled out of the broken window. The Master of Sinanju plucked it from air like a piece of ripe fruit and sent it sailing back whence it came.

The explosion burst windows throughout the apartment building, sending glittering shards of glass to the street. Inside, men howled in pain while others barked orders in a tongue Remo did not know but recognized as Arabic.

"You go front, I'll go back," Remo said.

"Have a care, my son," Chiun cautioned.

The old Korean spun in a flurry of kimono hems, bounding up the front steps. One foot lashed out and the fortified door cracked in two, broken sections wiping out the pair of terrorists who were waiting in the foyer. Chiun flounced inside to the sound of automatic weapons fire.

As Chiun stormed the front, Remo headed for the back.

A locked steel door was the only entrance to the side alley but Remo sensed no explosives wired to the door and in a spray of mortar and falling bricks, he tore it from its hinges.

The door was not wired to explode because there were five men inside guarding it. Remo used the door to crush two against the wall of the basement hallway before they could even finger their triggers. The remaining three, seeing their comrades turned to mushy central masses possessed of human arms and legs, and seeing the figure of legend who had killed them, tossed down their guns and threw up their hands.

"We surrender!"

Remo cast a cold eye over the three cowering figures, men who would gleefully murder innocents in the name of their cause, now quivering before him.

"Which one of you is Mohammed?" Remo asked.

Three shaking hands were raised. "Him too," one of the terrorists said, pointing toward a mangled corpse.

"Okay, now we're getting somewhere," Remo said. "Now which one of you is Mustafa's brother?"

Two hands lowered.

"Mustafa who was busted before he could fly a plane into the White House in 2001?" Remo asked.

The terrorist had to think for a moment. "Did you say 2001?" he asked. Remo nodded. "Oh." The terrorist lowered his hand and shook his head.

None of these was the man he was after.

"I will let all of you live if just one of you knows the meaning of the word mercy," Remo said coldly.

The three startled terrorists huddled like game show contestants. When they had decided on an answer, their spokesman turned hopefully to Remo.

"It means 'thank you' in French."

Remo left the bodies near the alley door and headed for the basement stairs.

Halfway up the steps, another grenade bounced down toward him. "Hah!" a triumphant terrorist shouted down from the first floor landing. His cry of victory turned into a split second of horrified gagging as his tossed grenade was returned to his open mouth. Then his head was a gray and red balloon bursting against the hallway walls and Remo was racing up onto the first floor of the apartment building.

He met the Master of Sinanju in the hallway.

"Must you make a racket wherever you go?" Chiun complained. "Some of us are trying to work."

Remo glanced back toward the street entrance. Apartment doors were splintered open. Bodies and weapons of terrorists littered the hallway where Chiun had passed.

"I don't suppose you took the time to find out if any of them was the guy we're after," Remo said.

The old Korean fixed him with a withering eye. Wordlessly, the Master of Sinanju swept past his pupil toward the staircase. Remo bounded up after him.

The grenade that Chiun had tossed from the street had devastated two apartments. Small fires were growing larger, catching curtains and cheap furniture. A few bodies littered the apartment's floor. Remo sensed no life on this floor. The third floor was another story. Even from the stairway, he could hear the distinct sound of more than a dozen heartbeats.

"INS raid," Remo called up the stairs. "Toss down your guns and green cards and come out with your dishrags up."

Above, a voice whispered out of sight and was shushed by several angry growls.

"Ambush," Remo said softly.

"Yes," Chiun agreed, nodding. "And thoughtful is it of them to allow us to ambush them so easily."

Avoiding the stairs, the old Korean ducked into the ruined apartment. Dodging growing flames, the two Masters of Sinanju made for the shattered windows.

The ledge outside the windows was charred and missing bricks. Remo and Chiun sensed the weaknesses in the mortar and avoided those spots where bricks risked falling loose. Fingertips found holds in the grooves between bricks. With swift, certain moves, the two men scaled the sheer face of the building up to the third floor. They slipped through an open window at the end of the hallway.

Thirteen terrorists were pressed against the walls near the staircase. Thirteen gun barrels were directed at the stairwell. Necks craned as they tried to hear the first sounds of the intruders mounting the staircases.

"Do you hear anything?" one frightened terrorist asked. Sweat stained his underarms and covered his face. "Perhaps they are dead, praise Allah," another said.

"Boo," said Remo.

The terrorists jumped at the American's voice at their backs. Several squeezed triggers reflexively as they wheeled toward the strange voice. Bullets chewed through flesh. Unfortunately for the terrorists it was the wrong flesh, their own.

Terrorists shrieked and dropped to the hardwood floor, bellies filled with lead fired from the screaming barrels of their comrades' guns. When the panicked firing was over, only two men remained upright. Smoke curled from the spent barrels of their empty automatic weapons.

"Achmed Mohammed?" Remo asked.

Two frightened fingers pointed to the fourth floor. Their faces did not lie.

Remo slapped the butts of the guns, launching barrels into soft tissue beneath jaws and burying them deep in brains. The last two men joined their fellows amid the bloody ruins.

Remo and Chiun flew up the last flight of stairs.

Achmed Mohammed smelled the smoke from the burning lower floors. When the gunfire stopped abruptly, he was afraid that it could not be good news. Achmed Mohammed was too unlucky to ever be on the receiving end of good news.

A decade of captivity in an Iraqi weapons lab watching his family members slaughtered one by one had been bad enough but even the miracle of his eventual escape had been marred by his family's dark past.

Mustafa. Somehow it always came back to his idiot brother. After the 9/11 attacks on America, Mustafa had become a celebrity in the al-Khobar terrorist organization and for all the wrong reasons. The only hijacker to oversleep and miss his flight. The only man from that day to live to trial. The only 9/11 al-Khobar terrorist to be sent to an American prison. The shame of his brother reflected on Achmed. It was a disgrace he would have to overcome himself.

Achmed could not see in the dark, but he could feel his body shaking. He held the weapon tight in his hand and listened. Not a sound in the nearby room.

The smell of smoke grew stronger. In the distance he could hear the noise of approaching sirens.

This was not the end that was meant for Achmed. It was supposed to be his duty to erase the shame Mustafa had brought to his family, to al-Khobar, to their glorious religion of peace and love.

Achmed's mission was to strike a glorious blow for al-Khobar in the heart of America. There would be bodies, yes, for it was his duty to kill unbelievers, but the dead were of secondary importance. More significant was the symbolism of the target that had been selected.

The smoke was growing thick. There was a vent at his back that seemed to be carrying it directly up from the floors below. He held his breath, and when that did no good he pulled up his shirt and breathed through the cotton.

Still no noise outside the door.

Perhaps the danger had passed. Achmed had been alone upstairs when the commotion broke out. The moment he heard the first gunshot he had hidden himself away.

On hands and knees he crawled to the door. He drew it open a careful inch, allowing but a sliver of light to enter. Holding his breath, he pressed one eye and his gun barrel carefully to the crack.

Although he had not heard a noise in the outer room, someone had obviously entered, for the moment Achmed's face was firmly against the door crack the door suddenly burst open. Achmed was slammed hard in the face and he toppled backward, flopping into a pile of dirty laundry in the back of his closet hiding place. His gun went sailing.

He looked up, blood gushing from his shattered nose.

Framed in the door was a thin young American with an irritated look on his face.

"Achmed Mohammed?" Remo asked the cowering little fat man in the plaid shirt and jeans.

"Yes, yes. Please," Achmed cried, "do not kill me."

"This is your unlucky day," Remo said. "Because you get to live. For now." Kicking soiled underwear off Achmed's head, he grabbed the quivering terrorist by the ear and dragged him out into the room. "Where's your brother?"

"I do not know."

Remo shook Achmed by the ear while Achmed's toes were dangling six inches from the floor. He brought his lips very close to Achmed's tearing ear.

"You super sure about that?" Remo asked.

"For the love of all that is holy, yes. I do not know."

It was clear Achmed was telling the truth. Remo dropped the terrorist to the floor.

"What is this place?" Remo asked.

Achmed realized that the question was not directed to him but to another man in the room. When he saw the tiny Asian in the kimono over by the tables in the middle of the floor, Achmed suddenly understood precisely who he was dealing with and he let out a tiny squeak of sheer terror.

"Hold that thought," Remo said.

Chiun was examining a heap of material that was spread out across several tables.

The rest of the fourth floor appeared to be abandoned. Daily life had been lived on the floors below. This one loft was the center of planning for as-yet unrealized terrorist acts. Nearby Colorado Springs Airport was the base from which the attacks would be launched. On the tables at which Chiun stood were spread maps, brochures and diagrams.

There were plans to hijack commercial jets from Colorado Springs Airport and fly them into Disneyland and the Golden Gate Bridge. There were plans to hijack commercial jets from Colorado Springs Airport and fly them into the St. Louis Arch and Boulder Dam. There were plans to hijack commercial jets from Colorado Springs Airport and fly them into the Rock and Roll Hall of Fame and Seattle's Space Needle.

There was an aborted plan to hijack commercial jets from Colorado Springs Airport and fly them into the Grand Canyon. In the margin someone had doodled in Arabic: "Already hole. Need bigger planes? Pray question to Allah."

One plan had apparently gotten the blessing of the local al-Khobar franchise.

An entire table had been devoted to Mount Rushmore. There were photographs of the great monument taken from every imaginable angle on the ground, as well as many from above. There were pictures of some of the men Remo had encountered downstairs wearing Mount Rushmore sweatshirts while standing amid the pines beneath the great granite presidential faces in the Black Hills of South Dakota.

There were plane schedules and four recently purchased tickets. Remo noted the date was four days away.

Remo turned back to Achmed Mohammed, who was still cowering on the floor. Achmed winced.

"Want to play a quick round of kick the terrorist, Little Father?" Remo asked, eyes dead.

"No," Achmed shouted.

"I am not wearing the right shoes," Chiun said.

"I can help you find him," Achmed pleaded. "His lawyer called yesterday. She said he claimed to have a weapon. My brother is worse than an idiot, he is a dangerous idiot. And if he has some kind of weapon, he is even more dangerous. Please, I can help you. He trusts me. I will help you set a trap. I beg you, show mercy."

"What do you think, Little Father?" Remo asked. "Guy's willing to sell out his brother, but on the other hand, he apparently knows the definition of mercy. That puts him one up on everybody else around here."

Chiun shrugged bony shoulders. "He grovels now but given a chance he will stick a dagger in your back. It is their way. But if you want him, he is yours to take care of. I am not feeding or walking him."

The smoke was rising thick from the stairwell. Remo could hear the sirens from police and rescue vehicles in the street below. With locals muscling in on the scene, Smith could keep the FBI away for just so long.

"Okay, we got a deal," Remo said.

"Praise Allah," Achmed Mohammed sang.

"Yeah, well, you might just want to rethink that, Omar," Remo said. Afraid Mohammed's loose ear might come off, he dragged the terrorist out the door by his hair.

11

Hitchhiking was too dangerous. Mustafa had been lucky the first time but that luck would not hold. There were too many police on the roads in Colorado. Fortunately, the Almighty One was still on his side.

After the Wilcox family dropped him off in Kansas, Mustafa walked only a mile before he spied a little old lady struggling to carry groceries into her house from her car. He offered to help her cart her bags into her neat little ranch and she gladly accepted his assistance.

"Aren't you nice. It's so difficult to find people who are willing to help out others these days."

Mustafa learned that she was a widow, with a daughter who lived in Oregon but who rarely called.

"What do I owe you?" she asked, reaching an arthritic hand into her ragged purse.

Mustafa strangled the woman at her kitchen table and stole her car. With luck, the old infidel's body would not be discovered for days. By then New York City would be gone.

He had settled on New York while still in that insufferable

family's minivan. The Prophet had given him a choice of cities to destroy and he had decided that it would be best to revisit the scene of al-Khobar's greatest triumph.

Mustafa had gotten as far as Missouri, the old Mohammed family Koran on the front seat beside him, when a police car flew up behind him, lights flashing. For an instant, he panicked. His instinct was to try to outrun the cruiser but his foot along with the rest of his body was frozen in place.

In those terrified seconds of hesitation, the state police car flew right past him and raced down an off-ramp, disappearing from sight.

His fear, he knew, had saved him. However, he might not be so lucky next time. He was a fugitive in an unholy land. Already he had nearly been caught by the two American killers of legend. New York might not be as easy for him to enter as he had hoped.

Mustafa realized that if he was going to succeed in his great mission, he would need help. And what better help than family? His brother Achmed was the answer. While they might have had disagreements in the past, blood was important and he knew that he could count totally on his brother in this savage land.

At a roadside diner he tried to phone his brother. He had learned from Constance Arnold that his brother had come to America on what she called "another great mission" and she had given him Achmed's phone number. But when he called, Mustafa got only an automated message telling him that the number was currently out of service.

Desperate, unsure what to do next, Mustafa remembered another phone number Constance had given him after the Elite Incursion Martyrdom Brigade failed to liberate him eight months before. He had jotted it down inside his Koran. Mustafa cracked the book, found the number and stabbed it into the pay phone.

The male voice that answered spoke Arabic and offered no pleasantries. "Where are you?" He was cold and efficient. Mustafa had not realized the line his lawyer had given him was one that had been set up exclusively for his use. He told the forceful voice his location.

"Stay where you are," Alawi Sulayam commanded. "I will be there shortly." After he disconnected the call, Sulayam turned to his Iranian lieutenants with a smile on his face. "This Iraqi fool has turned himself in to us. Soon, we will have this magical weapon of his. And we will know what to do with it."

Smith had made arrangements for Remo to get a special cell phone, its number the same as that of Achmed Mohammed's number in Security, Colorado, so that if Mustafa tried calling his brother, the phone Remo carried would ring.

The first time the phone buzzed in Remo's pants pocket he thought Achmed was trying to steal his wallet so he slapped the terrorist in his broken nose.

"It is your phone," Achmed cried, his nose re-gushing blood.

"Oh. Yeah," Remo said, fishing out the phone. He tried to open it. He had seen people on TV open cell phones a million times. There was a little bit that looked like the bit that should snap open. He snapped it open. The phone stopped ringing. That was because it was in two pieces.

"Crap," said Remo.

"Dyou broke dyour phobe in happ," Achmed said. He had pulled a Kleenex apart and was stuffing the pieces up his nostrils to stanch the flow of blood.

"Keep talking and you're next, Abu Ben Bubbie," Remo said.

When he called Smith from a pay phone to see if Mustafa had tried to contact his brother, the CURE director said that it was he who had been testing Remo's phone.

"There was a problem transferring the line over after his brother's building burned down. Pick up another from the nearest electronics store immediately," Smith ordered. "I will reroute Achmed's number to it."

When that phone rang and Remo still could not open it, he told Achmed to go borrow a screwdriver from a hotdog vendor so that he could use it to jimmy open the side.

"Give me that, nitwit," Chiun said, impatiently snatching the cell phone from his pupil. "The device works, Emperor Smith," he said, answering the phone. "To ensure that it continues to do so, I will keep it."

Chiun hung up the phone and it disappeared inside the voluminous folds of his kimono.

"Showoff," Remo said. Pausing on the sidewalk, he sighed. "We can't keep wandering around hoping to get lucky. I guess we should find a hotel or something until Smitty gets a handle on Mustafa." He turned to Achmed. "You sure you don't know what this weapon of your brother's is?"

"Dno," Achmed said.

"That's getting real tired real fast," Remo said. Reaching out, he pinched the bridge of Achmed's nose between two fingers. There was a soft crack and a gush of blood that launched Kleenex fragments. Achmed didn't have time to howl in pain before he realized that the pain was gone. His nose felt as good as new.

"Thank you, blessed one," Achmed said.

"Only thank me on those days I might not kill you," Remo said, tossing the terrorist in the backseat of his car.

"He calls you blessed now, but that is only because you were nice to him this minute," Chiun confided to Remo as they drove. "The only thing shorter than an Arab's gratitude is his memory, unless they are talking about the Crusades, and even then they still get everything wrong. Trust me, Remo, two minutes from now he will be cursing you for not worshiping as he does as he tries to crash our car into the nearest synagogue. Do not give him the wheel."

"Not a problem, Little Father," Remo said. To Achmed he said, "Now this weapon your brother, Dumbo the Magnificent, has . . . where did he get it from?"

"A weapons lab in Iraq. They were secret, buried under the sand, but they were there."

"No kidding," Remo said. "I was killed in one of them once. So what is it? Pills, injections? Did he keister something into prison and now he's going to bran muffin us all to death?"

"I honestly do not know," Achmed said. "At the laboratories there was much testing of many different things. There was a breakthrough or so they said but I cared not. I only wanted to escape. Mustafa knew. He is the one who made the deal with the devil that bought our freedom. He is an idiot."

"So he made a deal with the devil but you're the one planning to fly a plane into Mount Rushmore," Remo said.

When he looked in the rearview mirror, Remo was surprised to see that Achmed was not shrinking from his tone. The terrorist was looking out the window.

Achmed was staring at the passing scenery without seeing it, a faraway look on his face. In the deep worry lines hidden in his five o'clock shadow was a glimmer of a fear greater than any Remo could inspire in Achmed Mohammed.

"There are devils greater than you know," Achmed said softly. And the brother of the twentieth hijacker fell silent.

Mustafa Mohammed took a little booth near the restrooms at the back of Bill's Diner.

The little old lady he had murdered had not had much money in her purse, so he ordered only one plate of french fries and two glasses of water. He picked at the fries as he watched the entrance.

Mustafa knew nothing of the Elite Incursion Martyrdom Brigade except that they had hoped to liberate him from prison. He wondered if they knew about the wonderful weapon in his possession. He tried to recall if he had told anyone about it.

Constance had told him that the first Martyrdom Brigade were Iranians and had come to rescue him from federal prison only in order to blacken the eye of the United States. Not even his fellow Iraqis in al-Khobar knew about the weapon until Mustafa had used it on the prison.

Mustafa was not certain if this great weapon in his possession would change the attitude of the Martyrdom Brigade. There was also a chance that he was being set up and it would be the FBI that would show up at Bill's Diner. That was why he had ordered two glasses of water. One was for drinking with his french fries, the other was insurance.

In his sweating hand, Mustafa gripped a small scrap of parchment torn from his Koran. If things got difficult he would drop the parchment in the clean glass, and as the bodies fell he would get up and walk out the door.

There was one waitress on duty, an American harlot in early middle age. A fat man worked at the counter grill. A handful of people sat in booths and on stools. Everyone seemed to know everyone else. They all smiled big toothy American smiles and talked about the weather and about friends and family members. Every once in a while the waitress would glance in his direction and narrow her eyes and Mustafa would hunch down in his booth and gobble a cold french fry. When the bell over the door finally tinkled, the plate of fries was nearly empty.

Not one man but three had come to collect Mustafa Mohammed. The leader was a little man with powerful shoulders and thick forearms. A huge man shadowed him.

Mustafa had never seen a human being so large. The bodyguard had to turn sideways to fit through the door. The top of his shaved head dinged the hanging light fixtures, and he had to tip his neck to avoid them.

The booths were too small for the big man to sit. As Alawi Sulayam and the second bodyguard slipped into Mustafa's booth, the giant remained standing. Alawi's seated companion would have looked big in other company, but in the shadow of the massive bodyguard he appeared small. The big man obviously did not see Mustafa as a threat. He did not even look down across his barrel chest at the seated Iraqi. He watched the parking lot through the window where Mustafa saw a fourth man waiting behind the wheel of a sedan.

"Where is the weapon?" the Iranian agent demanded by way of greeting.

Mustafa had been watching the big bodyguard and was taken aback by the man's directness. "Forgive me, friend, but that is not for you to know. You were sent to liberate me but I am free. Your mission has changed. I require your assistance in a new, great mission that will glorify Allah."

Alawi snickered. "I was sent to this wretched land to free you, yes. I have spent seven miserable months washing the poodles of rich Americans while we awaited our opportunity to do so. But if you think that I care anything about you, you are grossly mistaken. I care about disgracing America as your liberation would have done. But now you are free and my superiors want to know how. They want your weapon, Mustafa Mohammed, so that it can be duplicated and used worldwide against the infidels. They and I care nothing about assisting you in some fool scheme."

Mustafa gripped the parchment more tightly in his hand. He moved his leg and was comforted when his knee bumped the big Koran on the seat beside him.

"You do not know my mission or who has given it to me," Mustafa said, "for if you did, you would be bearing me out on your shoulders and singing his praises." He leaned across the table. "The Prophet himself has chosen me."

Alawi glanced at the man seated next to him. The Elite Incursion Martyrdom Brigade foot soldier did not take his eyes from Mustafa across the table. He was particularly interested in Mustafa's hand which had remained hidden from view since the three men entered the diner.

"Ah, yes, the Prophet," Alawi said. He shook his head. "They told me you were like an idiot child. Why did you agree to fly the plane into the White House if you had this great mission?"

"I thought the Prophet had abandoned me," Mustafa said. "But he came to visit me in my cell and told me now was the time. He is with me now again and will be with you if you but join me in our great cause."

Alawi shook his head. "Enough of this. You will tell us where the weapon is or you will die."

Mustafa shook his head. "I am sorry that you feel that way. It was a poor decision to contact you. When you see the Prophet in Paradise, tell him that I do not want you to be judged too harshly for your shortsightedness."

When he started to lift his hidden hand, Mustafa felt something press against his belly. Across the table, Alawi's bodyguard had lowered a shoulder and was leaning forward.

Alawi took a toothpick from a table dispenser and tore the wrapper off.

"That is a gun barrel," the Iranian said. Sticking the toothpick between his front teeth, he looked out the window at the small parking lot and sighed. "You think, fool, we do not know when someone is holding a weapon? Let us see it. Bring your hand to the table. Slowly."

Mustafa hesitated. The gun pressed deeper into his gut. Jaw clenching, he did as he was told.

Alawi was surprised to see that the Iraqi was not holding a gun. In fact, whatever he held in his hands was so small that none of it was visible. Mustafa's hand was clenched so tight his fingers were white.

"Is this the weapon?" Alawi asked.

Mustafa said nothing.

"Watch him closely," Alawi hissed to his man. "He is an Iraqi and therefore stupid by nature." The eyes of the guard with the gun did not waver, did not blink. They bored through Mustafa's skull. The gun under the table was pressed tight to Mustafa's abdomen.

Alawi licked his lips. With eager eyes, he stared at the clenched fist of Mustafa Mohammed.

"Put the back of your hand on the table," Alawi ordered. Mustafa did as he was instructed. "Now, listen to me, Mustafa Mohammed, for you do not want a bullet in your belly and I swear to Allah I will order you shot dead if you move suddenly. Carefully open your hand."

Very slowly, Mustafa unclenched his fingers. When he

saw the object in the twentieth hijacker's sweaty hand, Alawi raised a surprised eyebrow at the piece of old parchment.

Alawi could not make out the words written on it. The scrap of damp parchment had turned a bright blue.

Alawi scowled and shook his head. "You pitiful little fool. Take him," he ordered the man seated beside him.

The gun nudged deeper in Mustafa's belly and the would-be hijacker got to his feet, the poisoned parchment still in his open hand. He slowly lifted his hand, making no sudden movements, until it was just above the glass. Alawi did not seem to notice. A scrap of paper could do him no harm.

The movement of men seemed to have awakened the standing giant. Yawning a mouth like a cave, he glanced to his superior for instruction. Alawi muttered something soft.

The moment Alawi was not watching, Mustafa turned his hand over. The sweat had glued the blue parchment to his palm. Sipping a panicked breath, he flicked at it with his other hand and it fell into the glass and sank.

Alawi glanced from the counter where the waitress and two customers were looking in his direction. Alawi flashed them a reassuring smile before turning to Mustafa.

"What do you think you are doing?"

Mustafa was holding his breath and waiting for the men to collapse to the floor, skin blistering and bodies writhing in final agony. In the prison, the results had been instantaneous. This close, these men should have dropped the moment the parchment touched the water.

But something was wrong.

Alawi picked up Mustafa's glass. Bringing it to nose level, he peered at the scrap of blue-stained parchment. The piece of folded parchment had blossomed open. Alawi swished the water for a moment before putting the glass down.

"The mind of a child," he said. "Bring him."

Mustafa tried to flee but with one massive paw the giant

grabbed him by the back of the neck and lifted him in the air. Mustafa kicked madly and screamed as the big man carried him smoothly to the door. As they hustled along, Alawi took out his wallet and waved it over his head, careful to make certain no one got a good look at it.

"FBI," the Iranian announced. "Do not be alarmed."

Mustafa kicked over stools and grabbed at the door frame. "My Koran," he cried.

"It will not help you," Alawi hissed in Mustafa's ear. At the windows, the patrons and employees of Bill's Diner watched the huge man stuff the screaming terrorist in the backseat of a car. The other men piled in and the car quickly sped off.

"No surprise to me," the waitress griped. "I could've told you an hour ago he wasn't going to leave a tip."

Remo returned to the room he had rented in the Colorado Springs First Western Hotel to find Achmed whimpering under the desk and the Master of Sinanju sitting placidly in front of the television. It was late afternoon and the TV was blaring the final strains of the *Judge Ruth* theme song.

Remo placed the cardboard takeout containers on a table, noting the Achmed-shaped outline in the wall where Chiun had apparently hurled the terrorist. He saw the distinct shapes of arms and legs, as well as what looked like a little of Achmed's hair. The sheetrock had buckled and there was glass spread on the floor where pictures had shattered.

Achmed's wide eyes darted hopefully to Remo.

"Somebody talked during *Judge Ruth*," Remo said. "Naughty-naughty."

Chiun reached out and snapped off the television. "He lives," he said. "Which is more than he deserves. Be sure to tell Smith of my forbearance. I deserve a reward for the sacrifices I make for the Emperor's crown."

They ate rice and fish. Remo felt bad for Achmed cowering under the desk so he tossed him some bones.

"So what did Judge Ruth have on today?" Remo asked as

they ate. "I bet there was at least one case with two twenty-somethings who were living together, but aren't anymore, and the girl paid the rent and now she wants him to pay his share even though he wasn't on the lease. And I bet he coun-tersued for his videogame console but she left it out on the porch in the rain and it got stolen."

Chiun's eyes narrowed. "That is why my supper is cold. You were watching in the lobby."

"Just a lucky guess, Little Father," Remo said.

Chiun studied his pupil's face to detect a lie but seeing none turned his attention back to his rice.

"Judge Ruth performs a valuable service. Nothing else has stopped this so-called society of yours from collapsing around your ears. She is the lone voice of sanity crying out in the wilderness."

"Screaming out in the wilderness," Remo said. "She's got a voice that could peel paint."

"Master Nuk, while visiting the land of the Luzu in Africa, once said, 'In order to be heard when hyenas shriek, even the lion must roar.' America is filled with hyenas."

At mention of the Luzu tribe and Africa, Remo grunted and focused his attention on his cardboard rice container.

"I have seen Judge Ruth before," said a timid voice from the floor. Achmed was squatting amid his fish bones and looking fearfully at the two Masters of Sinanju. "She is very fair. She reminds me of a judge I knew in Iraq."

"Perhaps I misjudged this one, Remo," Chiun said.

"Yes, very fair. He ordered that my uncle's hands be cut off for stealing bread from a vendor's stall." Achmed nod-ded. "Most fair."

"See, Remo? Even he sees." As reward for taking his side against Remo, Chiun tossed Achmed some scraps.

An hour later, when dinner was finished and the televi-sion was turned to the evening news to see if there had been any new developments in the Mustafa Mohammed prison break story, Chiun's cell phone sang to life. At some point while Remo was out, the Master of Sinanju had programmed the phone to play the *Judge Ruth* theme music, a techno version of the *1812 Overture*.

Chiun answered the phone without speaking to Smith and handed it off to his pupil.

"It's getting more complicated," Smith said.

"Tell me about it. I've got the brother but he doesn't know anything but I'm keeping him around 'cause he's a dirtbag and he'll hand up his brother without even a second thought."

"I'll trust you on that one, Remo. The brother . . . Mustafa . . . has been spotted in Missouri. Five men of Middle Eastern appearance were seen at a diner. Four of them kidnapped the fifth. No one knows yet that it was Mustafa, not even the FBI. I will keep them away as long as I can. There is a flight leaving in twenty minutes. I've already booked you on it."

"Any idea who grabbed him?" Remo asked.

"Mark has been tracing activity all day," Smith said. "He says that the Elite Martyrdom Brigade has made an appearance. It might be them."

"That's the gang we met in New Mexico, right?" Remo said.

"Yes."

"Then we really do have problems because they're not Iraqis. Chiun said they were Iranians because they smelled different."

"Iranians," Smith said softly. "Is Chiun sure?"

"Smitty, he's the Master of Sinanju. His family was working for Iranians back when they were fighting Alexander the Great. If he says they're Iranians, they're Iranians."

"Then that is a complication."

"Looks that way."

"They're even more irresponsible and dangerous than the Iraqis."

"I call it dead even," Remo said. "And they both smell bad."

"Be on that plane. Find these people," Smith ordered.

Remo glanced at Achmed, sleeping under the desk amid

his fish bones. The terrorist was obviously dreaming of stomping the infidel and driving the Jews into the sea because he smiled amid his stubble and his feet made little kicking motions.

"The airline takes pets?" Remo asked.

12

For almost an hour the Tuesday Peace Brigade enjoyed protesting outside Berkwood Federal Penitentiary, but eventually the family and friends of murdered guards began drifting off to make funeral arrangements, and when the press was allowed inside the first ring of barbed-wire fences, taking their cameras with them, Loretta Sanders-Parker gave up and herded her people back aboard their battered school bus.

"What do we do now?" one disappointed member asked.

"It's a safe bet we're not getting Mustafa's weapon, whatever it was," Loretta groused. "It's in the hands of America's military-industrial complex by now. We'll have to go to the Rally for a Free Kabul without it."

"Not me," Sally McAvoy said. "I should really get back to my ditch. The president-select will probably get out of Washington and head to Texas while the rally is going on." She was thinking longingly of the cameras that followed the president's every movement. The press corps used to make a beeline for Sally whenever the president came to town, but for a long time now they mostly avoided Camp Craig. Still, a lone reporter might stop by, and Sally did not want to leave her ditch vacant too long lest upon her return she find Susan Sarandon roosting in it.

Steve Sanders-Parker suggested that before they took Sally back and headed to the rally they could first sneak onto Fort Devens in his native Massachusetts and, in the name of peace and love and harmony, cut the strings on the chutes of some paratroopers. They were on their way there when someone remembered that Fort Devens had closed during some budget cuts and, like many former military bases around the country, was being developed into strip malls and low income housing.

The despondent Tuesday Peace Brigade pulled their bus to the side of the road. Maps were broken out to try to find the nearest available Army base. Unfortunately they found that nearly all of them were closed.

"Darn those warmongers," Steve griped.

While the others pored over maps, Sally McAvoy stepped out into the cold January evening air.

They were parked on some desolate forgotten highway somewhere in Missouri.

A car raced past as Sally stepped to the ground. The bus rocked from the displaced air. Red taillights disappeared around a bend and were gone.

Through the bare winter trees Sally glimpsed the yellow lights of a few scattered houses. Another road must be near. Although she could not see it, the steady engine hum of speeding cars rose above the sighing branches of the dark woods.

Sally did not like cars very much. Cars needed oil to run, and American oil companies were responsible for enslaving the people of the Middle East, people who yearned only to shuck off the tyrannical yoke of the American oppressors. She was wondering how difficult it would be to blow up every oil production facility in the Middle East and return the peace-loving indigenous peoples to the harmony of perfect brotherhood they had enjoyed before the wicked days of Halliburton when she noticed something in the near woods.

The figure rose up out of the darkness. It seemed to float as it approached her. The robes that hung from the man—for she could begin to see the outlines of a male face—were dazzling white, and seemed to glow from within.

Sally did not run back inside the bus. Mouth agape, eyes wide open with wonder, she watched as the figure floated out of the woods and came to be before her.

"Sally McAvoy," the man said. He had a calm, soothing voice, like the narrator on a Chrysler commercial.

The man had a perfect brown beard, a swimmer's build and idealized white features. And Sally McAvoy, who had known all her life that she was special even if no one else ever noticed, knew who it was that stood before her.

"Here I am, Lord," she said, the Almighty's perfect voice still echoing in her ears. "Is it I, Lord?"

"I just said your name, didn't I?" said the figure that Sally was certain was her Lord and savior. "Listen, we don't have a lot of time. I've got a mission for you."

Sally could not contain her joy. She fell to her knees before the glowing figure. "I am yours to command, my Lord."

"Yeah, great. I need you to go get something for me."

And the Lord told her of a special book that had been left at a nearby small diner by a disciple who had failed to do as he had been commanded. The Lord gave her directions to the diner which was only about two miles away and told her exactly what she should say to get the book back.

"Do this and you will be special in my eyes, and sit at my right hand come Judgment Day."

"I always knew I would, Lord," Sally said.

"Of course you did. And for God's sake, whatever you do, don't get it wet."

Sally scrunched up her face, puzzled. "Don't you mean for your Father's sake, my Lord?"

"Don't get smart with me, lady," the Lord snapped. "Get that book. I will send thou . . . thee . . . on thy mission then."

There was no dazzling flash of light. Sally assumed that when the Lord vanished, he did so in a flash like a stage magician or maybe like on *Star Trek*. But one minute he was there, the next he was gone and she was blinking the remembered brightness from her overwhelmed retinas.

"Thy will be done," Sally McAvoy squealed.

She stumbled up the stairs and onto the bus.

Remo had wanted to check Achmed as carry-on luggage, but there was no time to stop by the pet store to get a big enough plastic dog kennel. As it was, he made the terrorist sit on one side of the aisle while he and the Master of Sinanju took their seats on the other.

Passing flight attendants made a show of not looking directly at Achmed even as they gave the terrorist surreptitious glances. Several men on the flight, including a burly former professional football player, were less subtle than the stewardesses. They kept sharp eyes trained on the twitchy, sweating Middle Eastern man.

"So what's the story with this brother of yours anyway?" Remo said across the aisle once they were in the air. "How does he manage to walk out of prison alive when everyone else drops dead?"

"It is the curse of my family," Achmed said. "We are all possessed of perfect health. For generations there is not one of us who has ever gotten a cold, cancer or any other illness that befalls normal men."

Remo glanced at the Master of Sinanju but Chiun's attention was directed out the window at the left wing of the plane, as if glaring alone could keep it from tearing off the fuselage. Remo turned his attention back to Achmed.

"That doesn't exactly sound like a curse to me."

"There were eighty-four of us brought to the lab for testing," Achmed said. "By the time they were finished with their experiments only two of us were left alive. It is a curse, brought down upon the descendants of a foolish man who thought to tame the devil."

Remo assumed as soon as he heard "devil" that Achmed would now lead them back to American imperialism, Exxon Mobil, and how extracting goo from the ground somehow justified blowing a building out from under an accountant who had just sat down with his morning bagel and cup of coffee.

"If you can't die," Remo said skeptically, "how is it there's only two of you that survived?"

"I never said we could not die, only that we can't become ill. We live long lives and die old men. And so has it been for more than a hundred years."

"Your whole family gets slaughtered by fellow Arabs but rather than take it out on them you're over here planning to blow up Mount Rushmore?"

"I am an instrument of Allah," Achmed said. "This life has brought me much suffering, yes, but one great act at its end can bring me eternal happiness."

"So as usual the good ol' U.S.A. is all that stands between you and your reward of seventy-two virgins," Remo said. "Dress it up in all the sad-sack schlubbery you want, it's still murdering innocents."

Achmed feared to respond as he had been trained and so he remained mute.

Remo sighed. "Okay, say I believe you about this whole perfect health thing. That would explain how your brother was able to keep this big mystery weapon of his for so long without it getting him sick. But if no one else at that prison got killed until now, it must have an on-off switch. He must have activated it somehow."

Achmed shrugged. "I know nothing about that."

Just to be sure, Remo reached across the aisle, pinched Achmed's ear and asked him again. Achmed shrieked no as he jumped out of his seat.

A screaming Arab in midair was all the men on the flight needed. Led by the retired linebacker, the men tackled Achmed where he stood rubbing his ear in the middle of the aisle. Through the grunts and punches, Remo turned to the

Master of Sinanju. Chiun had turned from the wing and, with a bored eye, was watching the floor show.

"Ever hear of people who can't get sick, Little Father? Besides us, I mean."

"Do not think yourself invincible," Chiun warned. "We get sick, my son. We who have bested armies have been felled by things too small for the eye to see."

"For the love of Allah, help me!" Achmed yelled.

"I think he's got a bomb in his shoe," Remo called over his shoulder to the linebacker.

Achmed's shoes were torn off and tossed away.

Chiun stroked his thread of beard thoughtfully. "There have been stories throughout our history of individuals who are impervious to illness. Most have been proven false."

"Most?"

"Oh, here and there a Master may have encountered men who seemed immortal. The last was recorded in the histories by Master Loo-Koo but we pay attention to very little that he had to say."

"Name rings a bell, but I can't remember offhand. Why's Loo-Koo on the shit list again?"

"The times in which he lived were uninteresting and so he was sometimes creative when it came time to record his histories in the Sacred Scrolls."

"Oh, yeah," Remo said. "Loo-Koo the Storyteller. Pupil of the Great Wang, who eventually succeeded Wang's apprentice Ung as Master. Lied a lot. I remember now."

Remo knew well of the Great Wang. Wang was discoverer of the Sun Source and the first Master of the new age, as well as the only Master in Sinanju's history thus far to be credited with the honorific "Great." Wang's accomplishments were the stuff of legend, and all these centuries later the masterhood of the Great Wang was the yardstick by which all succeeding Masters of Sinanju were measured. It must not have been easy for Loo-Koo to walk so soon in the shadow of the greatest of all Masters of Sinanju.

"Loo-Koo is last to claim to have met mortal men who had gained immortality," Chiun said. "Supposedly they could not get sick, as this Arab says of his clan, but according to Loo-Koo the men he encountered could also not be killed. This creature makes no such boast."

Chiun aimed his chin toward the aisle where a bloodied Achmed had curled into a fetal position.

"So we're in uncharted territory," Remo said.

"However unlikely that may seem, it is possible," Chiun admitted. "In five thousand years of Sinanju history never has there been a story of one man surviving a prison plague that has claimed the lives of all others."

"Lucky us. I wish these were Loo-Koo's uninteresting times, Little Father," Remo said. He folded his arms across his chest and closed his eyes. "I'm going to take a nap. Make sure they pick up all of Achmed's teeth when they're finished playing with him. He had four."

Bill's Diner had not seen such excitement since way back in the 1980s when Ricardo Montalban had stopped in to ask for directions.

"Course, that was different," Bill Carstow confided.

At this late hour the owner of Bill's was leaning at the far end of the counter talking to two of his regulars, men who had missed the earlier excitement.

"Montalban, he's a real class act. Signed all kinds of autographs and even posed for pictures." He stabbed a thumb to a photograph on the wall in which a much younger and thinner Bill Carstow stood with his arm around the *Fantasy Island* star. "He sure as hell wasn't dragged out of here kicking and screaming like some mental patient. You should've seen the stink this crazy guy put up today for the feds. Don't know what his major malfunction was."

"I'm not sure they were feds, Bill," Kimberly Tawl said.

Kimberly, who had been Mustafa Mohammed's waitress, was at the other end of the counter. She was counting bills from the register and making notes in a pad. She had convinced Bill to phone the local police about the incident with the strange men, but the cops had not yet arrived.

"Whichever, that crap's bad for business," Bill said.

Several high school boys entered the diner and Kimberly and Bill fell into their usual routines. Bill was grilling burgers in the back when the bell over the door tinkled and a middle-aged woman entered the diner. Kimberly was filling a dozen sugar dispensers which were lined up on the counter like little soldiers. She glanced up at the customer.

"Have a seat anywhere, I'll be with you in a sec."

"I'm not here to eat," the woman said. "I'm here to pick up a book my husband left here."

Kimberly put down the Domino's Sugar bag. She cast a skeptical eye over the frumpy woman in the saggy "There Is No War" sweatshirt.

"Your husband?" Kimberly asked.

Sally McAvoy was no good at subterfuge. If she had been on her own, she might have panicked and run out the door. But, like Joan of Arc before her, the Lord was on Sally McAvoy's side. Not only that, but He had told her just what to say if she was greeted with skepticism.

"Yes, he's my husband," Sally said, allowing an indignant edge in her tone. "Why? Because he's not Anglo? Is that why? You're saying that I should only love white men? Well, I love all men equally."

Kimberly shook her head. "I didn't mean—"

"No one means," Sally snapped. "You all just assume. The men who took him told me my husband left his book here and I'm supposed to get it so if you'd kindly put your racist assumptions aside, I'd like my husband's property, please." Sally folded her arms angrily across her chest.

The waitress, who was not paid enough to put up with abuse from customers or their indignant wives, grunted and went to the register. Reaching down, she lifted a very old book from a hidden shelf. "Your husband's a lousy tipper," Kimberly muttered as she passed the book to Sally.

Sally slapped greedy hands on the ancient Koran, but the waitress did not release it.

"Wait a minute," Kimberly said, her eyes narrowing. "Don't I know you?"

"Gimme!" Sally snarled. Like an angry child she yanked the book from Kimberly's hands.

"Jesus, lady, take a chill pill, why don't you?"

Sally slapped the weapon that was capable of wiping out an entire major metropolis to her chest and bared her teeth. "I'll let Him know you're a blasphemer," she said.

Koran in hand, she hustled back outside.

The Tuesday Peace Brigade bus was parked around the corner. Sally ran to it as if the Devil himself was nipping at her heels and stumbled up the stairs.

Steve Sanders-Parker was holding court from the driver's seat. "I think we should sneak onto the nearest army base and pour cement in those big boomy phallic things they have on tanks," he was saying to several of the others. "It was a blast when we did it last Easter."

"Drive," Sally commanded.

Her tone might have raised the hackles of another, less progressive man. But his wife had long ago removed the last pesky vestiges of spine and testosterone from Steve's body and so when the order came he dutifully snapped to. The doors shut and the bus lurched away from the curb.

"Is that what you made us detour here for?" Loretta Sanders-Parker asked as Sally stumbled past her up the aisle. Clearly Loretta was not pleased to have her mission derailed by anyone, even America's most famous anti-war activist.

"He told me," Sally chimed, scarcely noting the curious faces of the Peace Brigade members she passed. "I am the instrument through which He works His awesome will."

"Yeah, whatever," Loretta grunted.

At the back of the bus were the sleeping quarters. Sally bounced off seats and walls in her haste to get to the back. She drew a black curtain and was alone with the makeshift bunk beds and dirty sleeping bags.

"I got it," she sang softly.

And then she was not alone.

Although the bus doors were shut and the vehicle was moving, a figure stood in its midst.

The Lord's face shone bright, his robes were dazzling white. He gazed greedily at the book in her hands.

"Good girl."

She quickly tried to hand the book off to him but his hands seemed unable to accept it. The book passed sluggishly through the fingers. They were not entirely insubstantial but neither were they solid. It was as if she had tried to push the book through warm oatmeal.

"I can't take it," the Lord explained. "I can only guide others in its use. Direct action is against the rules."

In the ethereal glow of her Lord and savior, Sally finally noted the writing on the book's cover. "It's not a Christian Bible, Lord," she said, confused.

"You don't own the exclusive on me. Am I not everyone's savior? Now, take the book east."

Sally scrunched her face up in confusion. "You want me to spread the word from this book? But I don't even know the language. What is it?" She riffled through some pages, glancing at the Arabic text. "Is this Latin?"

"Unbelievable."

"What, O Lord?"

"Nothing. Just take it east. To a big city."

The most evil city on the east coast was the first to spring to mind. "Washington, Lord?"

"Hey, why not? I'll see you there."

"Wait, Lord. There was a blasphemer back at the diner. Her name tag said she was Kimberly." Sally smiled wetly, like an eager-to-please first grader.

"Here's an eleventh commandment for you," the Lord said. "Thou shalt not be a tattletale."

Thus did the Lord depart from the sight of Sally McAvoy, America's Joan of Arc.

13

On orders of their leader Alawi Sulayam, the Irani-
ans of the Elite Incursion Martyrdom Brigade 2 drove to a
seedy motel on the outskirts of town.

Alawi had rented the room before going to collect Mustafa
at Bill's Diner. One of his men who had been a mall security
guard in nearby St. Louis had confirmed the motel as an ideal
al-Khobar safe house. The motel had been family-owned for
decades and was managed by a derelict son who was interested in gambling and drink and supremely uninterested in
whatever his customers were up to in his rooms.

The Martyrdom Brigade had taken the last room in the
strip motel, around the corner from the office, near the Dump-
ster and the broken ice machine. When the car stopped amid
the potholes of the parking space in front of the warped motel
door, Mustafa Mohammed lunged for the car door.

"Quiet him," Sulayam commanded.

Mustafa was stilled by a revolver butt to the temple.

The men carried the unconscious twentieth hijacker
inside.

Mustafa was awakened from his untroubled slumber minutes later by several sharp slaps to his cheek. He found himself staring groggily into the cold eyes of Alawi Sulayam.

Alawi crouched so that the two men were at eye level. Mustafa realized that they had sat him in a chair. When he tried to move his hands and feet he could not. Clothesline bound him in place.

"Are you awake?" Alawi asked. "It is important that you be awake for this. Are you? Good."

The Iranian stood.

"The West is weak," Alawi said as he stripped off his jacket and rolled up his sleeves. "That has become a mantra for us in this holy war. So much so that I wonder sometimes if the truth of it is forgotten on both sides. They have had great successes against us. It is an undeniable fact that in these past several years we have bled much more than they. But in the end we will be victorious. Take, for example, their view of torture. They shut the lights off and leave prisoners in darkness for just a few days and it is condemned in their major newspapers. They dunk the heads of prisoners under water—men with information that would save American lives—and their own senators decry the practice."

Alawi Sulayam leaned forward, bringing his nose to Mustafa's. "We have, my friend, much more effective methods to extract information. They take far less time, they are far more successful, and they do not end up being criticized in our newspapers or by our politicians."

Alawi started simple. A pair of pliers was produced to pull out Mustafa's fingernails and toenails. The giant bodyguard stood in the corner of the room and watched gleefully as Alawi first harvested fingernails. He clapped happy hands which were as big as throw pillows and laughed loudly as each bloody nail was ripped loose.

A rubber ball was stuffed in Mustafa's mouth, tied in place with a pillowcase. Each time a nail was removed and the muffled screaming stopped, the gag was removed and Alawi asked Mustafa the same question.

"Where is the weapon?"

Mustafa broke on the third fingernail.

"The restaurant," he gasped. "I left it . . . I left it at the restaurant!"

"Where in the restaurant?"

"The table where I was sitting. It's in my Koran. On the seat, the seat."

Alawi nodded to one of his men. The young man, a college student from Saudi Arabia who had been studying comparative religion in New York when the Martyrdom Brigade call came, nodded in reply and slipped out of the hotel room.

"This will seem repetitive," Alawi said to Mustafa, "but you should understand that I am not being needlessly cruel. I merely need to be sure you are not lying to me and wasting my time."

The rest of Mustafa's nails were pulled out in order to confirm the terrorist's truthfulness.

It was slow and brutal and blood was dripping on the cheap motel carpeting but when he was finished Alawi was convinced that Mustafa was telling the truth about the location of the weapon. Next was fire. A cheap cigarette lighter, picked up at a 7-Eleven, was a most effective tool in the extraction of information.

Alawi worked the forearms and by the time the sickly sweet stink of burning human flesh filled the motel room, Mustafa had surrendered everything.

"What is in your Koran?" Alawi asked. "Is it a virus?"

"I do not know."

"Is it chemical?"

"I do not know."

It seemed so wild a story. Could it be possible that an old family Koran left in the little diner across town was the weapon his terror masters sought?

The Iranian needed to confirm the information. He did so

by tearing the wires from a table lamp and applying electric shocks to Mustafa's genitals and fillings.

"Call Ibrahim," Alawi barked to the waiting Martyrdom Brigade behemoth once he was satisfied that he had extracted the truth from the whimpering man before him. "Tell him that it is indeed the Koran we want. Retrieve it by any means."

The big man, Ayir, pulled out his cell phone and with huge fingers phoned Ibrahim, the man who had returned to the diner. When Ibrahim answered the phone, Ayir barely had time to pass on the information about the Koran before the young man was chattering urgently on the other end of the line.

"He says he could not get inside the restaurant," Ayir said. "He says that the police are there and that it looks as if the federal authorities have arrived as well."

"Give that to me."

As Ibrahim continued to babble, Alawi reached a hand for the phone. Before he could take it, a smile of anticipation broke wide on Ayir's face.

"That is not all, Alawi," Ayir said. His voice was so full of excitement, he practically sang the words. "The old Chinaman and the white. The devils who killed so many of our fellows, Alawi. I can finally deliver the justice to those that deserve it. They have just arrived as well."

Remo noted the young Arab on the street corner as he pulled into the space a block from Bill's Diner. The man was hunched away from Remo but his darting eyes betrayed fear and guilt. He looked like he was whispering into his elbow.

"That your brother?" Remo asked Achmed.

"No," squeaked a voice from the backseat.

"Didn't think so. Give me a minute, Little Father."

Leaving Chiun and Achmed in his rental car, Remo strolled up to Ibrahim.

Ibrahim had been momentarily turned away from Remo

and was startled when he turned back to find the young white man with the thick wrists standing directly behind him.

"Didn't your mullah tell you it's not polite to stare?" Remo said, flashing a disarming smile.

He took the young man by the elbow. From across the street it would have looked like a friendly gesture, an old acquaintance greeting a friend he had not seen in years. Ibrahim gasped at the white-hot pain in his elbow joint. It was as if his marrow had been replaced with molten lead. The cell phone he had been whispering into dropped from his hand and clattered to the sidewalk.

"I am so sick of these things," Remo said.

He picked up the cell phone. All he heard on the other end of the line was heavy breathing and soft Arabic chatter. Remo did not speak Arabic but fortunately he knew better than Arabic for he knew the universal language of peace and love and human understanding.

"America is number one. Accept no substitutes. Suck on that one, Saladin." He crushed the phone under his heel.

"You're one of the Iranian thugs, right?" Remo asked Ibrahim. Through gritted teeth and watering eyes, the young man nodded. Remo dragged him over to the rental car.

"Chiun, this guy Iranian?" Remo asked.

"He smells like one. The faint whiff of tahini, tabouleh and goat is unmistakable."

"Thank you," Remo said. He dragged Ibrahim back away from the car.

"All right. Now let's see if you're smarter than a fifth grader. You guys have Mustafa. Where is he?"

"Please, sir, I do not know the address."

"That's not a good start," Remo said.

"But they are coming. They are coming here. For you."

"Well, then, I don't need you, do I?"

"I can help. I will be your assistant. I never liked them anyway."

"Not big on loyalty, are we?" Remo said. "What a thought. I'll tell you what. I'll keep you in the maybe pile."

For Ibrahim, the maybe pile was a filthy tin trash can at the dark end of the nearest alley. Remo stuffed him in head first and folded the terrorist's legs in order to get the lid to fit. He was whistling "You're A Grand Old Flag" when he returned to the car.

"Who was that?" Achmed asked from the backseat. He was a little the worse for wear from his ordeal on the airplane. A great purple bruise adorned his forehead and his upper lip was split and bleeding.

"Some guy," Remo said. "Who knows? Who cares? Anyway, he didn't have your brother with him. He must've tracked him here though. Looks like everyone else has too."

It had not taken long after the initial call to police for Bill's Diner to become the center for the manhunt for Mustafa Mohammed. The street was filling up with police cars and the plain sedans of federal agents. Through the long windows at the diner's side, Remo could see many men inside. They appeared to be questioning an overweight man in a stained white T-shirt.

"He has escaped again," the Master of Sinanju said, noting the tension in the shoulders of the agents questioning the diner employee. "They do not know where he is."

"Mustafa can't have gotten too far," Remo said. "Maybe they missed something. Let's have a look-see."

When they reached for their door handles, Achmed grabbed for his as well. "Three's a crowd," Remo said. A knuckle to the side of the Iraqi's temple sent the terrorist to slumberland on the floor of the backseat.

On the sidewalk, Remo had a pang of conscience. "You think I should maybe crack a window, Little Father?"

"If you do not wish it to suffocate, yes," Chiun replied. "If you are asking if I care if it lives or dies, no. And neither should you." He turned on his heel and marched up the sidewalk.

Remo thought of Mount Rushmore and a planeful of dead Americans lying in burning ruins in the Black Hills of South

Dakota. It was bad enough that Achmed was Mustafa's brother but it was even worse that Achmed had his own plans to destroy Americans. Didn't any of these mutts ever go to law school or become accountants or even something useful? Was all they knew based upon killing innocent people?

"Screw him," Remo mumbled and left the windows rolled up tight and wished he could have stuffed socks in the air vents.

14

Of all the terrorists that Alawi Sulayam had encoun-
tered over the past several years, only one did not fear the
secret task force that America had been sending around the
world to tear up the organization by its roots.

Ayir was like a giddy child in the passenger seat of Sulayam's Toyota Maxima.

"They say the Chinaman is a little thing," the hulking
Ayir said. "As little as a little girl. And the American they
say is nothing special."

"Trust me," Alawi said. "He is special. He has killed hundreds of our brothers. That makes him very dangerous despite his outward appearance."

Ayir waved a huge, dismissive paw. "I cannot be fooled.
They are both little men. If they have killed as many as has
been claimed, it is only because they have not met me. Did
I tell you, Alawi, about the men who shot me in Iraq?"

Alawi tried to answer that, yes, he had heard the story
several times, but in all things Ayir was like an avalanche.
Once he was started, there was no stopping him.

"It was in Kuwait when the Americans attacked us for taking back the land that was ours. I was there from Iran helping my Islamic brothers. My men and I were at the zoo in Kuwait City when the Americans came. They were part of the most elite American forces. Five times they shot me." He held up a hand with fingers extended. They looked like five fat salamis swiped from a deli window. "I did not even know it until I was told later. I killed three of them with my hands." Ayir made little twisting motions, as if he were wringing water from an invisible dishrag.

Alawi had heard of Ayir's exploits. How the Americans had been forced to break into the Kuwait City zoo's supply sheds and employ netting that was ordinarily used to capture rhinos in order to snag the rampaging Ayir. He could not be housed with other prisoners so they kept him in the gorilla cage. There was no problem with the gorillas being upset since the hungry Iraqi army had already eaten most of the zoo's population. Not that in a fight between Ayir and a gorilla would Alawi have bet on the genuine ape.

Ayir's sheer brute strength was the main reason Alawi had recruited him when he was assembling the second Martyrdom Brigade to infiltrate America. If the day ever came that Alawi was forced to die for his cause, he would gladly do so. But until that day came, he would remain safe, protected by a mastodon with huge shoulders, massive fists, barrel chest and a brain the size of a thimble.

Alawi parked his car half a mile from the diner, well away from the police activity. It took many long minutes to get Ayir to understand his instructions. So eager was he to get out of the car, Alawi had to repeat them several times.

"Do you have your gun?" he asked.

"Yes, but I do not need it."

The big man was positively giddy. He clenched and unclenched his fists. If he had possessed a neck, he would have craned it to see if he could spy the two American agents down the road. As it was, his piggy eyes stared hopefully.

"Ayir, I know that you like to use your hands but do not hesitate to use your gun. Get inside the restaurant and get that Koran. That is all that is important. If you see those two, remove them. Do not search for a fight, especially once you have the Koran. Do you understand your orders?"

The giant nodded sharply. He nearly tore the handle off the door in his haste to get out. The car bounced at the shift of his great weight.

"May Allah be with you," Alawi said, knowing that he was probably sending his bodyguard on a suicide mission.

Ayir lumbered off down the street, a dancing bear in an ill-fitting suit.

Alawi drove around the block and parked one street over. He retrieved a small valise from the trunk and headed inside the nearest building, where he climbed five stories to the roof. He thought that he might have to kill a janitor to gain access, but the roof door swung open. Bill's Diner was half a block away, illuminated at this late hour by bright street-lights. The entire street was bathed in light.

From this vantage, Alawi had a perfect view. He removed a pair of powerful binoculars from the valise and trained them on the street below.

Ayir was marching toward the diner. Even from this distance and without binoculars, the man was an imposing mountain of flesh. Passersby who did not yield the sidewalk to him were launched from his path.

When he got to the police line, officers ordered him to stop. Alawi could not hear what they were saying but he saw their faces grow angry, saw them remove sidearms.

Guns popped. People screamed. Ayir did not slow down.

One policeman got in his way. The man became a bloody smear of broken arms and legs tossed through the wind-shield of a parked police car.

Ayir was an unstoppable force, charging headlong at the diner. And then the side door of the diner opened and two men came hopping lightly out to the pavement.

One was white and appeared to be young, the other an elderly Asian.

Ayir lowered his head and charged. From the roof, Alawi turned his binoculars to the two American killers.

Rather than run from the path of the rampaging beast, the two of them stood their ground. The old one's hands were tucked inside the sleeves of his kimono, the young one's arms were folded over his chest. He yawned.

At this distance, Alawi could not hear what anyone said.

Far away, on the ground, Ayir asked Remo, "Are you the one?"

"I am Ivan Skavinsky Skavar," Remo said. "I do so hope you are Abdul the Bulbul Emir, fatso."

From his rooftop, Alawi heard none of this. All his field of vision showed was a living wall of enraged Iranian giant who, more than ever now, Alawi knew was moments away from entering Islam's eternal paradise.

Ayir charged at Remo like a bull, head low, eyes fierce, hot air snorting from his nostrils.

At the last second, Remo skipped a little sidestep. Ayir, unable to stop his forward momentum, continued charging straight past Remo and smack into the side of Bill's Diner.

"Ole!" Remo called. He gave what he considered an impressive little matador flourish.

The Master of Sinanju flounced up beside his pupil.

"First was that other mangy thing, and now this blubbery bovine," Chiun said. "If you think I am letting you bring home another pet, think again."

"I don't think this one's a keeper, Little Father."

Ayir pulled himself up out of some bushes. There was a dent perfectly shaped to his skull in the metal side of the diner. He shook the cobwebs from his head.

Screaming rage, he charged Remo once more. This time Remo directed him into a telephone pole. Ayir's shoulder struck with such force that the streetlight atop the pole cracked and fell to the pavement.

"It is a good thing you do not want this one too," Chiun said. "With that other one I would only worry about getting fleas on the carpets. The food bills for this one would bankrupt us."

Ayir was drawn to the old Korean's singsong voice. His attention diverted momentarily from Remo, who was proving to be surprisingly agile, he decided to go after what appeared to be the less problematic target. Racing to the Master of Sinanju, the giant threw out both arms and encircled the tiny Asian in a crushing bearhug.

Fortunately there were no reporters present and the line of sight of the police on the scene was largely obscured by a panel truck parked at the side of the road.

For a moment Ayir was apparently squeezing the life out of the helpless little Asian; the next he was rising up into the air as if his four-hundred-pound frame had been pumped full of helium. For a split second, those few who had an unobstructed view saw something that was surely impossible. The huge man who, it would later be learned, had been shot twelve times and did not flinch, appeared to be balanced on the Asian's extended index finger.

Ayir, his shoes dangling off the ground, finally realized that for the first time in his life, brute strength might not win the day. He pulled his gun from his holster. In his big mitt it looked like a cheap child's toy. Before he could fire, his hand went numb, and the gun was gone.

Chiun, still balancing Ayir on one hand, bounced the pistol in his free hand.

"Always guns," he said to Remo, his face a mask of disgust. "They used to use rocks. Why ever did your people go over there and tell them that oil was valuable? Now these morons have the wealth to buy guns and nuclear booms and poisons that kill whole prisons."

He looked up at Ayir, still lofted overhead, and said, "Tsk-tsk. You should have tried hitting me with a rock, something your moron people know how to use. Instead, you fall back on the tools of those you claim to hate. Shame, young man, shame." He snapped the gun in half one-handed and tossed the useless weapon away.

"Quit playing with that one, Chiun. There's another one of these numbnuts up on the roof." Remo glanced over his shoulder. "Damn." The man with the binoculars was gone. "It might have been Mustafa. Hurry up, Little Father."

Remo was already racing down the street.

Ayir was trying to grab Chiun's head in his hands.

"You once were smart enough to use rocks in your hands," the old Asian said. "Now, they are all in your skulls."

A sharp push sent one fingernail through soft tissue, neatly severing spinal cord from brain. Ayir became a limp rag doll. Chiun dumped the big Arab to the ground and set off at a sprint after his pupil.

The bastard Iranian torturer had said he might have need to question Mustafa again and so the twentieth hijacker had been kept alive for now. Two Martyrdom Brigade soldiers had been left at the motel to watch over the whimpering terrorist. There were guns and explosives in the room as well. The men had been given instructions to kill Mustafa and themselves if the American authorities arrived.

Mustafa was certain that he would not make it out of the motel room alive. Briefly there had been talk of sneaking him across the border into Canada and then carting him back to Iran. There would be tests there, like those dark days back in Iraq. But then, as he had overheard, the two American agents had been spotted at the diner where Mustafa's Koran had been left and Mustafa's torturer had rushed to meet them.

Mustafa felt ill. He had thrown up on the front of his shirt. The vomit had turned cold. His hands and feet where his nails had been torn out had gone from twenty individual, screaming pains to four massive aches. He hardly felt the burned flesh of his forearms, so great was the pain in his extremities. And he was thirsty.

"Water," Mustafa croaked.

His guards ignored him. The two men sat on the edge of a bed, eyes glued to the cheap motel television. A caption on the screen read *Little Lovers*. The talk show episode was devoted to full-grown women who were having illicit affairs with midgets. Profanity and body parts were covered over for the more sensitive members of the home audience.

The two Martyrdom Brigade members leered at the pixilated cleavage.

"Water, please," Mustafa repeated.

"Shut up," one of the men snapped.

Mustafa's mouth was dry. His tongue felt swollen. He pleaded for water a few more times and the men watching the TV grew increasingly angry. When a commercial finally came on, one of the men stomped over to the bathroom.

Mustafa heard water running. A moment later, the man reappeared with a dirty glass in his hand. Rather than hold the glass to Mustafa's parched lips, he upended the glass over the twentieth hijacker's head.

Mustafa shivered as the water ran down his face and neck. He would have cursed his tormentors but he did not want to inspire them to anger.

And then the water reached Mustafa's prison-issued undershirt and a very strange thing happened.

On his way back to the television, the man who had poured the water over Mustafa's head tipped over. Mustafa thought the man had tripped but then the next man slipped off the edge of the bed and joined the first on the floor.

As Mustafa watched, the eyes of his captors bulged and bled. A red rash erupted on their skin. For a moment they tore at their own throats, and then their hands dropped lifeless to the floor. After that, the only movements from them were the feeble spastic kicks of dead limbs.

For a stunned moment, Mustafa had no idea what had happened. He thought that perhaps the Prophet had intervened to save him from his tormentors. But as the minutes went by and the mysterious figure did not materialize as he had in the past, Mustafa realized something else was at work.

The water that had been poured on him chilled his skin and he shivered. His clothes were soaked all the way down to his prison-issued undershirt, and suddenly he knew.

The T-shirt. He had wrapped his Koran in this very shirt for months, and had only unwrapped it and put the shirt on clean the previous morning. The shirt had somehow been blessed by contact with Mustafa's old family Koran. It must have absorbed some of the potent poison the book contained.

Mustafa bounced the chair to which he was bound into the corner of the room. It took several agonizing minutes, and with each loud thump he was afraid someone would come rolling through the front door.

Once he was positioned in the corner, Mustafa rocked forward onto his feet until he was planted flat-footed on the floor and the rear legs of the chair were sticking out in the air. With all his might he pushed back hard.

He had not expected the chair to shatter on the first try. The rear legs broke on impact with the floor and the chair fell against the wall. The back snapped off, Mustafa's head hit the wall, and when he woke up a few seconds later he was lying amid chair fragments and loose knots.

Mustafa shook off the chunks of chair. Despite his ordeal, he felt energized. He scurried to his feet. The pain from his missing toenails shot like blinding electricity up his legs. Gasping, he stumbled for the door. He peered outside. No one was there.

There was only one car parked near the motel room. Mustafa tested the lock with a key he had taken from one of the dead men inside. The door opened and he quickly loaded the car with weapons and explosives from the room.

As he drove past the motel office, he saw the manager through the window. The middle-aged man was sprawled across the counter, his skin blistering red.

Mustafa took a chance and hobbled inside. In a private bathroom he found Band-Aids, which he wrapped carefully around the wounds where his missing nails had been. The tighter he wrapped them, the better they felt.

There was nothing he could do for the burns on his arms. He rolled down his sleeves, put on his shoes and hobbled back out to the car.

His kidnappers had not blindfolded him and Mustafa had paid careful attention on his trip across town. He quickly found his way back to Bill's Diner.

It was nearing midnight when he returned. The streets were devoid of life but for the commotion around the diner. Police attention was focused on a large dead animal lying on the sidewalk. At first, Mustafa thought it was a rhinoceros. Then he saw the giant hands and realized that the animal was Ayir, Alawi Sulayam's huge and vicious bodyguard.

Before he reached the restaurant, Mustafa turned down a side street, pulled over and turned off the engine.

Mustafa had not seen the white or Asian anywhere but he was certain they must have been there. Ayir was the biggest man Mustafa had ever met and now he was dead. Surely, those two legendary murderers had killed him.

Mustafa gripped the steering wheel to stop his hands from shaking. The pain from his missing nails shot from his fingertips and he released the wheel as if shocked. And in the face of pain and failure and death at the hands of the wicked American agents, a great swelling pit of fear and despair welled up inside Mustafa Mohammed, the Prophet's chosen one. Had he come this far only to fail?

The metal door hung wide open. Even before they had gotten to the top of the staircase Remo had sensed there was no one on the roof.

"Whoever he was, he's gone," Remo said.

Chiun's button nose was turned to the air. He sniffed delicately, drawing in tiny sips of cool January air.

"Another Iranian," the Master of Sinanju announced.

"You're sure?"

The elderly Korean fixed his pupil with a withering glare.

"Okay, so you're sure. Well, this whole thing stinks. We don't have Mustafa. We don't have his weapon. All we've got is that monstrosity out there in the parking lot and a lot of corpses that smell of goat. This has not been a good day."

He sensed something small and electronic. Sitting on the roof ledge and aimed toward the door was a cell phone. Remo did not understand the annoying gadgets but this one was already open as if it had been left there in anticipation of his and Chiun's arrival on the roof.

"I think we're being recorded," Remo said. He smashed the phone and tossed it over the roof's edge. "God, how I hate those things."

There were scuffmarks on the roof where the man with the binoculars had stood. Near the footprints, Remo noticed a scrap of paper with writing on it tucked under the corner of a loose flap of rubber roofing material. Remo snapped it up.

"Why don't I think it's a love letter?"

The note was written in English. Remo assumed it was left for them. It read simply, "Everyone can be killed." He flipped it over. The back was blank. Shrugging, he passed the note over to Chiun and said, "Reads weird. You think maybe it's about the bomb or whatever it is Mustafa's got? Some kind of warning to infidel America or something?"

"No," the Master of Sinanju said, eyes narrowing. "This was left for us."

"Great. Nice to have a fan club." Remo glanced around the empty roof. "Well, whoever he was, he's gone. We'd better get back downstairs."

For a moment after Remo had ducked through the roof door the Master of Sinanju lagged behind. He frowned as he cast a lingering eye over the note one last time. The small scrap of paper disappeared up the voluminous sleeve of his kimono, then Chiun hustled out the door after his pupil.

For a few fearful moments Mustafa Mohammed considered leaving his book in the diner. But dedication to his cause soon returned and he shook his head firmly. No.

It was his destiny. The Prophet had selected him out of all for this great task. Even though Mustafa was no good at formulating plans and his escape from prison had taxed his brain power to its limits, the Prophet expected him to succeed.

But he needed a plan. In the backseat of his car were weapons and explosives. Perhaps he could drive the car into the side of the diner and then, in the confusion, slip inside and grab the book. He had guns. He could take the waitress hostage, steal a police car.

Yes, it would work. It must work.

Mustafa grabbed a gun from the backseat. He was about to turn the key in the ignition when a great coldness came over his hand and he saw with amazement what appeared to be a skeletal human hand materialize over his own.

Heart soaring, Mustafa spun to the passenger seat.

The Prophet sat beside him. It was the same man, Mustafa was certain, yet he looked different somehow. His skin was waxier, his face more sunken over protruding bone.

The Prophet shook his head. "I know what you're thinking and don't bother. The book isn't in there. You dropped the ball, so I've had to pass it on to someone else."

The words were like a physical blow, worse even than the torture Mustafa had endured in the seedy motel.

"But-but . . . this was my mission, Prophet."

"And you blew it. Listen, I can see you're upset. Think how I feel. I had such high hopes for you and you go off and disappoint me like this. But, hey, I'm not a bad guy. So this shouldn't be a total loss for me, why don't you go make yourself a martyr to whatever cause you're into?"

"I do all to praise Allah's name, Prophet."

"Yeah, that's right. You're one of those. Hard to keep all these sects straight sometimes."

"Prophet?" Mustafa asked, confusion on his face.

"Nothing. Forget it. So we're done. But that doesn't mean you can't go out and bravely blow yourself up on a bus or in a disco or something. Small scale's okay too. Not as good as a city, mind you, but not all bad either."

Mustafa's mind was swirling. In the darkest days in Berkwood Federal Penitentiary his worst assumption was that the Prophet had forgotten about him. He had never imagined that his destiny would be handed over to another.

As his limited brain tried to understand how one could be fired from one's destiny, two distinct things occurred to completely overtax Mustafa Mohammed's cognitive abilities.

The first was the head that suddenly appeared in the backseat of the car in front of his. Someone had apparently been taking a nap all this time and had just awakened. When the man turned groggily to get his bearings, Mustafa was astonished to see that it was his brother Achmed.

The second shock was the sudden appearance of two men, a young white and a very old Asian, coming around the corner.

Mustafa's brother had noticed the two men nearly simultaneous with spotting Mustafa in the neighboring car. To Mustafa's further bewilderment, his beloved brother winced, shrank in fear from the two men, and began pointing desperately at Mustafa's car.

"That is him, that is him," Achmed's muffled voice cried. When he glanced back at the near car once more, he squinted. For the first time he noticed the figure in the seat beside his brother. Achmed's eyes sprang wide with terror and he dropped from sight once more.

America's killers were already racing for Mustafa's parked car. The twentieth hijacker was paralyzed with fear and shock. Fortunately at this dark hour of fear and betrayal, Mustafa Mohammed was not alone.

"Those two," the figure in black said coolly. There was no fear on his sunken face, only intense irritation.

And then somehow he was out of the car and standing beside Mustafa's window.

"Get out of here. I'll handle these two pests."

Reason returned, fear propelled him, and Mustafa threw the car into gear. Smashing cars in front and behind, he crashed out of the space. He turned a wide arc, sideswiping a parked car across the street in a spray of metal sparks, then tore off down the road.

In the rearview mirror he saw the Prophet standing his ground in the dead center of the road, the shapes of the two infidel murderers growing larger even as he sped away.

15

Remo spied Achmed pointing frantically at the car
behind Remo's rental. There were two figures inside. When
he saw Mustafa Mohammed behind the wheel, Remo ignored the second man and tore off straight at Mustafa.

But then suddenly, somehow, the figure in the passenger
seat was outside the car. Remo had not heard the door close.

The man was tall and thin and looked to be one wheezing
breath away from a long slab nap at the mortuary.

"Get the cadaver, Chiun," Remo called back.

Remo knew that the Master of Sinanju could snag the
man in the black robes easily. Or should have been able to.

But in the moment it took him to shout to his teacher, the
man who had been beside Mustafa's car was suddenly no
longer standing passively at the roadside.

Remo had seen men who could move quickly before but
since becoming one with Sinanju, he understood there was
always a logic to all movement. Even those trained in the
deadliest of all the martial arts adhered to basic physical

rules. Sinanju masters moved with a fluidity that was the
logical extension of the human form trained to the pinnacle
of perfection and harnessing perfect, harmonious coordina-
tion of muscle, sinew, tendon and limb. But this new man
moved illogically.

From the side of the road he slid sideways into the street.
There was no hint of motion beneath his robes. Arms and
legs were there, but seemed uninterested in involving themselves in the activities of the rest of the body. Reality too
seemed to bend around the figure in black, so that before
Remo could blink amazement, the robed man was standing
in the middle of the road directly in Remo's path. Beyond
him were Mustafa's speeding taillights.

Fine. If that was how this weirdo wanted to play it, so be
it. Not only did Remo not slow, he picked up speed.

The guy was dirty. He was obviously in this with Mustafa.
Remo would tear through him to get to the twentieth hijacker, to get whatever deadly poison it was Mustafa had, to
put this whole episode behind him.

"Remo, stop!" Chiun cried.

Remo was stunned to hear a hint of fear in his teacher's
voice. When he glanced back, the worry was evident in the
deep furrows of the Master of Sinanju's parchment face.

"I got it, Little Fa. . . ."

A wave of cold rolled over Remo like a rush of freezing
water and the words died in his throat. His breath left his
lungs and he gasped. Still at a sprint, he turned to see the
figure before him had grown larger.

It was impossible, of course. Just an optical illusion.

As Remo ran toward him, the man in black spread his
arms wide and his draping robes became bat's wings. But
they seemed to grow even wider than his arms could stretch,
out well beyond his body, beyond all laws of nature that
Remo understood. It was almost as if they were elongating,
like sheets of stretched black rubber.

And then Remo was upon him, ready to deal a lethal blow.

But before Remo's blow could register, the figure moved again and it was once more not the movement of a normal mortal. Remo could not stop, could not slow. He could only continue to run into the swelling cloud of cold and black. And the blackness of the man's robes seemed to wrap around Remo like a cocoon of suffocating night, but darker than the darkest midnight, and for a moment Remo had a sensation of running in slow-motion through what felt like a waterfall of freezing cold molasses, his limbs suddenly sluggish and useless. And just as quickly he was collapsing out the other side, falling to the ground, sucking air and trying in his bewildered mind to understand how it was possible that he had just run straight through that which his senses had told him was a solid human being.

And then Remo heard a terrible cry of distress, as of one suffering the worst human torment. It was Chiun.

For an instant Remo feared for the safety of his teacher, but he soon found the Master of Sinanju's wail of concern was not for himself.

"Remo," Chiun cried again and ran up beside his pupil. Slender fingers searched for wounds.

"I'm okay, Little Father," Remo said. He was already on his feet, already moving. Mustafa's car was gone. Remo spun to the robed man.

Seeing that his pupil was safe, the Master of Sinanju too directed his attention to the figure in black.

"Oh, please," the figure said as the two Masters of Sinanju slowly circled him. "Get over it. The one thing on this earth that you two can't kill is me."

"Not according to your buddy's note on the roof," Remo said. " 'Everyone can be killed.' Let's test that theory."

Remo threw out a flat hand for the man's throat. It was a perfect move, delivered flawlessly. For an instant when he should have brushed flesh, Remo felt something that was nearly substantial but it was like catching smoke. His hand numbed as it flashed through the neck and came cleanly out the other side. The figure in black merely smiled placidly at the killing blow and nodded.

"Nice moves, son of Wang. Oh, yes, you needn't look surprised. I know you. Both of you."

Remo shot a glance at the Master of Sinanju. Chiun was behind the strange man. The old Korean shook his head.

"Doubtful," Remo said.

"Let's see. I know you visit a grave that's marked with your name. A grave that is a lie where another sleeps in moist earth on a bed of roots and worms."

To Remo it felt as if a cold fist had enveloped his heart. He scarcely noticed the sandalled foot that the Master of Sinanju launched into the tall man's back. There should have been the snap of brittle bone and a body folding in half from collapsing vertebrae. Instead, the man turned calmly, offering Chiun a lugubrious frown.

"Eiichi Sumita," the man in black said.

"What?" Remo asked.

"Silence," the Master of Sinanju hissed, a look of fresh worry on his weathered face.

"It was his first kill," the robed figure said over his shoulder to Remo. His dead man's eyes never left the hot gaze of the Master of Sinanju. "A Japanese soldier who was unlucky enough to find his way into your village. Not that I'm complaining, mind you. I take what I can get from you two. I'm sure there are those who've thought that because of your body count the two of you are splatter-happy. But I know the truth. Because of your actions throughout the years you've prevented the deaths of millions. Billions even, considering those times you saved the world. You can understand why I'm not too thrilled with either of you."

Remo sent multiple blows, fist and heel, into the back of the robed man's skull. Every time was something almost like an impact, followed by the same biting cold. Across from his pupil, the Master of Sinanju had stopped fighting. The old Korean's hands were tucked deep inside the sleeves of his kimono as he contemplated the figure before him.

"The old one knows," the robed creature said. "No sense fighting. You can't fight Death." He turned to Remo, flashing a smile that split his face into two ugly hemispheres.

For a brief instant, another image seemed to be super-imposed over the tall man's face, like the double exposure on an old roll of film. A grinning white skull with long yellow teeth and barren eye sockets. In the moment it took Remo to blink, the chilling image was gone.

Any hopes Remo had that he had imagined the skull were dashed when he saw the look of bewilderment on the face of the Master of Sinanju. Chiun had seen it too.

"I don't care about the souls of the dead, mind you," the man continued, with the wave of a hand, as if unaware of the grotesque mask his face had briefly become. "Whatever it is that animates them or comes after they breathe their last I leave to the philosophers. I only care about gathering corpses. The rotting harvest is the thrill for me. And you two have been mucking up the works for me for years now."

"Chiun?" Remo asked.

But the Master of Sinanju remained silent, the leather mask of his face now betraying no emotion.

The robed figure turned full attention to Remo. "You know, you're the one who should be ashamed most of all. Passing off a perfectly good grave to someone else." He leaned in close, a cloud of foul breath passing between desiccated lips. "Do you even know his name?" The skull-face flashed again, grinning broadly. "Because I do."

One last time Remo sent a fist flying, this one aimed dead center at the bleached skull, a blow of such precise ferocity that it could shatter bone and turn brain into gray puree. But at the point when bone should have snapped and grinning face should have collapsed, the man abruptly vanished. Skull, robes and all were swallowed up by the chill January night, as if he had never existed.

Remo found his hand flying through empty air. In his younger years, the momentum alone would have torn ligaments and tendons. As it was, he barely caught his movement in time. Twirling on the ball of one foot to safely release the energy, Remo spun to a dumbfounded stop before his teacher.

High above, a pair of shrieking crows took flight from the telephone wires where they had been perched. Remo noted the big black birds for the first time as they too vanished into the night.

"What the hell was that?" Remo demanded.

Chiun stood quietly in the street, hands clasping opposing wrists in the sleeves of his kimono, a stone statue with expressionless countenance. When he spoke, the Master of Sinanju's voice was lifeless.

"It is the end of our association with Smith, the madman," Chiun intoned. "We are leaving America forever."

The rattling old bus scarcely slowed for traffic lights and stop signs in its haste to reach the highway. The black strip of the interstate carried them far from the Missouri diner where the Lord himself had guided Sally McAvoy on a sacred, albeit puzzling, mission. Unbeknownst to Sally or her comrades, the weapon that could murder millions was stashed away in a little cupboard, and oblivious to the great killing instrument in their midst, the Tuesday Peace Brigade sped quietly into Ohio in the dead of night without incident.

The curtain was drawn in the back of the bus. Soft snores mingled with the sound of the engine and the gentle hum of tires on asphalt. Every now and then Loretta Sanders-Parker spoke in her sleep, berating God for sending His only begotten son to talk to someone other than her.

Sally McAvoy was too excited to sleep. She sat alone in the little kitchen compartment and with glassy eyes watched the highway lights go by.

Thus it was that Sally McAvoy became aware that her Lord was once more before her. The figure in dazzling white glowed with spectral energy.

"Lord," Sally said, bowing her head, "we have traveled far and fast. We should be in Washington tomorrow."

The Lord seemed a little more agitated than He had the first two times He had manifested Himself to her.

"Great," He said. "But we're going to have trouble. Someone is going to try to stop you from glorifying my name."

"The U.S. government?" Sally asked.

Sally McAvoy blamed the U.S. government if the tire on her hybrid Prius went flat or if her morning paper was damp or if she got to the movies late and there was a fat man sitting in her favorite aisle seat. She was positively delighted when the Lord told her that this time, for the first time, she was actually right.

"They've got two guys coming after you. You need to do something to slow them down. Just a little thing."

"I am yours to command, Lord."

"Great," the Lord said. His perfect, slender white fingers drummed the kitchenette table anxiously, yet made no sound. "Get some picks and shovels."

"What do you mean we're leaving?"

"I mean that we are leaving," the Master of Sinanju said, as if that settled the matter. There was a look of grim determination on his face. Turning on one sandalled heel, he marched back to their car.

"I'm not leaving," Remo said.

"Yes, you are."

"Like hell. And you're not either. We can beat this whatever-it-is, Chiun. Did you see the look on Achmed's face? Whoever this Johnny Cash wannabe was, Achmed recognized him. We'll find out what it is from him and we'll clean his clock like we always do."

But when Remo rounded his rental car to ask Achmed who the strange disappearing figure in the black robes was, he found the rear door hanging open wide. Achmed Mohammed was nowhere to be found.

"Dammit, he got away. Everybody's skipping on us."

"It no longer matters," Chiun said. "We are leaving."

"Stop saying that," Remo snapped.

"Stop being pigheaded," Chiun snapped back. "This creature has never been encountered in five thousand years of Sinanju history. I will not march headlong into battle with a thing unknown. We retreat now to fight later."

"I don't think this guy is any great shakes, Little Father. Yeah, we can't hit him, but it's pretty obvious that he can't hurt us either."

"Oh? This is obvious?" Chiun's hands appeared from his sleeves, waving wildly in the air above his head. The shouting on the street below turned a few lights on in the apartments high above. "You—you, Remo Williams—are now telling me obvious things that I, lowly Reigning Master Emeritus of the House of Sinanju, your father and teacher, have somehow missed in my dotage. Explain, Remo, this obvious thing missed by your aged Master." Arms folded sharply across his narrow chest.

Remo hesitated. "Well if he could have killed us, don't you think he would have?"

"You say it is obvious but now you ask it like a timid child. And my answer is, no, I do not know that and neither do you. The only obvious thing here is that we have encountered something that no Master before us has ever recorded in our histories and that is enough cause for us to leave."

"He mentioned the Great Wang. Maybe Wang met with him before."

"He called us sons of Wang and, as Masters to follow the greatest Sinanju Master, we are all his sons. But in all his long masterhood, Wang recorded nothing about a creature such as this one. As sons of Wang we must all be students of Wang so you should know this."

Chiun was right. Like all Masters who had come before him since the time of Wang, Remo had been forced to study the exploits of the greatest of all Masters of Sinanju. He racked his brain but could come up with nothing like this in the long histories recorded by the Great Wang.

"Okay, so this is new," Remo said. "Better to blaze a trail than follow one."

Chiun had been getting in the car. He wheeled on his pupil, hazel eyes like fire. "Who told you such nonsense? Who? Those wimple wearers who had you for the first eighteen years of your life? O, would that I could reach into your brain and extract all the foolishness those dowagers planted in your skull. Since they taught you everything wrong as a child, it is up to me yet again to teach you in adulthood that which you should have learned since before you could walk. It is always preferable to follow a trail since the road has been tested and smoothed beneath your sandals. Blaze a trail only when absolutely necessary, for it could lead you off the side of a mountain. But I see that you would gladly march off a cliff. Bah! You are uneducable."

Chiun pulled the hems of his kimono tight and hopped in the car, slamming the door. Remo shut Achmed's open door and climbed behind the wheel.

For a moment Remo sat there, not turning on the engine. Lights clicked back off in the apartments around them.

"Little Father," Remo said softly, "that Japanese soldier he mentioned. The first man you killed. And my grave in Newark. How could he know those things?"

"I do not know. Which is why we are leaving."

"There was also something weird about his face. And he had that black robe and that hood. He almost looked like—"

Chiun tapped his long nails on the dashboard. "Drive," he commanded.

Remo did as he was told. There was still commotion on the main drag. Down the block, men fussed around the massive body of Ayir Ali. Remo turned back onto the main road and headed away from Bill's Diner.

Briefly Remo wondered if one of the last images he would see before abandoning his native land forever would not be the flag or an apple pie or the Statue of Liberty raising her torch for freedom, but a skull face grinning from within a shroud of midnight-black robes.

16

The emergency meeting was called in the Pentagon War Room in the dead of night. The directors of CIA and FBI were present along with the military's Joint Chiefs of Staff. A classified report from the Centers for Disease Control and Prevention was passed out to each man as he entered the room. The information had been digested and the room now buzzed with anxious chatter.

So troubled were they by the ramifications of the report, no one present took note of the unassuming young man who had entered the room last and taken a seat among the lowly assistants and scientific experts, far away from the big table.

When someone offered him a copy of the report, Mark Howard took it but did not even glance at it. He did not need to read the report since he had seen it before anyone else in this room. He was here now only to see if there was anything not in the written reports, any small scrap of information overlooked that might help catch Mustafa Mohammed and his doomsday weapon before it was too late.

The chattering continued for several minutes. All talk abruptly ceased when the president of the United States entered the room, accompanied by the vice president and the director of the Department of Homeland Security. Men shot to their feet.

"Let's make this fast," the president said to those assembled. "What have we got?"

"Mr. President," the FBI director said, "as you know, Mustafa Mohammed escaped from federal custody yesterday. Until now it was unknown if he alone managed to kill everyone at the facility where he was detained or if he had the ability to duplicate that act, perhaps on a larger scale. I am afraid, sir, that the answer to both questions is yes."

"How?" the president demanded.

"He apparently had the means to escape all along," the FBI director said. "Mohammed was allowed to take his Koran with him into prison. I am informed that it was checked several times and cleared for the prisoner's use."

"I don't understand," the president said. "What does his Koran have to do with this?"

The chief executive was quickly briefed about the Koran page that had been found floating in Mustafa's toilet and how the Koran itself was the only item missing from the cell.

In the back of the room, Mark Howard could have mentioned that Dr. Harold W. Smith, toiling in silent constant anonymity in his office in Folcroft Sanitarium, had been studying the photographs of Mustafa's cell taken over the course of the terrorist's months of incarceration. Mark could have told them that it was Dr. Smith who noticed that the only thing missing in the photos taken after his escape was Mustafa's Koran, and that Smith had, through circuitous means, fast-tracked the analysis of the Koran page that had been discovered in Mustafa's toilet so that now everyone knew the true problem they were dealing with. All of this Mark Howard could have mentioned but instead he stayed at the back of the room, out of the limelight, listening, hoping to hear something he didn't already know.

A CDC scientist was introduced.

"We haven't been able to identify the virus that's contained in the pages of the Koran," the scientist said. He was a young man, with thinning hair and a suit jacket that did not match his trousers. He was obviously nervous to be the center of attention, particularly in a group as distinguished and powerful as this one.

"It's a virus?" the Homeland Security director asked, glancing at the other cabinet officers present. "Have we finally confirmed that?"

"Yes, sir," the CDC scientist said. He did not take offense at the Homeland Security head's use of the word "finally," as if the CDC had been working for months on this problem and had not had it dumped in their laps a mere six hours before. He expected such impatience from non-scientists who wanted all of their answers last week. Besides, the CDC man knew the danger this virus represented and that petty squabbling was useless in the face of the potential loss of millions of lives. "It is a virus. Although what it is exactly we don't yet know. It is nothing we have ever encountered before. We have, for simplicity's sake, been calling it either Virus X or supervirus."

"I thought a virus had to be passed from person to person," the president said. "How could it have gone through the prison population so quickly?"

The CDC scientist pushed back his thinning hair. This was where it got tricky. He was used to dealing with fellow scientists, not laymen.

"A virus is simply a submicroscopic infective agent," he explained. "It is capable of growth and multiplication, infecting individual living cells. What we are dealing with here is a virus capable of rapid localized mutation but which has been married to at least two chemical processes. The first was the one that has kept it dormant. At some point the book was bombarded on the submicroscopic level. A chemical agent was used to bind Virus X, the biological agent, to the page, keeping it in stasis."

"Like a freezer," the vice president said.

The CDC scientist seemed uncomfortable with the analogy.

"In a sense. But the freezing process itself can be harmful on the molecular level. The supervirus has not been harmed in the least. There is no evidence that it lost any potency during dormancy. No, this is more like a perfect vacuum has been created around each molecule, locking them safely in perfect suspension until release. And the reactive agent, water, is brilliant. Dangerous, but brilliant."

The president pursed his lips, irritated that anyone would characterize something so deadly as "brilliant." "Okay, so what's the second chemical process?" he asked.

"The delivery system. It is similar to how gasses dissipate in the air. In fact, it essentially is a gas. Once released from stasis by H_2O, the biological agent remains married to the chemical agent and is carried until it reaches a host. It then infects person to person, multiplying as it goes along just like a regular virus, only at a greatly accelerated rate."

"So the entire world is in danger?"

"Fortunately, no," the CDC scientist said. "Not unless there's another source of the virus. The process itself has a weakening effect on the supervirus. It loses potency the farther it travels from the point of initial infection. That's why it was contained in the prison. There you had a small localized community, isolated from the general population. Even if Virus X reached beyond the prison—and we continue to test the surrounding terrain—it found no hosts and so it quickly died out. Autopsies of the prison victims have found only dead virus. After just one day we have determined that the prison is no longer hot."

"There has been, Mr. President, another incident," the FBI director said. "This one at a motel in Missouri. Only five people dead, the manager, a couple in one of the rooms, and a pair of al-Khobar terrorists. Blood was found at the scene, and it's being DNA tested to see if it matches Mohammed's.

So far no trace of parchment from Mohammed's Koran has been found in or around the motel."

"But a piece of parchment was found at the diner where suspected al-Khobar agents grabbed Mohammed," the CIA director interjected. "For some reason, despite the fact that it was found in a glass of water, no one was harmed." All eyes turned to the CDC man for an explanation. The scientist shifted uncomfortably at the renewed attention, pushing at the strings of hair on his balding pate. In the back of the room Mark Howard felt a twinge of sympathy.

"We're still analyzing the piece of parchment found in the diner," the CDC man said. "It's possible that it was not infected with the virus. Maybe only some of the pages of the book were. Unfortunately we can only know that when we can put the whole book under a microscope. Which we'll do so as soon as you deliver it to us."

A few more questions were asked, but it soon became clear that there was nothing more that the scientist could offer without Mustafa Mohammed's Koran in hand. The CDC scientist was nodded from the room.

"What's the latest on the manhunt?" the vice president demanded once the CDC man was gone.

"It's only a matter of time," the FBI director said. "We've set up a hotline and we're being flooded with tips. We're following up on the best ones. We will get him, sir."

"We might not have time," the president said. "He only has to drop it in a puddle of water to release all this so-called supervirus, correct?"

"Yes, sir."

"He could do that anywhere."

"Yes, sir, he could," the FBI director said, "but so far he has exercised restraint. Just one page in the prison, one small scrap at the diner. We suspect he is keeping his powder dry, so to speak. It is likely that he's after a larger target."

"He escaped in Colorado and was last seen in Missouri," the CIA director interjected, "so we figure he's heading east. It's doubtful he'd double back or turn north or south."

"Unless he's trying to evade capture," the president suggested.

"We think, Mr. President, that that's unlikely. Al-Khobar is singleminded. They tried to bring down the Twin Towers a decade before they finally succeeded. They have always had two preferred targets. We think that he is most likely heading for Washington or New York City."

The FBI director nodded agreement, his face and voice becoming somber. "You're going to have to get out of Washington, Mr. President."

The president's face soured.

"Just until we capture Mustafa and his book, sir," the Homeland Security director quickly added.

"And what if you don't capture him?" the president asked. "He's been pretty lucky so far. What if he manages to slip past us and uses that thing?"

"Lights," the CIA director called.

The room lights dimmed and the big panel maps on the walls lit up. Generally the world was spread out across the screens, but this day Asia, Europe, Africa, Australia and North and South America had been replaced with new images. On each of the big screens were computerized pictures of a major city in the eastern United States. Boston, Philadelphia and other potential targets were off to the sides. The two central maps were close-ups of New York City and Washington, D.C.

"In this projection, sir, we assume Manhattan is the primary target," the CIA director said. "For this demonstration, Mohammed has reached Central Park."

He nodded to a soldier at a console. The young officer tapped a few commands into a keyboard.

On the New York map, a red dot appeared dead center in the green rectangle at the heart of Manhattan. It was small at first, barely visible. It quickly grew, spilling out of the box that was Central Park. The expanding dot became a crimson circle that in seconds had extended across Park Avenue in one direction and threatened Broadway in the other.

"We've sped this up, as you can see, sir," the CIA director said. "Right now we're at five minutes."

A digital timer in the lower right of the screen kept track of elapsed time. The dot quickly expanded, growing to an oval shape as it extended beyond the island.

"We can't be sure of wind currents," the FBI head said. "A strong wind could take it up to Yonkers or down to Jersey City. For the purpose of this demonstration, we've assumed winds from the west. Manhattan, as you can see, sir, would now be gone."

Twenty seconds longer and the red oval had stretched into a larger blob that reached the Hudson River to the west and was rolling into Queens to the east. The digital timer read thirteen minutes.

"You can see that the cloud is weakening. See the pinkishness around the edges? As CDC has indicated, it will lose potency as it travels but it will still remain deadly. Red deaths are virtually instantaneous but even those hit in the pink zone will die lingering, agonizing deaths."

The blob was stretching from its red center out to a half-dozen elongated pinkish points, blunted on the ends. A rounded tip extended far onto Long Island.

"Twenty-five minutes," the FBI director said. "The only way off Long Island now would be by boat. Drive into the cloud and you are dead. Wait and you might be dead anyway. Second scenario," he called to the soldier at the console.

A red dot appeared on the map of Washington. The McMillan Reservoir near Howard University had been chosen as ground zero.

"Mr. President, the initial attack doesn't have to come from a well-known location," explained the Homeland Security chief, who had chosen the reservoir to illustrate his point. "Unlike a conventional bomb or a 9/11-style attack, he could do this at a distance, fly under the radar if you will."

It took only minutes for the red cloud to extend down

from the reservoir to the tourist section of the city. The White House was quickly bathed in red, and the moving blob inexorably crossed the Potomac into Arlington and Alexandria.

"As you can see, sir, D.C. is not safe. We have no way of knowing for sure the potency of the supervirus. The good news is that the virus dies quickly so you would not have to stay away long."

The president leaned back in his chair. He had remained active in late middle age, and was still in excellent shape for a man in his sixties. Still, despite his best efforts, the years were finally catching up with him. Some of his predecessors in the Oval Office had been able to coast through their terms, pushing history aside, kicking the can down the road. But not only had history not waited for him, it had been relentless, crashing in successive waves throughout his two terms in Washington. The strain had taken its toll. The president was ready to leave. He felt tired. But here was another crisis, delivered to his doorstep.

The president sighed. "How do we issue a warning to the public about this?" he asked those assembled. "There's a maniac on the loose with the ability to kill millions who may or may not be coming to their city?"

"We've discussed this and we don't think there's any way you can issue any kind of warning, sir," the Homeland Security director said. "We don't know for sure that he's heading for New York or Washington. Those are just best guesses. We can't cause mass panic in both of those cities only to have him attack Jersey City. In fact, an alert in those two cities would probably warn him off and inspire him to select another random target. The only option we have, sir, is to ride this out and hope we catch him before he acts. In the meantime, for safety's sake, you need to get out of here. Your ranch would be a safe enough distance."

The president thought longingly of his Texas ranch and of the day he could retire there and leave the insanity of the world and Washington politics behind him forever. That day would come soon enough but it was not today. He was a leader and a leader did not turn tail and run.

The president stood. "I'm staying," he said firmly. He held up a silencing hand. "Issue a terror alert to the media. Highest level. If we can't specify a threat, we can at least let the people know they should be on guard."

"The Rally for a Free Kabul starts tomorrow, sir," the vice president warned. "They'll say you're only putting us on red alert to undermine the protest."

"Let them think what they want. I'm their president too whether they like it or not and I'll do my best to protect them, whether they like that or not too." The president placed a hand on the older man's shoulder. "Get out of town for a couple of days. Take the wife. I hear Wyoming's okay. Not as nice as Texas, but what is?"

The vice president knew enough not to argue when this president made up his mind. Eyes moist, he nodded understanding. They shook hands, two weary warriors who had seen days more terrible than either could ever have anticipated when they came together to Washington seven years before.

Mark Howard sat in the back of the room silently. They were all missing something; he knew it, but he didn't know where the answer was. The Koran that contained the virus had not just vanished. It was somewhere but where was it?

After, the president hurried from the War Room. The presidential motorcade returned him through empty post-midnight streets to the White House where he hustled up the stairs to his private residence and hurried to his bedroom. His wife was out of town. The president sat on the edge of the bed and removed a cherry red phone from the bottom drawer of the nightstand.

Even though it was nearing three in the morning, he knew that someone would pick up. The man at the other end of the dedicated phone line was always on duty.

The phone was answered on the first ring.

"I assume this is about the Mustafa Mohammed matter,"

the lemony voice on the other end of the line said by way of greeting. "My special people are on it."

"You might not know the latest, Smith," the president said. "He has the means to destroy a major U.S. city."

"Mr. President, CURE would not be involved if this were merely an escaped felon. We know about the book and about the supervirus. I strongly suggest, sir, that you reconsider your decision not to leave Washington."

The president blinked surprise. "How could you possibly know that? I made that decision not ten minutes ago."

"I had a man at your Pentagon meeting. You should leave Washington," Smith repeated. "There is no sense adding your death to the countless others should this terrorist succeed. Destroying Washington is horrifying enough but killing you as well would be a feather in al-Khobar's cap that we should not willingly give them."

"Smith, you're in Rye, aren't you?"

There was the slightest pause on the line. "Yes."

"I've seen the projections on that virus cloud. If he releases it in New York City, Rye isn't safe."

"CURE will remain operational if anything happens to me. I have just ordered my assistant to visit his family in the Midwest. However, I suspect you are not worried about operations here and that you're suggesting our situations are similar because we are both remaining in potential danger zones. But, sir, you are wrong. If I die, I will be a statistic. You will be a headline."

"No, Smith. I can't save my skin and leave everyone else behind, and I can't go on TV and create a panic by telling everyone that what happened at that prison could be happening in their city and that they should go out and pick up some duct tape. You're staying because you have to. So am I. End of discussion. Now what good news do you have?"

Smith sighed, but did not argue.

"Not much I'm afraid. Knowing about the virus and delivery system does us little good until we find Mohammed. The weapon is small and can be set off anywhere. According to what we have pieced together, it is likely that it originated in an Iraqi WMD lab which is now defunct. We will know more once we have the book in hand."

"What about your men? Those two?"

"I have not heard from them in several hours. I sent them to the diner in Missouri where the parchment segment was found. They should be checking in any minute now. I will let you know as soon as I have anything new to report."

The president had spoken to Smith enough to know when he was getting the brush-off. He almost wished Smith good luck but that seemed inadequate. This might be the last time the two men spoke. Each was within striking distance of one of the cities the experts had concluded were the likeliest al-Khobar targets. In light of all that Smith and CURE had done for the nation during this president's tenure and throughout the eight administrations prior to his own, and the ultimate sacrifice he was ready to make now, there was only one thing the president could think to say as his parting words.

"Thank you, Dr. Smith."

For the first time in their association, the president was first to hang up the phone.

He exhaled loudly as he got up from the edge of the bed and went to the window. The sky over the capital was black, yet the brilliant white lights around the White House, the Washington Monument, the Lincoln Memorial and other tourist sites illuminated official Washington like midday.

The tourists would come early as they did every day. So too would the Rally for a Free Kabul protesters. And at some point tomorrow, everything the president could see might be wasteland, littered with the corpses of those he had been unable to save, unable even to warn.

He returned to his bedside, this time collecting the normal outside line from the top of the nightstand. He did not go through the switchboard but called direct.

"Hey, it's me. I know it's late. Listen, honey, don't come

back here tomorrow. I know you were planning to but don't. And make sure the girls stay out of town too. No, I can't. No. I love you." He hung up the phone.

If things went badly tomorrow, the press would judge him harshly for forewarning his wife while others got no such warning. But the press had never been kind to him so he hardly expected them to change their attitude toward him postmortem. And in the face of his own death, saving his loved ones was the only power that the most powerful man on earth had left. America's best were on the case. There was nothing more the president could do.

Feeling the weight of the world on his shoulders, he pulled off his jacket and got ready for bed.

Smith was replacing the White House hotline in the bottom drawer of his desk when the blue contact phone jangled to life. He noted the time on his trusty Timex wristwatch even as he snapped up the phone.

"Remo, where the devil have you been?"

"Hey, Smitty," Remo said.

The lack of reaction from CURE's enforcement arm to Smith's unusual fit of temper sent up an immediate warning flare for Smith.

"What's wrong?"

"Everything. Nothing. Damned if I know. Listen, Smitty, I hate to be the bearer of bad tidings—"

Chiun's impatient voice cut in from the near background. "Give me that or we will be here all night." The Master of Sinanju came on the line. "It has been the great privilege of the House of Sinanju to serve you, Emperor Smith, but lamentably all things, even good ones, must end. Rest assured that even as we set sail from these shores we remain always with you in spirit. May your reign be long and free of distresses, large and small. Blessed are we who were fortunate to serve and honored to know that your crown and throne remained secure thanks in small part to our meager efforts. All hail to thee, Smith the Wise."

Smith was not sure what to say to the Master of Sinanju but fortunately Chiun had handed the phone back to Remo.

"I guess that says it all," Remo said.

"Says what? Remo, what on earth was Chiun saying?"

"Toodle-oo. As in, we quit. I guess." Remo did not sound entirely happy with his own words.

"Quit? What are you talking about? Remo, you can't quit. We have a major crisis here."

"Tell the ghost-face good-bye and hang up the phone," Chiun's voice hissed from nearby.

"We've all got a crisis, Smitty," Remo said. "You've got one there and I've got one here, and believe it or not mine might be bigger. But this might not be forever. Tell the kid to keep a light on in Folcroft's window. Sinanju might be ready to serve again in another couple of decades."

"I sent Mark home to Iowa," Smith said. "Remo, tell me what the problem is. Maybe we can deal with it after—"

"No can do. Too crazy. Sorry to bail like this, Smitty."

After a pause, Smith said, "Just one thing. Do they have newspapers in Sinanju?"

"No. Why?"

"I was just wondering if you'll be able to read about the millions of Americans killed in New York or Washington."

There was a long pause. "Jesus, Smith, that's low. Even for you," Remo said.

"I'm sorry you feel that way. But it's what we signed on for."

"I never signed on," Remo snapped. "I was shanghaied. Remember?"

"Only because you were the right one. The right one."

The phone went dead in Smith's hand. He did not hang it up. His arthritic knuckles were white on the blue receiver.

His brain, ordinarily as precise and logical as a computer, could not process this new information.

Remo and Chiun quitting.

Madmen were on the loose and America's giant cities were faced with destruction and the country's best chance for survival had just up and left without so much as an explanation.

As he sat clutching the receiver, Smith heard a muted thudding and wondered for a moment who would be banging nails at Folcroft in the dead of night. Then he realized that the pounding was the blood in his own ears.

Woodenly, he replaced the phone in its cradle and looked at his computer monitor, a single accusing eye staring up at him from the depths of his desk. And for the first time in over forty years as head of CURE, Dr. Harold W. Smith had not a clue what to do next.

So he did the only thing he had always known how to do. He called up the reports on his computer and began to study them again. Maybe something, somewhere, somehow, there was some answer in the endless flood of paper reports.

The holy pilgrims of the Tuesday Peace Brigade
drove through the night and into the next day, stopping only
for gas and Twinkies on their sacred mission to America's
east coast. The traffic had grown heavy with the new day. It
was afternoon by the time they arrived in New Jersey.

Sally McAvoy told the others that the Lord had instructed
her to buy picks and shovels and wait for cover of darkness.
After they had gathered their tools they parked in a Home
Depot parking lot and slept and sang songs about love and
about fighting wars for peace until the sun finally dropped
below the horizon.

In darkness the bus at last stopped beside the high fence
to which, Sally said, the Lord had guided her.

"The Lord has guided me, the Lord has guided me, the
Lord has guided me," Loretta Sanders-Parker snarled. "Em-
broider it on a pillow, why don't you?"

Loretta had not joined in the songs of brotherhood, opt-
ing instead to sulk in the corner of the kitchenette.

"I forgive you your jealousy, sister," Sally said, placing a hand on Loretta's shoulder. "The sinners who put Joan of Arc to death were doubters just like you."

"Yeah and you're the Maid of Orleans, right?"

Sally hesitated. "I'm not from New Orleans. I'm from South Dakota," she said.

Loretta rolled her eyes and shook Sally's hand off her shoulder. "What do we have to do now?"

Shovels were passed out and the Peace Brigade climbed out of the bus. The gate was locked. Steve Sanders-Parker tried to break the chain with his shovel but after a few frustrated "gosh-darn-its" his wife shoved him aside.

"Jesus, you're such a wimp," Loretta said.

Loretta reveled in the gasps and whispers of blasphemy as she whacked at the chain with her spade. The rusty chain snapped and the gates creaked open.

Flashlight beams guided them. They followed the directions the Lord had given Sally on the narrow roads and pathways and when they stopped, Sally McAvoy's flashlight shone across a plain granite block in which were carved two simple words: Remo Williams.

"Who the hell is Remo Williams? What's so special about this guy?" Loretta asked as the others began to chip away at the hard earth.

"It is not my place to question my Lord," Sally said.

"Christ," Loretta cursed and turned from the digging. Annoyed, she tossed her flashlight beam around the immediate area until it fell across the neighboring grave. "Craig McAvoy," she read. "Craig McAvoy? Isn't that your kid?"

Sally glanced at the messy grave. "I guess."

"You mean you don't know?"

"Well, I haven't had the time to visit it. The last couple of years have been so busy. Anti-war protests don't organize themselves, you know. But, yes, I think he was buried in New Jersey somewhere. His warmonger father was from here but he's dead now. I think a grandmother or aunt may have paid to have him buried here," she added vaguely. Sally turned her back on her only son's grave. The next chunk of frozen earth she heaved over her shoulder knocked over her son's pathetic little wooden marker.

It was hours before the cold ground surrendered the coffin of Remo Williams. The Peace Brigade dragged the sturdy old box up into the winter air.

"Now what?" Loretta asked, panting.

"The Lord will guide me," Sally said. "Stay here."

The others remained with the musty coffin while Sally, shovel in hand, marched off to a cluster of trees that formed the eastern border of Wildwood Cemetery. And, as He had told her, her Lord waited there for her.

The figure in white sat on a log and stared at the stars through the tangled branches of winter trees.

"All finished, Lord," Sally said brightly.

"Great," the Lord said. "I'll take this from here. Now I want you to get that book to Washington." The Lord never took His eyes off the stars. "It's a funny thing. The chance for my biggest score in a hundred years and those damned Sinanju meddlers have to stick their noses in. How great will it be when I beat them by using a nitwit as a weapon."

His words were not directed at her but at the stars.

"This time, them. Before them, long ago, the Great Wang. And now my chance."

Sally was confused by the Lord's words but before she could ask what He meant, a sudden sound at the edge of the woods surprised them both. Heads spun to the noise.

Sally saw the shocked face of Loretta Sanders-Parker peering through a laurel thicket.

Loretta was not looking at Sally, but at the Lord. Rather than reflecting the jubilation her soul should have felt at glimpsing the splendor of her Savior, Loretta's face was a mask of sheer horror. Blood draining from her ashen cheeks, she stumbled to her feet and turned to run. Her toe snagged a root and she pitched forward, falling into the cemetery. Her head struck hard against a headstone.

Sally ran to Loretta's side.

"Skull . . . skull . . . he's a monster . . . ," Loretta was muttering, eyes rolling in a ghostly white face.

The Lord floated up behind Sally. An irritated frown formed within His perfectly trimmed beard and mustache. "Complications. Always with the complications."

"Why did she run from you, Lord?" Sally asked.

The Lord gazed down upon the semiconscious Loretta and sighed. "Because the unrighteous flee from judgment, yadda, yadda. I've seen into her soul. She's not one of ours."

Sally glanced down at Loretta.

". . . a monster . . . skull . . . worms for eyes . . . ," Loretta babbled. Blood trickled from the wound on her forehead.

"There's nothing else we can do for this lost sheep," the Lord said. "You're going to have to kill her."

There was no horror on Sally's face. She merely turned to the Lord, eyebrows raised questioningly. "Why?"

"She's an infidel and must be destroyed."

"An infidel?" Sally asked, puzzled.

"Oh, right. You're not one of those. A heretic, she's a heretic."

Sally had not heard Loretta say anything heretical per se but she had blasphemed this very night. And she was certainly no stranger to the seven deadly sins. Her jealousy that the Lord had chosen to speak not to her but to Sally had been on full display this whole past day.

Sally thought of Abraham being told by God to sacrifice his son Isaac. Just before he could do the deed, an angel had stayed Abraham's hand. Sally hauled back and sank the tip of her spade deep in the back of Loretta's head. Since no angel tried to stop her, she assumed Loretta, the jealous, blaspheming heretic, had it coming to her. Afterward, she rolled the body into the woods and covered it with leaves.

The figure in white sat on a headstone and watched her work. "I love your naiveté," he remarked.

"I love your Nativity too, O Lord," said Sally, spooning a handful of wet, frosty leaves over her friend's face.

"God, what an idiot."

"What?"

"Nothing. You've done well. Leave that Remo Williams coffin where it is. I'll handle the rest."

There were only two steps from the side door to the driveway, and Agnes Whiteman took each of them with great care. She held on tight to the railing. She did not want to have another incident like last winter when she fell on the first step and bruised her chin.

The driveway was empty. She used to have a car but it was gone now. No point since the cataracts had gotten so bad that her doctor had her declared legally blind. There was apparently an operation available but it was with those laser things that Agnes didn't understand and besides she could see well enough for TV and the senior center bus took her to the grocery store and Mrs. Aubrey down the street took her to church on Sundays, so what need did she really have for a car?

Actually there was one need. She would have liked the old car back in the driveway just to have something to use for balance on her long daily trek down to the mailbox.

She took slow, careful steps and eventually made it to the street. Agnes was collecting the mail when a minivan pulled into the driveway across the road. The young woman who got out smiled and waved.

"How you doing today, Mrs. Whiteman?"

"I'm fine, thank you. I've got something over here for Kyle when he comes home from school."

"It's not money, is it?"

This was an old argument with the neighbors. Agnes liked to pay her way but the nice young couple across the street refused to accept money for the little odd jobs their family did to help out their elderly neighbor.

"No, it's not," Agnes said, smiling.

"Okay. Do you need a hand with that?"

Agnes pulled the rolled up bundle of mail from her box

and was trying to put down the flag. "No, thank you," she said. "You've got better things to do than worry about an old pest like me." She got the flag down on the third try, thankful that it clicked before the poor young thing had to come running across the street.

The young neighbor was carting in bundles of groceries as Agnes hobbled back up the driveway.

The stairs were a struggle. Some days were so much worse than others. Once she was up, she fought for several frustrating minutes with the doorknob. Her hands were so swollen from arthritis that it was getting harder for her to do simple everyday tasks. She was worried that the young woman across the street would see her struggling with the doorknob and would come running over to help, but fortunately the knob finally turned and the heavy door opened.

Funny that she now thought of the door as heavy. For most of the nearly sixty years she had lived here, it had just been a regular door, worth scarcely a thought.

She carried the mail to the kitchen table and was grateful to sit down. She had poured herself a cup of tea but left it when she heard the mail truck and now it was tepid. It was too much of a struggle to get back up so she didn't bother to reheat it in the microwave.

She rolled the rubber band down from around the mail and laid the papers and envelopes out on the table, shifting a plate of gingersnaps wrapped in cellophane out of the way.

She had spent the entire morning baking a few dozen cookies. Agnes knew that her neighbors were trying to be nice by refusing cash payment for the little jobs they did around her house, and so she frequently baked things for them to show her gratitude. But it was getting so hard just to mix the dough. Sometimes on days like today when her hands were practically useless, she wished they would accept money.

Of course things would be so much easier for her if John were still around.

Agnes was the youngest of four children, all the rest boys. Her last brother, Randolph, had died two years before. Agnes had been alone since her husband died many years before and when she had become a widow it was her brothers who had looked out for her. But Randolph was the last and once he was gone, her nephews and nieces had begun talking about putting Agnes in a home.

She would hear none of it. As long as she could live on her own in the house where she had raised her only child, she was going to do so. But John would have made things so much easier for her, especially in these sad, long, lonely years.

Agnes sorted through the mail. There were a few store flyers, junk mail from credit card companies, some mass cards from the Marian Helpers, and a phone bill. She wondered as she did every month why she kept paying for the phone. No one ever called her these days. But there was one reason to keep the phone, one overriding justification to hold onto the same number she'd had for decades.

A flimsy paper slipped from one of the store ads. It was a blue and white postcard, on which was printed the picture of two people, a man and a child.

Agnes stared at the card, marked "resident," from the National Missing Children Network, and began to cry.

Thirty-seven years. That was how long it would be, come June. Thirty-seven long years since her little John had been taken from her. He had been twenty years old when he vanished. A good boy, but troubled. He had fallen in with the wrong crowd. All the boys were into the drugs back then. John would have straightened his life out, Agnes knew, if only he'd had the chance. It was not unusual for him to disappear for weeks on end, only to resurface, more disheveled than ever. But the last time had stretched from weeks to months and none of his friends knew where he was. Her only child had simply vanished forever, leaving his poor widowed mother to wonder all her life where he had gone.

She sobbed alone in her little kitchen but eventually the tears dried as they always did. Her tea was cold now. She had no choice but to warm it in the microwave even though the numbers were hard to push. She was reaching for the cup when she felt something at her back.

A presence. Someone was with her in the kitchen.

It was as cold as the darkest hours of night when she cried to herself and wondered why she had lingered so long. But it was familiar as well, welcoming. She had been waiting for it to claim her for a long time now.

There was a mirror on the wall, with a wooden frame that read "welcome guests" in interwoven stenciled vines. Her eyes were poor but good enough to see the figure that stood behind her. He was like a shadow, not quite real. He was tall with robes of long, dazzling white. The face was broad and kindly. Above a shock of yellow hair was a nimbus of gold-tinged white. Stretching wide—from the Whirlpool fridge on one wall to the knickknack shelf with the Thimbles of the World collection on the other—were two huge, fluttering white wings.

It was a creature of staggering beauty and the wash of cold comfort that emanated from the figure quelled any fears Agnes might have had. This was an old friend.

Agnes stiffened her age-curved spine. It was time.

"I'm ready," Agnes Whiteman said softly.

It was more a sensation, a thing understood on an instinctive level. She had lived in its shadow for a long time but had never imagined that when the Angel of Death at last came to claim her that it would be something that would talk back.

"Not yet," said a soothing voice. The light of his halo glinted brightly off the silver toaster. "Your time is coming very soon but I can't take you until you've finished your work here. I sense you have a question, something that's been bothering you for years."

Agnes had thought the answers would come later, after she had passed into the light. She could not believe it. She held her small fists up to her chest as if to slow the beating of her disbelieving heart.

"My boy," Agnes said. "My little Johnny. I never knew . . . what happened to my John?"

The kindly Angel of Death gave his massive wings a happy little fluttering flap.

"Well, babe, I think we might be able to help you out there," said the warm, heaven-sent voice.

18

The Master of Sinanju was in the next room packing and Remo was flipping between *Green Acres* and the local noon news at their Connecticut home when he caught a glimpse of a reporter standing before the gates of Wildwood Cemetery. The caption at the bottom of the screen read, "GRAVE MATTER."

For a moment Remo was shocked, but then he remembered that Craig McAvoy was interred at Wildwood so he assumed the story had to do with the pitiful condition of the young hero's grave. Curious to see if something was being done to right such a shameful wrong, he nudged up the volume on the remote.

". . . a former police officer, Williams was the last man executed in New Jersey."

For a moment Remo sat stunned. His ears rang. He had to have misheard. Yet the next instant the camera cut and there was his familiar headstone, his name chiselled out in granite for all the world to see. The earth had been chipped away. Remo's grave was an open hole. There was no coffin.

"Everyone thought this story had ended decades ago but a strange twist to this old true crime drama has thrown doubt on who was truly buried in this grave."

Another quick cut and the camera was inside a kitchen where a little old lady sat at a table, hands resting on the tablecloth, the joints of her hands bulging white and lined with heavy blue veins. She held a framed picture of a young man to the camera. The boy's hair was long and dark, the picture old.

"He told me it was my John buried in that grave," the old lady said. "All these years he's been missing and I never knew where he'd disappeared to."

A reporter off-camera asked the woman, "And how would it make you feel if the man in that grave is your son?"

The old hands fidgeted around the picture. Tears glistened in the corners of her eyes. "It would be nice to finally know what happened to John. It's been so long."

The camera cut back to Wildwood Cemetery. The reporter who had been outside the gates now stood inside, rows of markers spread out behind her. In the far distance Remo saw tape strung around the area where his grave had been. Men moved around the hole, a few unmarked cars parked nearby.

"Agnes Whiteman has been looking for answers to her son's whereabouts for decades and the mysterious phone call that has directed her here on the very day this grave has been desecrated by vandals could be a cruel hoax. But if it turns out that John Whiteman has been here all along, we will have more than just an open grave. We'll have an open grave . . . that has opened many questions. Back to you."

Before the picture cut back to the anchors in the studio, Remo snapped off the TV and shot to his feet. He had the phone in hand and was stabbing out the multiple 1 code that would connect him to Smith when a sharp voice called from the doorway.

"Hold!" the Master of Sinanju commanded.

"I've got to call Smitty, Chiun," Remo said.

The old Korean flounced into the room and snatched the phone from his pupil. "Do not be a fool." Chiun paused to listen, but the connection had not yet been made. He quickly replaced the phone in the cradle. The instant he did so, the phone began ringing. His first instinct was to rip the phone from the wall but he'd have need of it later. Picking it up quickly, he hung it back up. The moment he did so, the *Judge Ruth* theme music sounded from within his kimono. Exhaling angrily, he produced his cell phone and smashed it to pieces. "We are well rid of this lunatic," he muttered, tossing the cell phone fragments into the cold fireplace.

"You don't understand, Little Father. Wildwood Cemetery was just on the news. Someone dug up my grave."

"I understand better than you. I heard the pretty talkers blathering about that grave that is not yours. Did it not occur to you, Remo, that this is the handiwork of the creature who claimed to know who was truly buried there, that this is a warning from him for us to hie from this nation?"

"Yeah, but I've still got to tell Smitty. If that wasn't what he was just calling about, he's going to stroke out when he sees this."

"Tell Smith what?" Chiun challenged. "Tell him that we have encountered a being who revels in death, who knows the secrets of the dead, and who can use those secrets against his enemies? Assume Smith did not think you madder than he is, Remo. Assume that he believes that we have seen the face of death. How long do you think he would keep us in his employ? You know Smith's insanity when it comes to secrecy. If he knew we faced an enemy that could turn against him the legions of dead we have slain at his command, would Smith still retain our services? No. He would likely try to kill us himself to cover all we have done and, failing that, kill himself and Prince Mark."

Remo had been hovering between listening to his teacher and reaching for the now-silent phone. When his hand fell back to his side, the Master of Sinanju nodded and marched from the room. Rotating his thick wrists absently, Remo dogged his teacher into the dining area and out the sliding glass doors to the patio.

"Smith is going to find out about the grave."

"That is his problem, not ours," Chiun replied.

"I don't like leaving him high and dry, Little Father. I'm not even sure that guy is who he claims to be. I felt something when I tried to hit him. Like something was there but it was just beyond my ability to touch it."

"I felt it as well," Chiun said. "But since we could not touch him, it is as good as meaningless."

"As good as, but not entirely?"

Chiun waved his hands, as if Remo's words were the most meaningless thing he had encountered in the past two days.

A row of hedges had once separated their patio from that of the neighboring condo. Initially, Chiun had a habit of tormenting everyone who tried to move in next door, to the point where the condo association was talking about giving Remo and Chiun the boot. Remo did not feel like moving and decided that it would be easier to buy the place next door than have to clean up the bodies of the condo board after Chiun got through reasoning with them. A path was now cut through the shrubs, connecting the two patios. Chiun marched into the connecting condo.

Several of Chiun's steamer trunks were scattered around the living and dining rooms. Chiun's kimonos had once hung on racks all around the condo. Most had been packed away already. Empty wooden hangers hung on lonely metal frames.

Chiun hustled over to a rack that was still filled. He pulled down a kimono and began to fold it carefully.

"So if you felt something too, that means we were maybe just too slow to touch him," Remo said as he watched his teacher work.

"That touch of flesh that was not there is not all you felt, my son," Chiun said without turning.

Remo knew what his teacher meant. It was true. He had

been trying to come to terms with what he had felt when he passed through the cadaverous creature. He had never before encountered anything like the numbing coldness that had chilled his marrow, yet despite its newness it had been familiar somehow. It was as if the creature had existed in a different dimension, but there had been something tangible to the limitless cold that dwelt within the creature in black. It gave the sense that one was touching the icy flesh of death. Both Masters of Sinanju had visited death upon so many over the years that they had developed an instinct for it. Death and Remo were not old friends but they had been companions for many years. Remo could not shake the feeling that he had stood in Death's cold shadow.

"How can it be, Little Father, that we of all people have never encountered this thing before?"

And because his pupil, who was now full Reigning Master himself yet was still so young in so many ways, had asked the question with such innocent sincerity, Chiun set aside the kimono he had been folding and sank cross-legged to the floor. He encouraged his pupil to do likewise.

"For us there is Sinanju," Chiun said. "We live it, breathe it, accept it as the center of all. Yet I ask you, how many throughout history have known of us?"

"Not many."

Chiun nodded. "And of that handful who have learned of us, most have carried that knowledge to a speedy grave. And so it is that we have lasted five thousand years, yet no books speak of us, no television programs detail our exploits, and no maps even show the true location of our village, though every carpenter in Palestine has a fan club. Yet although we remain hidden to the greater world, Sinanju remains the Sun Source of all the lesser martial arts. Without Sinanju, there would be no karate, no jujitsu, no tae kwon do. Many are the rays, but there is only one source of light. Because we are not seen by the world at large, because we are not a household name, that does not mean that we do not exist."

"But that's different, Little Father. Sinanju is real."

"Before becoming one with Sinanju would you not have thought it impossible for men to climb walls and dodge bullets? Think of the things you do with ease, Remo, and then think of describing them to another. Those who did not see for themselves would insist that Sinanju was not real."

Remo realized that his teacher spoke truth. "But we're talking about the Grim Reaper here."

"That is just one of his names. The Arabs call him Azrael or Malak al-Maut, the Angel of Death. Azrael has four faces and a thousand wings, with a body entirely consisting of eyes and tongues. It is he who collected the souls of the firstborn in the tenth and final plague on Egypt. The Mexicans have Santo Muerto, their Saint Death. The Vikings had Hel, queen of their underworld who has authority over all who die of sickness and old age since, Remo, Viking honor goes only to those who are hacked to pieces on some desolate slab of ice while wearing one of those stupid horned helmets of theirs. The Lord of death in Hinduism is Yama, ruler of the departed, who is subordinate to Shiva, the Destroyer." Pausing, the old Korean raised a thin eyebrow.

"If Yamaha called me, the phone must have been off the hook, Little Father," Remo said. "And could you keep the Viking bashing to a minimum? My daughter happens to be one."

"Half Viking," Chiun corrected. "The good half is Sinanju which has made up for her barbarian side. There is still hope for her." The old Asian waved a dismissive hand. "And this is not about my beautiful granddaughter." He fussed with his robes. "There was Mot, who was the Semitic god of death and whose throne was a pit and whose land was filth. The Egyptians had Sekhem Em Pet, the guide of the dead and guardian of their underworld. Tartarus ruled a vile place of the same name, lower than Hades for the Greeks."

"All right," Remo said. "Good list. But what's the point?"

"The point is that all of these, Remo, were gods of death

and dying, rulers of the deepest pits in the darkest realms. All civilizations have come to know of similar beasts of the abyss. Is it unreasonable to think that, like our art of Sinanju, there might not be a single entity that is sun source to these creatures as well?"

Remo could see the logic to his teacher's words. At an earlier time, when he was younger in the discipline of death, Remo might have dismissed Chiun's argument with a smartass comment. But Remo was older now and had seen much since he had taken those first tentative steps into what would become for him the one universal truth. Maybe Chiun was right. Maybe this creature was death personified. Yet doubt still lingered.

"It just seems like some Master somewhere would have met him before," Remo said. "And he did mention Wang."

"As discoverer of the Sun Source, the Great Wang would be known to this beast. It was in Wang, after all, that Sinanju perfected the art of bringing death."

"But that's kind of my point. We've been whacking people for five thousand years, even before Wang. Don't you think we would have stepped on this thing's toes before now?"

"It is true, my son, that we have never seen the living face of death before but that does not disprove its existence. The blind man who never sees the stars simply fails to see, he does not extinguish their light. All I know for certain is that when I touched this creature, I felt the cold essence of death within him. If it was not Death, it is still a thing responsible for many deaths. Until we know what it is, we cannot hope to defeat it."

Remo shook his head, exasperated. "But, Little Father, if he is who he claims, then we can never hope to beat him."

"Possibly," Chiun admitted. His voice was low, the worry lines in his forehead dark with troubled thoughts.

"So if we retreat now from an enemy we can never beat, aren't we giving up Sinanju forever? Death will always be around, so if he's somehow suddenly got it in for us, the first time we try to show our faces he'll be there waiting like a Whack-A-Mole game. Not to mention we'll be abandoning our obligations not just to Smith but to the villagers of Sinanju. If we're out of the assassination business they're shit out of luck because we're their meal ticket."

For this Chiun had no answer so he rose to his feet and shook his head. "We do what we must so that Sinanju survives for now," he stated firmly. "All else will be for later generations to decide."

The wizened Korean returned to his packing. Remo sat in silence, watching his teacher's back. After many long minutes, Remo finally got up and returned to their living quarters. He did not turn the television on again.

When the phone began ringing desperately once more, Remo ignored it.

Smith let the phone ring two dozen times before he finally gave up. His hands were still shaking and it took two attempts to get the receiver back in the cradle.

A small black and white television sat on the edge of his desk. Smith had taken it down to watch for news of Mustafa, never dreaming that he would see an image of the open grave of Remo Williams in Wildwood Cemetery.

A quick, panicked check on his computer found that the story had been packaged for the local affiliates of a single network. So far the other networks had not picked it up and many outlets around the country had chosen not to run it. Under ordinary circumstances the story would die had it been based solely on the Whiteman woman's speculation. Authorities were not likely to order a grave reopened just because an elderly woman claimed her son was buried there, a woman who claimed—and was clearly lying— that she had been told about the mislabeled grave by a voice on the telephone. Unfortunately vandals had exhumed the body. Now, because the coffin was already unearthed and because Remo Williams had no known living relatives to object, a judge had ordered that the remains be

DNA tested, to be compared against the DNA of Mrs. Whiteman.

The day had started better than he expected. Smith had ordered Mark Howard out of town, then managed to get a few hours sleep and when he awoke to a cold sun and a new day, he was relieved. The fact that he was alive and that his laptop and cell phone had not awakened him meant that the East Coast had survived the night.

He had also sent his wife to visit their daughter in Vermont the previous day. Maude Smith did not know why her Harold suddenly wanted her out of town, to the point where he had gone against his usual tightwad nature and volunteered to pay for air fare. But Maude didn't care. Any excuse to see her daughter and three grandsons was a delight for Smith's wife.

So Maude and the East Coast were safe. Yes, Remo had quit CURE. That was a problem, but he had quit before and always come back. Smith had come to work thinking of ways he might persuade Remo to return. And then the bomb of Remo's open grave had exploded at midday, and a feeling of utter helplessness had settled over Smith once more.

Smith got up stiffly from his desk. He left the TV flickering, the volume turned down, and stepped from the office.

His secretary glanced up from her work and noted the ashen complexion of her employer. "Is something wrong, Dr. Smith?" she asked worriedly as he trudged past.

"Everything is fine, Mrs. Mikulka," he lied.

Mark Howard's office door was closed and locked. Smith walked past it to the boiler room stairs. Two flights down, he found tucked away in a corner a simple steel box, covered in a thick coat of dust. Smith stopped next to his coffin.

Early on there was a plan in place if CURE were ever compromised. Part of that would be the physical dismantling of CURE at Folcroft. Smith would erase all computer files and burn the Folcroft mainframes within their special sealed chamber behind the basement wall. He would then climb into

the steel box and take a poison pill. After, Mrs. Mikulka
would see to it that his body was sent for cremation.

In later years, Smith had amended the plan. The coffin
would be too suspicious. Better to have his body found lying on his office floor upstairs. At his age, and with his
preexisting heart condition, a sudden death would draw no
attention. But now with Mark Howard in the mix, things
were complicated again. Mark had his own poison pill and
if both the director and assistant director of Folcroft were
to die simultaneously, there would be questions. Still,
there would be no answers, for Smith and his assistant
would take CURE's secrets with them to their respective
graves. An imperfect plan, but one that would work well
enough.

But now, it seemed, the grave was not as silent a resting
place as Smith had imagined.

He ran a longing hand along the edge of the coffin. Slapping the dust from his palms, he turned and headed back
upstairs to wander the halls of Folcroft.

Staff who were unused to seeing their reclusive employer
in the public wing of the building watched with surprise as
the lanky, gray sanitarium director meandered past.

Smith could not recall the last time he had felt so alone.
For more years than he cared to count, Remo and Chiun had
almost always been only a phone call away. Chiun had
never particularly cared for talking on the phone and in recent years Remo had taken several extended trips to Africa
but even when Chiun was in one of his moods and would
not answer the phone or when Remo was out of the country,
Smith had Mark Howard to turn to. Even before those three
had come to work at CURE, Smith had had an old CIA
friend, Conrad MacCleary, working with him at Folcroft.
But now they were all gone, and Smith was more alone than
he had been in years.

The news that the grave with Remo's name on it had been
desecrated was shock enough. But seeing the name Whiteman connected to the story had struck Smith like a physical

blow. It was impossible, yet somehow the grave in Wild-wood Cemetery had been linked back to John Whiteman.

Conrad MacCleary had assured him this day would never come. Smith could remember the conversation almost ver-batim, as he could recall nearly everything of those critical days for CURE. They were embarking on something so dangerous back then, undermining the document that they had sworn to protect, subverting the Constitution in order to save it. The memory of his own voice echoed inside his head.

"The individual you, er, acquired," Smith said. "What steps have you taken to ensure that he is not linked to us?"

He could hear Conrad MacCleary's voice booming back at him through the years. "Well, first off I was in charge of his death."

Smith had winced. CURE had only recently been sanc-tioned to kill and Smith hated the thought. "I need to know," he pressed.

MacCleary was sprawled on a chair in his quarters at Folcroft, one leg hanging over a chair arm. In his right hand he held a bottle of rye, in place of his left hand was a hook which hugged a purple pillow. To Smith's distaste, the bed was unmade, mounds of clothes were heaped up like snow-drifts and rye bottles liberated from an eight-foot cabinet decorated every flat surface. There were no windows.

MacCleary produced a fat envelope which he tossed to Smith. "All you need to know is in there. Nothing anywhere to connect him to us or Williams. Father deceased. Guy was pushing junk on schoolkids to feed his own habit. A real doll, John Whiteman, of the Bristol, Connecticut, White-mans. The world won't miss him, Smitty."

"You didn't really kill him," Smith said.

"No, but I would have. Instead I just let him die. Forget it, it's over."

For more than thirty years MacCleary had been correct. After Remo's phony execution, MacCleary had switched the bodies and made sure it was Whiteman that was lowered into Remo's grave. It was a literal cover-up, with six feet of dirt packed down over a secret that, were it ever to surface, could doom the great American experiment in democracy.

How had Agnes Whiteman learned about her son's body? While the news reports claimed a voice on the phone had told her, the story seemed fishy to Smith. Who could possibly know the truth? MacCleary was as thorough an agent as Smith had ever worked with. Conn MacCleary had insisted there was nothing that could possibly connect Whiteman to CURE and Smith trusted implicitly the word of his old comrade in arms.

As he wandered back to the executive wing, Smith's thoughts drifted to Remo and Chiun. They would not quit CURE on a whim. The Master of Sinanju had been particularly agitated and Remo had sounded unnerved. Something had spooked the two of them. If Smith were a gambler he would bet that John Whiteman surfacing after all these years was somehow connected to Remo and Chiun's sudden departure.

When he returned to his office, Smith's computer was chirping, alerting him to some fresh information gathered by CURE's mainframes. He quickly settled in his leather chair, already fearing new information from Wildwood Cemetery, the beginning of a dotted line that would lead directly to CURE. Instead he saw that the mainframes had picked up a police report from outside St. Louis.

Mustafa Mohammed's brother, Achmed, had been captured. The news took Smith by surprise. Remo had not mentioned Achmed Mohammed in his brief phone call. The CURE director had assumed that Remo had eliminated Mustafa's brother.

Another loose end; another thread tearing away from a rapidly unraveling tapestry.

It might be possible to learn Mustafa's location from his brother, assuming the brother knew where the twentieth hijacker was. Smith would ordinarily send Remo to the jail to question Achmed, but Remo was not answering his phone.

Going through old-fashioned espionage channels would take too long. New York might be gone before the FBI learned from his brother where Mustafa was, assuming Congress did not step in to prevent the feds from questioning the terrorist.

At the corner of Smith's desk the little TV continued to flash silent black and white images.

The news was nearly over. The final story was of an anti-war protest. There had been so many similar stories in recent years that Smith might not have paid attention if not for the backdrop. The protestors were gathered in Lafayette Park in Washington, D.C. Across the street could be seen a high black fence, and beyond it the White House.

Smith could not blame the president for remaining in Washington despite the risk.

Smith had always thought it foolish romanticism that compelled a captain to remain aboard a sinking ship even after all hands had been saved. Yet here he was. If necessary Smith could have worked from his briefcase laptop computer from anywhere in the world. But if there was a problem with the mainframes, or if communications went down, or if any of a dozen other problems cropped up, Smith needed to be at Folcroft. And so in the face of doom, he remained at his post, staring at his old television with the tinfoil wrapped around the rabbit ears, and feeling more helpless than he had ever felt at any other time in his life.

In that moment of deepest despair, Smith spied something that made his heart leap inside his narrow chest.

He could not believe it. It had flashed by so quickly. Perhaps he had been wrong.

The TV was forgotten. Nimble fingers attacked his keyboard. Smith pulled up the raw footage of the peace rally from the network source. The picture was clearer on his monitor. He pulled in tight on a single image.

Eyes blinking furious disbelief behind his glasses, he pulled up the prison photographs from Mustafa Mohammed's cell taken weeks before the twentieth hijacker's escape.

"My God," Smith croaked.

The Washington Rally for a Free Kabul was being attended by many fringe groups, including an organization called the Tuesday Peace Brigade. On TV, the TPB's most famous member stood on an old crate waving a book over her head.

The domestic terrorism alert had been raised to red, and the nation's entire domestic security apparatus was still mobilized in search of Mustafa Mohammed, and no one realized that his book had already arrived in Washington and was a few hundred yards from the White House.

On Smith's television was Sally McAvoy, America's famous "peace mom," clutching Mustafa Mohammed's Koran as if it were a Bible and she a preacher at an old-time revival meeting, oblivious or uncaring that she held in her hand the power to obliterate more human life than all the wars she had ever protested against combined.

19

Mark Howard's folks had bought a thirty-acre farm in central Iowa the year before Mark was born. For a few years in the sixties Mark's father, who at the time owned a small regional chain of pharmacies, hired men to work the land but the profits were negligible and the government far too intrusive. Eventually he had given up on farming, which was not so great a sacrifice since he had bought the land not really for farming but as a place to raise his growing, young family.

Forest had reclaimed most of the old property except for a few acres devoted to pine trees which Mark's father grew as a hobby. Every year in December his father opened up an acre and allowed any locals with children under eighteen to cut down a free Christmas tree. For this Mr. Howard was revered by generations of kids in Higher Calling, Iowa, and had earned the nickname "Mr. Christmas." Mark had heard the name since childhood and so had never thought it strange to hear his father called that even in the heat of August at the Old Town Mall or in the parking lot at St. Benedict's, where

Mark had served as an altar boy and attended eight years of parochial school.

The crisp morning air smelled of pine as Mark stepped out onto the big wraparound porch of his parents' home. He was wearing jeans and a heavy sweater and carried his gleaming leather briefcase at his side. His sneakers were a little too new and white for his liking. He had left Rye in haste for his trip to Washington and had packed on the fly. After the War Room briefing at the Pentagon, Dr. Smith had insisted that it was too dangerous to risk returning to Rye. Mark could not pack properly for a trip home to Iowa and so had to purchase whatever he needed when he landed.

The new sneakers squeaked on the gravel drive on his way to the big red barn with the white trim.

The barn was hardly used these days. The busy season had just ended for Mr. Christmas and Mark's dad did not put much work into the trees he grew. He used to fuss for hours on weekends among his pines but as he had grown older the old man's motto had become, "I'll keep sticking 'em in the ground, and whatever grows grows and whatever doesn't doesn't." Mark suspected that his father would have liked to give up the aggravation altogether but the community had come to expect something of him and, unfortunately, the trees remained healthy despite the benign neglect of Mr. Christmas.

A room at the back of the barn had been converted to his father's home office. Mark's father had sold his dozen pharmacies for a hefty profit to a large national chain a decade before and had little need for the office since. It was mostly used for storing old paperwork that should have been tossed out years before.

Some dusty newspapers were piled in a basket near a pile of wood stacked next to the potbelly stove. Mark noted the date on the top paper was from four years ago. He crumpled a few sheets, arranged some kindling and started the stove.

At first when Dr. Smith had ordered him to leave town, Mark had refused.

"If you're staying, I'm staying, Dr. Smith."

Mark had been on his cell phone in a Pentagon parking lot.

"I appreciate your loyalty, Mark, but this is not a request," Smith had said. "We need to be sure that CURE remains operational. If both of us are here and New York is Mustafa's target, Folcroft could be finished. CURE would be as well for there would be no one left to direct Remo and Chiun. This is not open to debate. Visit your family. You'll be safe there. CURE will survive."

Mark could not remember the last order Dr. Smith had given him. Though separated by many years, the two men were generally on the same page. Reluctantly, Mark conceded that Dr. Smith was correct as usual. But just because he was not in his Folcroft office did not mean Mark would shirk his duties completely.

There was still a question to be answered, a puzzle to be solved.

Popping the hasps on his briefcase, Mark set his laptop computer on his father's old desk. He noticed that the briefcase made furrows in the dust. There was nothing in the room he could use as a rag so he lifted his laptop and blew as much dust away as he could, then swiped the rest with the sleeve of his sweater. Brushing the collected dust from his sleeve and thinking that his mother would kill him if she saw him clean the old desk with his new sweater, Mark sat down to work.

There were several e-mail messages waiting for him from Dr. Smith, updates on the Mustafa Mohammed crisis.

Mark pulled up the data he had been working on back in New York. Dr. Smith was concentrating on Mustafa while Mark had been following the brother.

Achmed Mohammed had escaped Remo's car only to be

captured by agents near St. Louis. Although it was doubtful that he could know his brother's present whereabouts, that did not mean something of value could not be learned from the brother of the twentieth hijacker.

Mark scanned the latest data on Mustafa's brother.

The British were already making diplomatic noises for Achmed Mohammed's extradition to face charges for his involvement in the 2005 London transportation attacks.

There were dozens of new reports on Achmed from the CIA and FBI, but Mark was not interested in the editorializing that might seep into the reports of individual agents.

The top secret transcripts of Achmed's interrogation sessions were now available. Using CURE's resources, Mark had circuitously ordered that the transcripts be fast-tracked. He saw that Achmed had already surrendered the names of nearly two dozen terrorists.

Mark did a quick check. While some of the bodies at the al-Khobar building Remo had cleaned out in Security, Colorado, had been identified, most still had not. Identification was slowgoing since most of the bodies had been burned beyond recognition in the fire that had destroyed the building. But thanks to Remo, five of the twenty-three men Achmed had given up were no longer threats to the American public.

The tough questions had not even started and Achmed was already surrendering all he knew. It seemed like every one of these great, fearless al-Khobar martyrs sang like the Celtic Women as soon as the handcuffs were slapped on them.

It was a good thing too, Mark noted, for the agents questioning the terrorist were not being as tough on their captive as the situation demanded.

"Where are you from?"

"What is your name?"

"What are your intentions?"

Mark shook his head as he read the inane questions. All that was left was "What's your sign?" for Mark to think he was reading the transcripts of a cheesy bar pickup rather than the questioning of a notorious terrorist. Not that it was much of a surprise. The politicians in Washington had made these agents fear even the imperative of the "ticking time bomb." It was often mentioned in the debate over the extraction of information from terror suspects that the rules could be relaxed if there was an imminent threat. But since no one knew how much to relax the rules and since terrorists seemed to get more slack than the men who were protecting the nation, the agents questioning Achmed had obviously decided to stick with the interrogation protocol that would not get them hauled before a congressional committee. While a major east coast city awaited obliteration, it took the agents two hour-long sessions to finally get around to Achmed's brother.

Agent L: Let's talk about your brother.
Agent P: Assuming that's all right with you.
Agent L: Yes, assuming that's all right with you. We don't want you to feel uncomfortable in any way. Would you like something to drink? I could get you a hot chocolate from the vending machine in the lobby.
Achmed: Yes, please.
Agent L: You got a dollar, Jim?

* * * BREAK TRANSCRIPT * * *

* * * RESUME TRANSCRIPT * * *

Agent L: Oh, shit. Did you want marshmallows on that?

* * * BREAK TRANSCRIPT * * *

In his father's old office, Mark Howard shook his head and decided that God must truly bless America for divine intervention was the only explanation why the nation that he loved had not already collapsed into the sinkhole of its own stupidity. He scanned the transcript, expecting little in

the way of useful information. When he saw half a page
devoted to acquiring the suspect a Butterfinger candy bar,
Mark was about to give up when something caught his eye.

Agent L: There's someone helping your brother?
Achmed: Not helping, guiding. My brother is not an
          intelligent man. He would not have gotten as
          far as he has alone.
Agent L: So who is he? Where can we find him?
Achmed: (laughter, unintelligible) . . . not someone you
          can place in custody. He is beyond human jus-
          tice. My brother is a fool who does his bid-
          ding. The monster guides his actions. He kills
          not for jihad, not for any human reason. He
          kills because that is what he does. It is who he
          is. He is the face of death, and death delights
          him.

The potbelly stove had warmed the room in his parents'
barn, yet despite the heat Mark felt a chill up his spine.

Mark quickly read the rest of the transcript. Achmed
talked more of a "monster" that was directing his brother's
actions, but apart from a few vague references to his family
would not elaborate further.

Abandoning the transcripts, Mark backtracked to the
agents' reports he had earlier passed over. In his notes Special Agent Simon Lindsay, one of the two FBI agents who
had questioned Achmed, described the terrorist's demeanor
as "anxious" and "fidgety" up until Achmed began describing the man who had apparently helped Mustafa escape a
WMD lab back in Iraq. At that point "subject became visi-
bly afraid, as if he expected unknown terror suspect A to
walk in cell . . . when assured that was impossible, subject
laughed."

Mark was often able to make intuitive leaps based on few
facts. He had described it once to Dr. Smith as being able to

see the puzzle as one picture, even when the pieces were scattered across the table. But this time he did not need to rely on his uncanny sixth sense.

Still there was something more important missing.

Where was the Koran?

He read back through all the police reports, the stilted formal language policemen used when they were afraid their reports would become public record. And suddenly it jumped off the page at him.

There had been a waitress in the restaurant where Mustafa had been abducted by the Iranians . . . yet no one had questioned her.

It took him three phone calls and five minutes before he was on the phone with Kimberly Tawl. She had gone home ill after all the ruckus at the restaurant and the idea of questioning her had just fallen through the cracks. Yes, of course, she remembered the book, and yes, of course, she knew what had happened to it. With her own hands she had given it to the woman who came in demanding it.

"What woman?" Mark asked.

"That silly bitch who's always on television hoping that Americans get killed," the waitress said.

"Sally McAvoy?" Mark asked, in a leap of intution.

"You got it, buddy," the waitress said. "It took me a little while but I'd know her anywhere. I've got a brother in Iraq."

Mark disconnected the call and, eyes fixed on his laptop screen, he pressed out the multiple 1 contact code. The phone was answered on the first ring.

"Smith."

"Dr. Smith, it's Mark. Sally McAvoy's got Mustafa's Koran. All those cops and agents kicking around and nobody talked to the waitress at that diner. She got sick and went home. I found her and she said that Sally McAvoy had come for the Koran."

"I just found out about the McAvoy woman myself. She's in Washington. I have to try to persuade Remo to come back."

"Another thing. I think Mustafa's brother knows more than he let on," Mark said. "I'll fill you in later, but for the time being, what about me? If the book's in D.C. can I come back to Rye now?"

"The sooner the better," Smith said.

The dark figure sat high up on the marble tomb and cast a contented eye across the limitless rows of beautiful dead.

A winter breeze carried across the Potomac and stirred the neatly trimmed grass of Arlington National Cemetery. The trailing ends of his robes were wisps of black spiderweb, but though wind bit deep he did not feel the sting of cold.

So many dead.

There were Union soldiers from the Civil War whose gangrenous limbs had been amputated near fields of glorious death, and who had limped home to ruined lives, dashed dreams, and eventually to small plots of moist earth.

Confederate soldiers who had fought brother against brother at last reached rapprochement amid the digging worms in the vast, silent forever of rich loam.

Marines from the Great War who had died while still in their teenage years in far-off places never heard of in Indianapolis or Kansas City, places with strange names like

Belleau Wood and Chateau Thierry, had been shipped back in simple coffins and placed in tidy rows of rotting dead.

Paratroopers from World War II, cut to ribbons by antiaircraft guns before they had even reached the ground, wounded men crushed by German tank treads at the Battle of the Bulge, and sailors asphyxiated in sunken submarines propped up row upon row of simple white crosses.

Soldiers conscripted to the battlefields of Southeast Asia were here. They were called at a time of great turmoil and did not flee for fear. And here they were now.

He had not known the names of any of them when they left home, but in that moment when the bullet struck, the bomb dropped or the mine exploded, he knew them all.

Not that he was limited to war dead. Fatal heart attacks, skiing accidents, backyard pool drownings, bus crashes. Every minute of every day when the light of life flickered out another name was added to the great list. He could walk blindfolded among the dead in any cemetery in the world and know the name of the rotting meat beneath his feet.

The marble tomb on which he sat was a simple block on which was carved the inscription, "Here rests in honored glory an American soldier known but to God."

There were other tombs of Unknown Soldiers around the world. Following the First World War, France and Italy, Britain and Belgium had built monuments to the war dead who could not be identified. Their nations might not know their names, but he knew them all.

In Paris, beneath the Arc de Triomphe where a flame was kept ever burning, was a young fellow named Maurice Fauroux. His parents had died when he was a baby, and his grandmother who raised him had never learned his fate.

Great Britain's Unknown Soldier was Reginald Tickel, born in a small town in Lincolnshire, died in a muddy ditch in the Ardennes and undiscovered for eight months. Rats had made young Mister Tickel impossible to identify, yet his name was not unknown to the gangly figure in black.

At the base of the Colonnade of the Congress in Brussels

was a career Belgian soldier who had lived to middle age only to have his face sheered off by German shrapnel. The family of Hugo Moreau might have wondered whatever happened to their long-lost son, but there was one who knew the truth.

In Rome, before the monument to Victor Emmanuel, thousands passed by the remains of Franco Andreotti never knowing that his unidentified body had almost made it home to the cemetery of his fathers in Civitavecchia on the Tyrrhenian Sea, a mere twenty-eight miles away.

And then there was the boy in the box below.

America's Tomb of the Unknown Soldier in Arlington National Cemetery was the final resting place of Pvt. William Clyde Latimer, an honest son of Alabama, who in 1950 had enlisted in the Army in order to see the world and who had died far away from Mobile, on a muddy hilltop in Korea.

The figure in black brushed a bony hand over the cold marble and smiled. "Don't tell me 'known but to God,'" he said, his voice a hoarse whisper fed to the soughing breeze. "I see you, Mr. Latimer. I see the strips of leather that were your skin. I see the yellow bone, brittle as a bird's. I see your dead mama and papa in the family plot way down in Mobile, with the empty plot next to your brokenhearted mama just in case her poor lost boy was ever found."

The shrieking caw of a crow was his reply.

A flock of the birds flapped up from the river, settling to cold monuments and barren trees.

Although it did not chill him, he felt the cold of the marble. It irritated him that the cold did not bother him and so he lifted his skeletal hand and looked off to the distance. Across the river Washington hummed, oblivious to the fate that was about to befall it.

More dead. More names on the list. And all was good.

As he often did when he visited the final homes of the wonderful dead, the figure in black thought of the little anonymous Iraqi tailor of long ago. Old Abdullah had only wanted vengeance against the Turks responsible for the suicide of his beloved daughter. But as always happened, Abdullah had not been specific with his wish.

Many had heard the tales, but most of those trusted that there was no wiggle room, that they would be smart enough to outwit the curse. But, bless the old fool, Abdullah had not even tried. So blinded was he by grief, so desperate was he for revenge, the little tailor was far more rash than most men. Abdullah had wished for perfect health for his family and for foreigners to go off and kill one another. And now, over one hundred years later, he would have been horrified to see the results of his wish.

Not that the wish ever worked the way it did in the movies. He could not wave his hand and change the world in a puff of smoke. It was far from magic and in truth was much more mathematical in nature. Very complex. It had all to do with probabilities and controlled outcomes. The strategic nudging of seemingly random, unconnected things in one direction or another to affect outcomes.

Still in the early stages of their great technological age, humans were only beginning to understand the nature of such things. They tried to be clever by talking of the multiverse and quantum physics—sometimes they even got close to the truth—but still they had really only scratched the surface of understanding the true nature of the universe. It was a simple enough thing if one lived outside the quotidian existence humans were mired in. In truth, he had no idea how they endured it, trudging day to day through pitifully limited lives, trapped in sacks of warm meat.

He was their liberator. He freed them from the daily drudgery. Death they called him and Death he was, for his was the name of Death and death delighted him.

Abdullah again. Thanks to the old Iraqi tailor he had become Death. He had not always been so called although his true name was unpronounceable in modern human tongues. But the power of the wish as it came across the ages, across the many dimensions of the real world, altered his nature, reshaping him in any way necessary to ensure that the wish was granted.

Many thought of him as some sort of a deity which made him laugh. He was just a shadow of what mankind itself was.

There was no spirituality involved in it; only science, although on a level that human beings were centuries away from comprehending. Not that he would ever make the mistake of trying to explain it to one of them. One of his fellows had attempted to impart some wisdom on a human many years ago and it had ended unhappily.

That had been a costly mistake, one that had resulted in the dispersal of his kind to even more distant dimensions and realms. He was the last, a gatekeeper of sorts. The last one to remain behind in this realm, who had answered the summons of the mortal Abdullah and was now trapped on this plane.

The pale bones that formed his grinning mouth contorted into a grimacing frown.

"The Great Wang," he growled to the wind.

Why was it that those pests from Sinanju always seemed to show up at the worst possible time? It was not enough to chase off the two current Masters. Sinanju had been an open wound for him for far too long. This time they would have to be removed entirely. After Washington was gone and he was through counting the dead, he would take care of them. They would settle back in their village in North Korea to lick their wounds. The end would come for them there. The madman who ran that country would be receptive to persuasion as had been Mustafa Mohammed and Sally McAvoy. Fools and lunatics always were. North Korea needed sites to test their nuclear bombs and, unbeknownst to the two current Masters, the village of Sinanju had just gotten painted with a great big bull's-eye. Game over.

His bony frown creaked to a wicked smile.

As he watched the white winter sun warm the sky over

the District of Columbia, a shudder of joy passed through his rattling bones. It was right. It was fitting. It was justice.

"No human like a dead human," he said. He patted the Tomb of the Unknown Soldier. "Sorry to cut in on your racket, Billy Clyde, but I'm afraid that after today there'll be a whole lot more unknown dead around these parts."

He stood amid his swirling black robes, tacked into a gust of wind and was gone.

21

The closer the Tuesday Peace Brigade bus got to the nation's capital, the more Sally McAvoy wished she had picked another city in which to do the Lord's good work.

Sally hated all things Washington, and that included George, Martha, the state, and the jelly cake. Most of all she hated the District of Columbia, which she had long ago decided was the center of evil in the modern world.

The Lord had only instructed her to get to Washington, with details to follow, and so Sally had spent the last several hours among the protestors in the massive Rally for a Free Kabul who had gathered in Lafayette Park across from the White House.

"Massive," of course, was a relative term. Only about eight hundred people had shown up so far but the news media had guaranteed that they would shoot from the right angles to make it look like there were millions. Sally knew from experience that these TV folks knew their business. She had once attended a rally with only forty other fringe protestors, yet when she watched it on television that night the evening news shows made it look like Woodstock.

Unfortunately for Sally, though there were news people present, they all seemed to be avoiding the small patch of grass that had been staked out by the Tuesday Peace Brigade. With no cameras to mug for, Sally had spent her time attempting to proselytize out of the book to which the Lord had guided her.

The rest of the Tuesday Peace Brigade were confused by the book, which did not appear to be a Bible. Sally had decided that it was, in fact, a Bible after all but that it was written in the language of angels that no mortal could understand.

"The president claims to believe in this great and holy book," Sally called to passersby. She had held the heavy book overhead so long her arm was growing sore. "Even as he sends the American war machine overseas to rape the land of the innocents of the Holy Land. It must stop. The American love affair with guns and pillage must end. The president's soul is lost, but even Satan might have been saved if he had repented. To save his soul the president must meet with me that I can pray with him out of this holiest of holy books to which the Lord Himself has guided me."

Sally's fire and brimstone sermon was not drawing the crowds her stirring oration had once merited. She had yelled herself hoarse all morning but had attracted only a handful of amused gawkers.

Two teenaged boys walking by exchanged delighted glances before bursting into laughter. A woman in her thirties pushing a baby carriage was more polite. She tried not to laugh but whispered to her husband to take a picture of Sally and her book. Afterward the couple walked off suppressing giggles.

Sally lowered the book and slouched. Her shoulder ached and her fingers hurt. In frustration, she blew away a clump of bangs hanging over one dull eye.

This was certainly not like those heady days of just a few

short years ago. She eyed longingly the cameras and reporters that were filming other areas of the protest. To the press Sally McAvoy was yesterday's news. Of course, in their defense they did not yet know that the Lord was now appearing in visions to her as He had recently done on that refrigerator in Mexico. And before that on an English muffin. And the back of a mud turtle. Miracles were everywhere if one would just believe.

With a heavy sigh she hefted the book over her head once more just as Steve Sanders-Parker came crawling out of one of the tents the Peace Brigade had set up on the grass.

"The Lord," Steve cried, stumbling to his feet and running over to Sally.

Nearby was one of the dozens of D.C. police who had been assigned to the Rally for a Free Kabul. When he saw Steve, disheveled and ranting, he brushed a cautious hand over the butt of his sidearm.

"He's one of us, fascist," Sally snapped at the cop.

The officer, his face etched in stone, turned his gaze back to the cars driving past the White House.

Running full out, Steve tripped over his own feet, wiping out in the grass. He got up, breathless.

For a second Sally thought he had somehow found out that his wife had not actually sneaked off on a covert mission to fill an ICBM silo in Kansas with cement, as Sally had told him, but was now in Purgatory with a shovel hole in her head trying to explain her blasphemy and heresy to a six-horned demon. But Steve was as uninterested in his wife now as he had been on their wedding night. He slid to a stop before Sally.

"He is here," Steve announced, ecstatic.

"Who?" Sally asked.

"The Lord," Steve said, panting. "In there." He pointed back to the shabby tent. "He's waiting for you."

Sally climbed down off her orange crate and book in hand hustled to the tent. She was stunned to find the Lord sitting on the nylon floor at the back of the tent.

"Shut the flap," He commanded.

Sally did as she was told.

It was a simple blue-and-white nylon tent bought by the Tuesday Peace Brigade at a Salvation Army store. Sally could barely stand upright. She hunched near the door, clutching the Koran to her chest.

"I have been spreading your word, Lord," she said.

"Yeah, that's swell. Damn, it's cramped in here. Where the hell's your bus?"

A cloud of soft confusion passed over Sally's face. "They wouldn't let us park it so close to the White House. America's occupations of Afghanistan and Iraq have inspired to action many brave Arab freedom fighters who might come here and blow the place up. But Cindy's from Maryland so we left the bus at her house and most of us took public transportation. Her car is here if you want to sit in that."

"No, this is fine," the Lord grunted unhappily.

"My Lord," Sally pouted, "why did you appear to Steve?"

"I waited for ages for you to get through yapping. I finally tossed that faggot a bone. After all, you did stick a shovel in the back of his wife's head."

Sally wondered briefly if she was going to have to send Steve to Purgatory as well but she would have to wait and see. She wondered if the Lord would chastise her for those thoughts but although the Lord should know all, including where the Tuesday Peace Brigade bus was parked, He did not seem much interested in Sally's dark thoughts.

The beatific vision slapped his hands silently together, rubbing them anxiously. "Okay, it's showtime. Get water. As much as you can. And a pan. Yeah, a pan would be about right. About so big. You have a pan?"

Fortunately the Tuesday Peace Brigade always had a pan on hand. Steve had last broken it out when he tried to wash the feet of the hitchhiker they had picked up in Oklahoma. Sally brought the pan along with several dozen bottles of Lubec Springs water back to the Lord's tent.

The savior instructed her to fill the pan with water and when she was at last finished, He commanded her to bring forth the book.

"Sink it," the Lord instructed.

Sally held Mustafa's Koran over the pan of water. "You want me to get it wet?" she asked, confused.

"Sure thing. How many people in the D.C. area? You got northern Virginia and Maryland within spitting distance. We're talking a couple million easy. Sink it."

Sally lowered the book to the pan. The closer it got to the water, the less angelic the Lord's face became until, two inches from the surface of the pan and just before Sally's clutching knuckles brushed the water, the glowing white aura around the Lord disappeared completely. For a flash, Sally was shocked to see something darkly sinister. A grinning white skull with sunken evil eyes.

She gasped and withdrew the book.

The figure crouching across the tent glanced up from the pan. "What are you doing? Sink it, you stupid bitch."

Sally pulled the book further away from the water. "I heard that," she said. She was studying the Lord's face.

The ethereal glow had returned. The frightening image that had briefly overlapped the handsome man's face was gone. Sally was not certain if her eyes were playing tricks on her. Suddenly Loretta Sanders-Parker's last words were pounding in her ears: He's a monster . . . worms for eyes . . . skull . . . skull. . . .

The Lord should have been able to read her mind, yet again the glowing figure seemed oblivious to her thoughts.

"Sorry," he said. "Sorry. My bad."

"The Lord wouldn't curse."

"It's more a tiny little swear than a full-blown curse," said the figure, glowing slightly less now.

"And some of the other things you've said weren't very nice either. And you should know all, like where our bus is parked, and that we always have a pan handy in case we

have to wash a leper's feet or cook gruel to feed the poor.
Why didn't you know that? And digging up that dead body.
What was that all about anyway?"

"Look, I said I was sorry about the stupid bitch thing,
okay? Remember how I work in mysterious ways. Are we
friends again? Now, please, sink the book."

Sally wrapped her arms around the book. "I'm starting
to think you're maybe not who you claim to be."

The otherworldly glow faded, and the bearded figure
Sally had thought was the Lord for two glorious days sank
back to the floor. He shook his head.

"You really don't have a clue, do you? You think by being
on the anti-war side that you're automatically on the side of
good. I love your sanctimony. It feeds me." His voice was
angered.

"What do you mean?" said Sally.

"You're so blinded by self-righteousness that you can't
see past the end of your holier-than-thou nose. God, I do
love it. Back in the day I used to feed off war. The times
they are a-changin'. Now I feed off the avoidance of war."

"War must be avoided at all costs," Sally insisted.

"Fine by me if you want to keep thinking that, sister. I
know it won't matter if I tell you but it isn't war, it's avoiding
war that has caused the greatest number of deaths in the past
century. But, like I said, believe what you want. In the meantime, I've got work to do and you are no longer the Lord's
vessel." He sighed, shaking his head. "No rest for the wicked.
See you soon."

Without so much as a pop or a flash he was gone. Long
after he was gone, Sally continued to stare at the vacant
spot where the bearded man had been sitting.

"If he wasn't the Lord, then maybe he was. . . ."

She thought of the shovel sticking from the back of
Loretta's head. She thought of damnation. She thought of
eternal punishment. And then she thought of how she was
without sin, just as she had always been.

"A test," she said firmly. "He is only testing me."

Now no longer sure what to do with the book, she considered leaving it in the tent. She almost placed it next to the pan of water, but then she changed her mind. What if the glowing figure returned and got someone else to take the book, just as she had gotten it from the diner? It was obviously important, even if he had not told her why.

When she stepped numbly from the tent, she found the rest of the Tuesday Peace Brigade watching the sky. A distant rumble, like the exploding Baghdad bombs she had once protested against but only when they were killing Saddam's thugs and murderers, rolled across official Washington.

"What was that?" Sally asked.

"Thunder," Steve Sanders-Parker said.

"Oh," Sally said, without hearing. She was wondering how many Hail Marys Father Billy back home would make her say for sticking a shovel in someone's brain.

Holding the book to her chest, she watched the dark rain clouds roll in.

Chiun had ordered a fleet of taxis to cart his luggage to the airport. The Master of Sinanju's fourteen lacquered steamer trunks were piled neatly in the living room. Remo had packed as well. His toothbrush and spare T-shirt were in a Blockbuster Video bag next to the front door.

The cabs had not yet arrived when Remo heard the sound of a single car engine driving up the hill out front. It stopped in their driveway. Remo recognized the distinctive heartbeat and creak of one knee as the driver hurried to the front door. So, apparently, had Chiun.

"It is Smith," Chiun hissed. "Quick, shut off the lights."

"It's daylight still, Little Father."

"Turn on the sprinklers."

"After last Halloween I shut them off."

Chiun had no time to whisper more instructions before Remo opened the front door and Smith spilled inside.

"Mustafa's Koran," Smith announced breathlessly. "It's in Washington. There is a military jet waiting. I can have you there in under an hour."

"You remember when people used to say hello, Little Father?" Remo asked.

The Master of Sinanju did not offer Smith even a perfunctory bow. Hooded hazel eyes regarded Smith as if the CURE director were a dead mouse that the cat had just dropped on the living room carpet. "Better was when people understood the meaning of good-bye," the old Korean droned.

"Remo, please," Smith said. "You were not answering your phone. You must get that Koran."

"I thought it was Mustafa I must get."

"Not any longer. Mustafa is out there somewhere but right now he's not our main problem." Smith quickly explained the weaponry potential of Mustafa Mohammed's family Koran and the danger it represented to millions and in whose hands it had wound up. "I have not alerted FBI or CIA yet," he finished, breathless. "Sally McAvoy is unstable, her behavior too unpredictable."

"Wait, Sally McAvoy? The mommy-of-the-year who's so busy protesting she doesn't have time to plant a friggin' geranium on her kid's craphole-of-a-grave?"

"Mark figured it out. She picked up the Koran back at that restaurant. There is no doubt she has the book. I saw it on the news."

"Good. Throw a butterfly net over her and that book and be done with it. The tinfoil in her hat's been screwing with our radio reception."

"I can't," Smith insisted. "It is too dangerous to trust anyone outside of CURE. She has friends in government. If she is tipped off that agents are closing in, or if she suspects it on her own, and assuming she knows the unique properties of the book, she could sink the Koran in water and kill everyone in Washington, including the president. She is protesting directly across from the White House."

"Tell him to get out of town," said Remo.

"He refuses to leave," Smith said. "Remo, you have to go to Washington. Until now Sally McAvoy has been a harmless simpleton on the fringes but now the devastation she can wreak is incalculable. Millions could die. You and Chiun must get that book from her."

Chiun drew back the curtains and glanced out the window. "Is that our ride?" he asked blandly.

"The cabs haven't arrived yet and you know it, Little Father," Remo said in Korean.

Smith could see that he had reached Remo. There was a look of troubled indecision in his dark eyes. Chiun saw it too and, releasing the curtain, the old man quickly drifted to his pupil's side.

"Remo cannot go," he said.

"But why?" Smith pleaded. "Why are you quitting? I think that after all this time I deserve an explanation."

"Trust me, Smitty, this is one of those things that you don't want to know about."

"At least tell me if it is connected with Wildwood Cemetery. It is, isn't it?"

Remo glanced down at the Master of Sinanju who stood at his pupil's side, arms crossed, expression stern. Remo glanced back at Smith. "Yes, it's Wildwood, yes it's us, no, it doesn't have anything to do with CURE. I doubt this guy knows anything beyond that cemetery plot. He knew I wasn't in it and he knows who really is. I mean, I assume so. Is Whiteman the guy you stuck in that hole?"

"Yes. MacCleary handled the Whiteman matter," Smith said. "So this individual you've encountered is a he?"

"Actually, he's more of an it. And this isn't twenty questions, Smitty. For your own sanity, drop it."

"Are you sure he knows nothing of CURE?"

"Not a hundred percent but it looks that way."

Visible relief settled on the shoulders of the CURE director. The stress of the past few days suddenly caught up to him and he took a seat in a simple wooden chair, the only piece of furniture in the room.

"We would love more than anything to assist you in this hour of need, as we have so many, many, many times in the past, Emperor Smith," Chiun said, "but lamentably we have more pressing private matters to contend with."

"I'm going to D.C.," Remo said quietly.

Chiun spun furiously on his pupil. "We are not going," the Master of Sinanju snapped in Korean.

Remo's expression was somber. "Chiun, I've tried to explain it to you before," he replied in the same language. "America is special to me the way Sinanju is special to you. I love my country and Washington is a symbol all the bad guys would love to wipe out. If these nutsos have something that can do that, I've got to help, no matter what."

Chiun folded his arms. "Then you go without me."

Rather than admit foolish error and surrender to the will of his teacher, Remo slowly shook his head.

"So be it," he said.

Chiun exhaled angry frustration. "Have you forgotten your obligations to the House?" he demanded. "You are Reigning Master now. I could forgive your impulsiveness when you were young but you can no longer run off on every fool's errand Smith throws in your path. Set aside for this moment the specter of death who stalks us. If Smith is correct, the poison in this book is enough to kill you. And for what? A city of politicians. Men you rightly deride nearly every day. Men who are, Remo, lower than prostitutes, for at least streetwalkers serve a useful function."

"Little Father, I do not expect you to understand. But if this woman destroys Washington, the worst scum of humanity will be dancing in the streets around the world. I can't give them that victory."

"So this is it? On the whim of a woman even Smith thinks is insane you would end the five-thousand-year Sinanju line?"

"If I die—and I don't plan on it—you've got a head start for the next time," Remo pointed out.

Chiun waved a hand. "The sand runs low for me. I do not have another thirty years to train a pupil, let alone the extra time I would need to unteach bad habits. I will accompany you. But if we die in this fool venture it will be entirely your doing."

The old Korean turned to Smith. The CURE director had been watching the two men bicker, head turning from side to side as the verbal ping-pong match escalated. Although he did not understand Korean, he knew that a resolution had been reached. When Chiun fixed him with a cancerous glare, it felt like the sort of glare one should stand for and Smith quickly clambered to his feet.

"We're both going, Smitty," Remo said.

"I'll drive you to the airport," Smith said.

"No," Chiun said. "Remo will take your vehicle. You will stay here and oversee the loading of my luggage, for I have arranged that it be shipped ahead to England, then home. For us to do this one last thing for you, you will do this for me, as well as pay for the taxis."

"Very well," Smith said. He handed Remo his keys and gave directions to a nearby municipal airport where a Navy helicopter was waiting to take them to the Army jet.

"Stop," Chiun commanded as Remo was heading for the door. To Smith he said, "Before we leave, you will agree to get me an autographed picture of Judge Ruth. This is a non-negotiable demand and you will guarantee it or we do not go."

"Little Father, this isn't the—"

"Silence," Chiun snapped.

"Done," Smith said.

Without any more acknowledgement, the old Korean marched out the door. Right behind his teacher, Remo offered Smith a shrug. "At least we have our priorities straight. You've got to say that about us."

Remo could see the worry writ large on his employer's face. Some were able to hide it better but all good men felt the same emotion when sending their troops into the waiting arms of death.

"Good luck, Remo," Smith said, expression ill.

Remo flashed a reassuring smile and lightly clapped

Smith on the shoulder. "Don't worry about a thing. Just tell the twits in Congress to light a candle in the window for the cavalry. Assuming they haven't figured out a way yet to tax flame."

Even when the Iraqi scientists under the leadership of the great Saddam had dragged his family away one by one for experimentation and death, Mustafa Mohammed had not felt so low. Even after he had overslept and failed to catch the plane he was supposed to fly into the White House he was not so despondent. The years he had spent in the infidel prison worrying that the Prophet had forgotten him were bad but even then there was always a glimmer of hope, for at least in Berkwood Federal Penitentiary he always had the Prophet's weaponized Koran.

For the thousandth time in two days Mustafa replayed in his head the events in Missouri. And for the thousandth time he knew that he could not have done anything differently.

He had been outnumbered. There was no way he could have gotten away from Alawi Sulayam's men.

He could have told them the truth right away. Even though they were Iranians, they were supposed to be on the same side as Mustafa, fighting the good fight for al-Khobar. But Mustafa knew that if he had surrendered the Koran at the diner, both the book and Mustafa within hours would have been across the border in Canada on their way to being delivered into the hands of the Iranian government.

Mustafa could not have done anything differently. Still in his mind he pictured himself the hero, killing Sulayam and his men, stealing their car keys, grabbing his book, driving east to glorious martyrdom, as he was destined to do.

But now his family Koran was in the hands of another—someone entirely unknown to Mustafa. The Prophet must have foreseen his failure and intervened which was why the parchment fragment had not worked at the diner. The Prophet had truly abandoned him for good this time and with him had vanished all chance for a great, heroic death.

After escaping from the two vicious American killers near the Missouri diner, Mustafa had been unsure what to do next. He had not felt so alone in all his life. For a time he parked by the side of the road and wept. His bandaged fingers and toes ached even more than the open wounds of his forearms where the flesh had been burned away.

Sniffling, rubbing mucus on the back of his injured hand, he at last came to a decision. Yes, the Prophet had taken away his great destiny, but in his final visit he had offered a small chance at redemption.

In the dark hours of the night Mustafa robbed a convenience store. He stole food and maps, as well as Band-Aids and aspirin for his wounds. Afterward he had driven to the heart of darkness in America, Washington, D.C.

Maybe the Prophet had not abandoned him entirely for the police did not stop Mustafa on his long trek east.

Once in D.C., he turned up the collar of his jacket and put on a pair of sunglasses he had stolen from the convenience store. He hunched behind his steering wheel and drove through streets where people lived, neighborhoods that were not part of the tourist section of the District of Columbia.

Mustafa was surprised to see so many faces darker than his own. His impression of America had always been that of a whites-only club with a few blacks allowed to compete in sports or act in movies and the rest locked away in prison. But here were many blacks, most well dressed and seemingly happy, living in homes that, while not palaces, were nicer than any dwelling in his native village.

Mustafa found a tidy brick building into which were streaming many young happy black faces. None of the happy faces was older than twelve. A sign out front read "Cornwall East Grammar School." A female police officer was directing traffic in the road in front of the school.

Mustafa held his breath when she held up her hand for him to stop. A dozen children with backpacks streamed across the street and through the gates of the school. They raced across the front driveway where buses and harried parents were dropping off more children and joined the stampede of students up the front steps.

Before allowing traffic to resume, the police officer squinted her eyes at Mustafa. Fortunately the sun was behind him, so if she had any suspicions they vanished the moment a few cars down the line started beeping horns.

Traffic resumed and Mustafa drove around the block. He parked in a wide alley next to a small abandoned warehouse. Engine idling, he hid behind the open trunk and took inventory of the supplies he had liberated from the Elite Incursion Martyrdom Brigade when he escaped back in Missouri.

He loaded a vest with explosives and taped a detonator to a waist that had grown two belt sizes during his time as a guest of the hated American government. It took a long time to get everything ready. The more intricate the task, the more difficult it was to use his injured fingers. He stuffed a gun in every pocket and slipped his jacket back on. When he checked the clock in the car, he was surprised that it had taken him nearly four hours. Sweat dotted his brow.

Classes had long been in session by the time he arrived back at the school. A late bus with students in the afternoon kindergarten class was parked across the street. Tiny children bounded down the steps and were ushered through the crosswalk in a skipping row by a female police officer. Mustafa noted that it was a different woman from the one who had been acting as crossing guard that morning.

The stop sign was extended on the side of the bus. Mustafa was at the front of the row of traffic and he dutifully obeyed the sign in order to get a good look at the school.

The building was four stories tall, ugly and cubelike. An explosion at the center of the ground floor would collapse the floor immediately above, and when that one went the next two would go as well. With luck, the whole building would collapse toward the middle and bury several hundred young students in the rubble-filled basement.

Others in this jihad would be delighted to take so many infidels with them in a final act of martyrdom. But Mustafa Mohammed was disappointed; he was supposed to obliterate millions and a few hundred infidel children, while enough to gain him glory in the afterlife, was nothing compared to the destiny that should have been his, the destiny that had been handed off to another. He doubted that he would even be invited to enjoy the seventy-two heavenly virgins that should be waiting for him. He thought of his fellow 9/11 hijackers. They would be eating sweet dates and honeyed cakes and taunting him mercilessly for missing his flight back in 2001. As he waited for the final children to step down from the bus, Mustafa Mohammed cursed for the thousandth time the man, doubtless an American, who had invented the snooze bar on an alarm clock. Mustafa would be lucky to get any virgins at all, much less six dozen of them.

The last child, a cute little girl of six, with purple beaded cornrows and a matching purple skirt, hopped to the sidewalk and skipped across the street.

He would have to kill the crossing guard. But the police officer had a sidearm and a walkie-talkie. When the bus pulled away from the curb, Mustafa spied her squad car tucked between two minivans a little ways up the road. There was no partner in the car, but she might still be able to call for help on her walkie-talkie. He would have to take her out fast. Then the school, an explosion, and an embarrassing eternity of taunts by murderers more successful than he.

The bus was halfway down the block and already turning a corner. An angry horn beeped behind him. Mustafa drew up tight beside a parked van. A few backed-up cars were nudging around him as he slipped a pistol into a bandaged hand. Sighing deeply, he reached for the door handle. When he exhaled, his breath was white steam.

It was cold outside, but the heater in the car was running high. Dark shadows passed over his hood. Two fat crows flapped to rest on the telephone wires a car length ahead. He shivered in his heavy coat.

"Okay, here's the thing," suddenly said a voice beside him.

When he turned, Mustafa felt his heart rejoice. The familiar visage of the Prophet once more blessed Mustafa Mohammed with his glorious presence. The Prophet seemed distracted and his voice was more nasal than usual, annoyed.

But even more joyous than the Prophet's return were the words next spoken by the glorified figure.

"I need you to get your book back." The Prophet's eyes were directed not at Mustafa but at the crossing guard.

Since Mustafa's first pass by the school, the sun had disappeared behind gloomy black clouds. No longer blinded by sunlight, the police officer had taken interest in Mustafa's double-parked car. She shouted something Mustafa could not hear and waved for him to move along.

"So this was all just a test after all, Prophet?" said Mustafa, practically singing the words.

"Yeah, right. A test. You passed. Straight A's. Just like the genius you are. Now hurry up and move it. This chick means business."

Rejoicing silently at his good fortune, Mustafa did as he was told.

The policewoman watched the car with the Missouri plates pull back into traffic. If she saw the Prophet sitting in the car she did not seem to care, nor did she appear to recognize the most wanted man in America behind the wheel. She waved an angry hand for Mustafa to keep moving and turned her attention at once to the car behind his, waving for the next man in line to hurry along as well.

"I am invincible with you to guide me, Prophet," Mustafa said proudly.

The figure in black shook his head. When he spoke, it was to himself, not Mustafa. "I don't need invincible, I just need *someone . . . anyone* to get this damn show on the road."

An entire runway at Ronald Reagan Washington
National Airport had been shut down for Remo's plane. The
Army jet was still rolling to a stop as Remo and Chiun
hopped down to the tarmac. Smith had arranged for a car
and driver to be waiting for them. The young man in the suit
and tie did not know what to expect, only that he was to de-
fer to every command of the men who got off the plane.
This he told Remo.

"Good," Remo said. "Keys."

"Um, sir, I'm supposed to be your driver."

"You're supposed to do everything I say?"

"Yes, sir."

"Stand on one foot, cluck like a chicken and give me the
car keys."

The confused young Department of Homeland Security
agent failed to follow the first two orders, but did finally,
with reluctance, hand over his keys.

"There's hope for you yet," Remo said as he hopped in
behind the wheel. "What are you doing in government?"

Chiun took the front passenger seat and they sped into the heart of Washington.

The traffic was no more clogged than usual. It was well before the end of the workday, so more traffic was streaming into D.C. than out. Despite the elevated terror threat that had been issued, this was just a normal day. The nation's capital had no idea that the end was nigh.

Remo found a blue siren bubble which he placed on the dashboard, but all he managed to turn on was the rear window defogger, the wipers, the AM radio which he then could not figure out how to shut off, and the wipers again.

"A little help, Little Father?" Remo asked.

Chiun tossed the non-flashing bubble out the window and under the wheels of a speeding tractor-trailer. "You're welcome," the Master of Sinanju said.

"You don't have to be so pissy."

"And you do not have to be so pigheaded. If Smith is correct, the bugs living in that book will kill millions. Will it make you feel better, Remo, if we are numbered with the dead?"

"It won't kill anyone if we stop it," Remo said.

"If this being truly is the face of Death, we cannot defeat it. Even if we thwart it this time it will return, angry that we failed to heed its warning."

Remo careered into the commuter lane and then lane-hopped back across two speeding traffic lanes.

"Big whoop," he said over a symphony of honking horns. "If digging up my grave was the ace up his sleeve, I'm not sweating it, Chiun. I'm beginning to think this guy can't do anything on his own. Mustafa had that book in prison for years and nothing happened. Now this dingbat Sally McAvoy has it and so far Washington's still standing. I don't think he can get directly involved. I think he can only get people to do what he wants and I think we lucked out that he picked a couple of prize-winning numbskulls to do his dirty work for him."

"There is no way you can know that."

"No, Little Father, there isn't. But what's your alternative? We sit in the dark with the lights off and the shades drawn and hope to hell we don't tick this guy off for the next ten centuries? 'Cause if that's the case Sinanju Masters may as well stop being assassins and take up basket weaving. I'd rather go out in a blaze of glory than sit in a rocking chair on the back porch waiting for the sun to set on Sinanju." They were speeding past the Pentagon.

"Spoken like a true American," Chiun said.

"Thank you, Little Father."

And seeing the look of misbegotten pride on his pupil's face, the old Korean grunted disgust and stared out at the passing cars.

Mustafa Mohammed was grateful to have the Prophet riding shotgun for the streets of America's capital were confusing to an Iraqi terrorist from the small village of Khwajah. Like most people, including many Americans, Mustafa thought Washington, D.C., to be nothing but a collection of limestone buildings, broken up by the occasional fountain or patch of green grass. He was happy to finally see the Washington Monument rise above the bland urban landscape.

The Prophet told him where he could find the old Mohammed family Koran, and with a final command to "get that damnable book by hook or by crook" vanished from the car.

Mustafa located the Tuesday Peace Brigade's small tent village at the edge of the Lafayette Park protest.

Across the street was the White House, throne of evil in a capital city of demons.

The building should have been in ruins. It was Mustafa's fault that it was not. The plane that he should have commandeered on 9/11 would have obliterated the White House and crippled American morale. But the White House stood because Mustafa had overslept that fateful day and he had overslept because he had been up late the night before visiting

two infidel strip clubs. Perhaps if he had not rented a porno-
graphic movie on the way home he might still have gotten
up on time. America was so decadent.

Now, finally, he had his chance to redeem himself.

Mustafa saw the frumpy woman in the saggy sweatshirt.
The Prophet had described her but did not have to. The entire al-Khobar network knew Sally McAvoy. After all, they
were all on the same side.

The woman and her fellow peace activists were milling
about amid banners that read "No Blood For Oil" and
"Amerikkka Loves Murdring Inocents." And then a fat man
with a long beard shifted out of the way and Mustafa saw
his Koran. Sally McAvoy was holding the book to her belly
as she watched some low storm clouds roll in.

Mustafa's first instinct was to kill the woman and snatch
the book. Unfortunately there was a police officer standing
near her group of protestors. Many more were positioned
around the periphery of the rally, as well as patrolling the
sidewalk in front of the White House.

His opportunity came when Sally walked out of sight of
the police in order to use the eight-foot-tall plastic Plop-
a-Poop portable toilet that had been rented for the protest.
Mustafa sneaked up around the back and lay in wait and just
when Sally was opening the door he jumped her.

Her attacker grabbed for the book in the crook of her arm.
Sally wrapped her arms around the book and held tight.

"What are you doing?" she cried.

"Let go!" Mustafa hissed. He punched her face.

Mustafa wasn't much of a fighter and the blow only dazed
Sally for an instant. She came back baring fangs and sank her
teeth in the back of his bandaged hand. Mustafa's howl
brought someone running.

"Oh dear," Steve Sanders-Parker said.

"Get this maniac off me," Sally snapped.

"I'm sorry but we took a pledge of nonviolence," Steve
whined. He held his shaking hands up near his chest like a
frightened woman shielding her purse from a mugger.

"He's trying to kill me!" Sally said.

Mustafa tried to pry away her fingers, but she kicked him in the knee. Mustafa found that the woman was wiry and strong. He had beaten women back in Iraq, of course, but none had put up any struggle at all, let alone reacted with violence. He tried wrapping his arms up under the Koran, hoping to peel it away. His hand brushed a small breast and Sally reacted like a wounded bear. Hauling back, she clouted the terrorist in the side of the head with the Koran.

Mustafa reeled. Sally dropped a hard heel down on his right foot. Missing toenails brought a fresh shock of white-hot pain and he gasped. When he threw his head back, Sally walloped him under the chin with the book. Mustafa fell back hard into the portable toilet, knocking the plastic booth over and slopping himself from banged head to bloody toe in the tofu and bean curd lunch that had been processed through the digestive systems of the Rally for a Free Kabul protesters.

Sally stood panting next to the toppled toilet. "You were a big help," she grunted at Steve.

"He looks like an Arab," Steve said defensively. "In any conflict that pits a brave Arab against an American or Jew, we must side with the poor, put-upon Arab."

Thunder rumbled in the distant sky. From inside the plastic container, Mustafa groaned.

Sally sighed. "Go start packing up. The rain's going to start any minute."

Steve did as he was told, disappearing around the tents. When she turned back around, Mustafa was climbing woozily out of the Plop-a-Poop.

She peered at his ordure-smeared face. "Do I know you?" The instant she asked the question, her eyes opened wide in recognition. "It's you, it's you," she said. "You're the Mustafa everybody was looking for."

"Shh," Mustafa hissed. "Give me my Koran."

"Your Koran? It's an angelic Bible that the Lord guided me to. At least I think He was the Lord."

"It is not your Lord, it is my Prophet," Mustafa insisted. "That is my family Koran and he has guided me back to it."

He started to reach for the Koran but Sally held it up as if to pummel him with it once more and Mustafa realized the risk was too great. The police might walk by at any moment. He had heard about Sally McAvoy's exploits even before his imprisonment at Berkwood, her denunciation of America, her trips abroad to embrace her nation's enemies. He leaned in close. "The book is a great weapon," he whispered. "Together we can use it to destroy America."

Sally scrunched up her face. "What are you talking about?" she said slowly.

For a moment she thought Mustafa was making a statement about all of Islam and not this particular Koran if that was indeed what it was. She assumed he had been turned in prison, probably by putting him on a leash and having a dog bark at his genitals. When she began to argue, Mustafa shook his head.

"Listen to me," he snapped.

Mustafa's voice was hoarse as he explained the true nature of the book Sally held in her hands. When he was finished, she blinked astonishment.

"This is what killed all those people at that prison?" Sally asked. Mustafa nodded sharply.

He could see that some doubt remained. "All you need to do is sink it in water," he said. "You hate this country as much as I. Place the book in water. Then all of our dreams will come true."

Sally hesitated. "He wanted me to do that too."

Mustafa nodded. "That was my Prophet."

"No," Sally said. "He didn't look Arab. He looked sort of like Niles from *Frasier* but with a beard. And Loretta said he had a skull for a face. Now, how could he look like three different things to three different people?"

"It is not our place to question the Prophet but to bow to his will. He wants us to do this thing. He has told you and he has told me."

Sally thought for a long moment, then shook her head. "I hate to be a Doubting Thomas but I think I've taken a little too much on faith these past few days. You're going to have to prove it. And besides, if everybody dies, I die with them. Then who'll be left to fight fascism? And this evil government that doesn't care about innocent lives?"

Still, Sally allowed Mustafa to tear a corner of one page from his Koran. When he suggested she sink it in water right then and there, Sally noted that he was staring greedily at the Koran. In a rare display of good sense, she suggested that he leave the scrap of paper on the grass.

Fat raindrops had started to pelt the ground as Sally and Mustafa hustled to the car of the local woman who had brought her to the protest.

For several tense minutes, Sally watched the raindrops fall. They smacked the road, tapped the roof of the car, and splattered here and there across the windshield. They struck everywhere, it seemed, but the bone-dry scrap of parchment lying on the grass of Lafayette Park. For a deep breath it appeared as if the threatening storm had stopped.

Then all at once the heavens opened up and a sudden downpour drenched the park. The instant water touched the parchment, bodies began to drop. Peace Brigade members who had been running from tent to tent clutched at throats and clawed at bleeding eyes. Farther away, other protesters began to fall. Sally saw Steve Sanders-Parker clutching his throat and toppling into a tent. His legs kicked feebly at the mud even as she threw the car in gear and stomped on the gas.

"Toss the book out in the rain," Mustafa insisted.

"No," Sally said. "No. That would kill too many people. I'm not a murderer. Not a mass-murderer," she quickly amended. "And by the looks of it, it'd kill me too, and suicide is a sure trip to Purgatory and there's no way I want to see Loretta before she has a few decades to cool off about that whole shovel-in-the-head oopsie. Besides, we've got the whole Rally to Free Kabul in town and if we wipe them all out there'll be no one to speak on behalf of the poor, downtrodden farmers of Afghanistan." She nodded, manly jaw set. "No. I know what we're going to do with this."

When Mustafa tried to snatch the book, Sally stuffed it under her fanny and squeezed his bandaged fingertips. His howl of anguish was swallowed by a clap of thunder.

By the time Remo and Chiun reached Lafayette Park, the rain had stopped, ambulances were on the scene, and the press was screaming for the president's scalp.

"What happened?" Remo asked a woman reporter with a microphone who was waiting for her cameraman to set up.

"Some poison gas or something was released. The terror warning has been on red alert for a day, but the president didn't tell us specifics. He obviously knew this was going to happen, and he let it happen anyway for political reasons. A domestic terror attack props up his sagging poll numbers."

"No, that's not it," insisted another network reporter near the first. The two blond-haired, blue-eyed, designer-clad girls might have been twins if not for the different logos on their microphones. "I heard this was the work of a presidential CIA hit squad out to silence opposition."

Remo looked both pretty young girls up and down. "Wellesley or Columbia School of Journalism?" he asked.

"Wellesley," said the first.

"Columbia," said the second.

"God save the Fourth Estate," said Remo and wandered off to find the Master of Sinanju.

Behind him, one of the newsettes asked the other, "Do you have an estate?"

"Yeah, but not four of them," the other said.

The first one sniffed. "What a dope he was."

Remo found Chiun standing on the sidewalk beyond the police barricades.

"Looks like the press is about equally divided between stupid conspiratorial option A and insane conspiratorial option B," Remo said.

Unlike the rest of the spectators, the old Korean was looking not at the bodies but at the White House. He did not directly answer his pupil.

"Only a fool does not flee when he has a chance," Chiun said. "The puppet president is lucky he is still alive."

"He's not a puppet, Little Father. I've told you a million times he isn't sitting in there just to keep the seat warm while Smith really runs the show behind the scenes. And I get your point and, no, I'm not running. Not anymore."

Chiun could see that his pupil was more determined than ever. The fact that an attack had occurred so close to the president's mansion, which was not even as nice as the palaces of France or Russia or India, stoked old patriotic embers that even Chiun had not been able to stamp out although he had tried to do so for many years.

Chiun shook his head. "Hopeless."

Remo flashed ID that got them within the police line. Two dozen protesters were dead. Others had taken ill and were being treated near ambulances while still more had already been taken off to hospitals.

Remo and Chiun did not find Mustafa, Sally McAvoy or the book anywhere. But Remo did find a scrap of parchment in the grass that had thus far been overlooked by investigators. He pointed it out to an FBI agent who bagged and tagged it and sent it off for analysis.

They left the crime scene and found a pay phone. Chiun glowered at scudding black clouds as Remo dialed.

"We were too late again, Smitty," Remo said when he had raised the CURE director. "The nuts escaped with the book."

"I was hoping you had succeeded when I saw the damage was so limited," Smith said, voice laced with disappointment.

"No such luck. Mustafa and Sally McAvoy were nowhere to be found. Assuming Mustafa was even here to begin with."

"He was," Smith said. "A man matching Mustafa's description, driving a car with Missouri plates, was spotted near a Washington elementary school. They found the car, filled with weapons and explosives, near the Washington Monument a few minutes ago."

"Hail, hail, the gang's all here," Remo muttered. "Well, the good news is he didn't use the whole book. We only found another small piece of parchment."

"I assumed that would be the case, given the low death count," Smith said. "There is some news on that front. At that diner in Missouri, you remember, nobody died when Mustafa dropped the parchment into water."

"Yeah. How'd that happen?"

"Our first tests say the virus was dead before it hit the water."

"How?"

"Sweat," Smith said. "Mustafa must have been clutching the parchment in his hand for some time. His perspiration killed the virus. The same traces were found on the page at the prison, although only on a small portion which was why it was still effective. He must have been sweating profusely and it was transferred to the parchment while he was handling it. His sweat killed the virus in a few small areas."

Remo recalled the blue whorl patterns of fingerprints on the parchment page found in Mustafa's prison toilet. "So whatever it is that keeps him immune from it also kills it?"

"So it would seem. The CDC is hoping that Mustafa himself can be employed to kill the virus. Assuming you can track down both Mustafa and the book."

"Well, we're at a dead end here, Smitty. Washington's still here so they must have given up on it for now. They could be heading up your way. Or they could be off to Miami or Tuscaloosa. Who knows with these maniacs?"

"I am not so sure," Smith said, thinking aloud. "Mustafa reached Washington. He would have used the whole book if given the chance. The fact that only a fragment was used suggests it was a demonstration. Since Sally McAvoy is not numbered among the dead, it is likely it was for her benefit." Smith hummed thoughtfully. "If he felt he had to make so dramatic a demonstration, probably he was proving the book's power to her. I assume then that the book is still in her possession. I will attempt to track her."

"You do that. I'm sick of being one step behind these clowns." Remo could already hear the sound of Smith's fingers drumming on his capacitor keyboard.

"Oh, and Mark has found something," Smith said as he worked. "I know that you would not tell me exactly what you encountered in Missouri, but it might help you that Mustafa's brother has been captured again and may know more than he told you."

"I doubt that," Remo said.

"Why?"

"Because I can be very persuasive."

"Perhaps this subject just never came up," Smith said. "He has mentioned several times a 'monster' that is bound somehow to his family. He claims that it is directing his brother's actions."

Remo glanced at the Master of Sinanju. He knew that Chiun could hear every word Smith was speaking. The old Korean glared at the clouds with fresh anger, shook his head and muttered imprecations even Remo could not hear.

"He say anything else?" Remo asked.

"Well, obviously none of this fanciful stuff can be taken literally. But given the extensive dealings the House of Sinanju has had in that area of the world, I thought that it might be possible the so-called monster that caused you to quit was merely some violent secret sect or villain Sinanju had encountered before. It has happened in the past."

"No, Smitty. Never met this guy before."

"Oh. I thought it might be important to you. Well, anyway, this brother Achmed said something about a great-great-grandfather, one Abdullah Mohammed, making some deal with an unknown entity."

Chiun's head whipped around so fast the far tips of his thin wisps of hair snapped like tiny firecrackers.

"Abdullah Mohammed?" Chiun hissed.

"Did Master Chiun say something?" Smith asked.

Before Remo could answer, the phone had been ripped from his hand and Chiun was snapping at Smith.

"Where is this knave being held?"

"Achmed? A jail in St. Louis," Smith answered. "But Mustafa's brother is a side problem, Master Chiun. Our main concern is still the brother and the book."

Smith would have said more, but Chiun had already hung up the phone. "Talk, talk, talk. Does the lunatic ever stop talking? Come, Remo, we must hie to St. Louis."

"Care to let me know why we must hie?" Remo asked.

"I must confirm that our enemy has given himself away."

Saying nothing more, Chiun spun on his heel and stomped off, a determined expression on his weathered face.

24

It did not take long for news to leak out that the brother of escaped terror suspect Mustafa Mohammed had been captured and was being questioned without the aid of legal counsel by federal authorities. Two congressmen and fifty lawyers, all crying about constitutional rights violations for a non-citizen illegal alien terrorist, descended on the downtown St. Louis police station where Achmed Mohammed was being temporarily held. When it was mentioned that the suspect had admitted to a plot to blow up Mount Rushmore, one United States congressman from New York City hailed the scheme.

"All them dead white men up there lookin' down their noses on us. About damn time someone blew it up."

His opinion was heralded as "visionary" and "brave" and the major weekly news magazines raced to get out cover stories touting the congressman as presidential timber, as "the man who speaks truth to power."

Amid all the madness, the questioning of Achmed Mohammed was suspended and the terrorist was taken to his dingy cell while authorities figured out what to do with him.

Achmed was sitting on a lower bunk, his knees pulled up to his chin. He found that if he pushed himself far back in the corner, the shadow of the upper bunk nearly hid him.

He was hiding thusly when he became aware of someone standing in the cell with him. Achmed had not heard the cell door open. For a moment he feared he knew who it was who could enter a prison cell so silently but when he saw the old Asian and the young white, his tense face relaxed.

"Thank Allah, it is you," he said, sighing relief.

"Not the reaction I'm used to getting," Remo said. "You want to tell me what exactly we're doing here, Chiun?"

The Master of Sinanju stepped forward. He grabbed Achmed by the ankle, bounced him to the cement floor and dragged him into the harsh cell light.

"You are from Khwajah?" Chiun demanded. When the answer didn't come fast enough, he slapped Achmed across the face.

"Yes, yes."

A look of angry understanding settled amid the old man's wrinkles. "Tell me about this monster to which you say your worthless family is bound," the old Korean commanded.

The spark of fear returned to Achmed's eyes. Remo could tell the terrorist was thinking of clamming up but a single touch to the side of his throat by the Master of Sinanju and Achmed's mouth opened wide in a howl of silent pain.

"It is the fault of an ancestor," Achmed gasped. "We do not know why but my great-great-grandfather Abdullah was angry at the Turk invaders. He used foreign magic to summon a spirit from the dark realms to do his bidding. But this creature would not be controlled. It killed him. It was supposed to be bound to a certain object, lost now. But Abdullah's sons feared the beast. Only one ever tried to summon it again and it is from him we learned what it looked like and of the requests Abdullah made of it. For generations all in my family had the wisdom to fear it, until my fool brother Mustafa."

In the middle of the cell, Chiun nodded slowly. Remo noted the look of cold understanding on his teacher's face.

"You know who this goomer is after all," Remo said.

"It is not a who, it is a what," Chiun said. "The spirit this one speaks of is a jinn."

Achmed recoiled at the word.

Remo frowned. "A jinn? You mean like a genie?"

"Sinanju has encountered their kind before," Chiun said darkly. "Until the time of the Great Wang the earth was plagued by them." The old Korean considered. "We will deal with Smith's problem first, then this creature."

Remo, who was still trying to wrap his brain around the concept that genies were walking the earth and interfering with the lives of men, shook his head. "You actually want to do Smith's work before personal business? I didn't see the Weather Channel today. Was there a frost last night in Hell?"

"What I need to defeat this spirit I do not have at the moment. When I do, it will pay for annoying the Master. For now we may do Smith's bidding. And at some point we will need to stop by the market. Peaches should suffice."

"Peaches," Remo said.

"Yes," said Chiun.

"And genies," Remo said.

"One jinn," Chiun corrected. "We may go now."

"That's it? No more quitting?"

"Why?" Chiun asked, frowning. "Do you want to quit?" Remo only rolled his eyes and followed his teacher. Behind them, still kneeling on the floor, Achmed relaxed.

At the cell door, Remo suddenly asked, "Hey, we still need the Sheik of Araby here?"

"No. And if you want to keep it, you will have to build a house for it in the backyard for it is not tracking mud across my clean floors."

Remo decided he had no interest in learning carpentry at this stage of his life so he tore up one bolted leg of Achmed's cot, stuck a squirming Achmed's head under it and let it spring down like a mousetrap.

"That's for Mount Rushmore," Remo said.

When Achmed was found with a cot leg through his brain, many in the media would howl about America's latest case of prisoner abuse but one university professor, who had received his doctorate in Native American studies by pretending to be a Cherokee Indian even though his entire family had come from Wales, would applaud the dead terrorist's exit. He said, "The determination of the man not to crack under torture by America's goons and the ingenious method by which Achmed Mohammed committed suicide is just one of many reasons why the American imperialist blood machine is destined to lose this so-called 'war on terror.'" A week later, his university awarded the professor lifetime tenure; the Cherokee nation meanwhile disowned him.

25

Sally McAvoy had hoped that the protester deaths in Washington would spark renewed interest in her one-woman show but when none of the press even called her for an interview, she decided to return to her regular stomping grounds in Texas. When she got there, she found that Camp Craig was the same desolate counterculture outpost it had been the past two years. She paced anxiously around the bus, Mustafa Mohammed's Koran under her arm, knowing that very soon she would do something that would change everything. Very soon she would achieve the end fondly wished but as yet unrealized by her movement.

She had retrieved the Tuesday Peace Brigade bus from the home where it had been parked in Maryland. Sally was afraid that her part in the D.C. Massacre—as it had been dubbed on TV—would be exposed but she had kept the kitchenette television tuned to the cable news channels for the entire trip and there had been no mention of her, which was a disappointment, but that had evaporated the moment she heard the good news.

"And in an act that some are calling cowardly," said a talk show host whose descent into vitriolic madness was counted down every night at nine, "the president intends to leave Washington in the wake of the activist murders. Some accuse him of fleeing the scene of the crime."

The president was coming to his Texas ranch.

"Will the range be enough?" Sally demanded of Mustafa Mohammed for the dozenth time.

The terrorist's hands were behind him and tied at the wrist around the leg of the small kitchen table.

"The Prophet told me it would kill for many miles in every direction. You told me the presidential devil's ranch is only five miles away. He will be close enough."

"My distance from his ranch was court-ordered," Sally complained. "Bite one little warmonger-in-chief and the secret service treats you like you're insane. I'll show him who's crazy."

She slapped the Koran down in the middle of the table. A barrel filled halfway with rainwater was waiting outside.

Mustafa craned his neck and eyed the book greedily.

Under ordinary circumstances Sally deplored killing but if Mustafa was right and the vision she had seen was his Prophet and not her Savior, she had already broken the fifth commandment when she stuck that shovel in Loretta Sanders-Parker's head. And the Almighty might suggest she had a hand in the protester deaths back in Washington. If she had managed to eradicate official Washington as well, He might have gone easy on her for that, being the same God who wiped out Sodom and Gomorrah. However, since she could not be certain of the Almighty's thoughts, she could not risk wiping out all of Washington, no matter how much she despised her nation's capital. No. Redemption for Sally McAvoy would come with the only single death that would wash clean her soul.

Sally suddenly heard the sound of a helicopter rumbling across the prairie.

Leaving Mustafa inside the bus, she hustled down to the

ditch that had been her home for much of the past few
years.

She had picked up a half-dozen Tuesday Peace Brigade
members on her way from Washington. The men were standing around the rusted water barrel in which Sally would sink
the great weapon of peace. None of the men owned guns, so
they were armed with whatever was at hand. They held plastic Wiffleball bats, wooden spoons and plastic Teflon spatu-
las. The eyes of the anti-war activists were trained on a small
black speck in the pale blue sky. The speck was growing
larger.

The president's helicopter never came within two miles
of Camp Craig. As usual, Marine One would fly straight to
the president's ranch, avoiding the site of Sally's ongoing
protest. But today, Sally knew, there was no longer safety in
distance. Today the true war criminal would see justice.

"I'll give him twenty minutes to get on the ground and
get settled," she said. "Then he will pay for his crimes."

It was an excellent plan but for one tiny flaw. Rather than
disappear in the direction of the president's ranch, the helicopter kept coming. By the time she finally saw that it was
not Marine One after all, the downdraft was hurling dust in
her shocked face and she could barely see the two figures
who jumped from the hovering aircraft. When the two men
hit the ground amid the swirling, blinding dust, they were
already running toward her ditch.

"Form a human shield!" Sally screamed to the remnants
of the Tuesday Peace Brigade.

She darted back into the bus to grab the Koran.

Mustafa had heard the helicopter closing in and knew he
was trapped. As trapped as he had been in his cage back in
Iraq. As trapped as he had been in prison, or in the hotel
room where the Iranian Alawi Sulayam had tortured him.

Mustafa chastised himself for giving up hope so easily,
for in this, the moment of his greatest despair, a familiar
face appeared before him.

The Prophet crouched in the aisle of the bus. A mouse poked its nose out of a cupboard and bounded to his ankles.

"Get up," he hissed. "This dingbat is going to blow the whole book on one isolated little ranch. I want millions not one guy and his staff. Hurry up and get up."

"My hands are bound, Prophet."

"Well, I can't deal with that so let me just take a look." The Prophet leaned forward, peering behind Mustafa. The terrorist felt the familiar icy chill that always came with closeness to the great apparition.

The Prophet dropped back to his haunches. "She ties knots like a girl," he insisted. "Pull loose."

Mustafa pulled. The pain in his fingers was fire. The helicopter was practically above the bus by now. The big vehicle rocked back and forth in the great artificial wind.

"Pull, damn you!" the Prophet shouted.

With a great wrench and a howl of pain, Mustafa slipped his right hand through the ropes, tearing off most of the gauze and Band-Aids in the process. He scrambled quickly to his feet, grabbing his Koran from the kitchenette table.

The Prophet had already vanished. A voice shouted a single word in Mustafa's head, and the terrorist was not certain if it was his own voice or the voice of the Prophet. The word was *Run!*

"There she goes, Little Father," Remo called as Sally McAvoy turned and scurried up the bus stairs like a startled rabbit from a coyote. The men near the door crowded in to block Remo and Chiun's way.

Racing close behind Sally, the two Masters of Sinanju fell in among the remnants of the Tuesday Peace Brigade.

"War is hell," Remo said as he upended the biggest man in the rain barrel. The man managed a few girlish kicks before his body went limp. He dropped his spatula to the ditch. "I've just declared it against all of you assholes. You want to stay and fight or you wanna retreat?"

As much as the Tuesday Peace Brigade did not like war,

they suddenly decided that they especially did not like being on the receiving end of one. Rededicating themselves to the ideals of nonviolence, they threw down their wooden spoons and plastic bats and retreated from the field of battle as fast as their flapping sandals would carry them.

Remo and Chiun flew up the bus steps where they found America's Joan of Arc wearing an "Israel Out Of Palestine!" sweatshirt and on her hands and knees searching desperately through the cupboards.

"Where's the book?" Remo demanded.

Sally looked up wild-eyed.

"I suppose you're going to toss me in your Cuban gulag and torture me now, you fascist stormtroopers," she snarled as she flung oatmeal and brownie mix to the floor.

"Nah," Remo said. "We ran an ad in *Fascist Stormtrooper Quarterly* but when they heard you'd be at the top of the naked pyramid all our applicants bailed. The book."

Sally stopped digging through the cupboards. She had given up hope that the Koran had somehow found its way behind the wheat germ and goat curd. "It's gone," she said.

Remo saw the ropes and some bloody bandages lying on the floor near a table leg. The rear side emergency door of the bus was open. It creaked on rusty hinges.

Smith was right. Sally McAvoy had briefly controlled the book, but its rightful owner had taken it back. Mustafa would not stop until he had laid waste an American city.

"He's not getting away this time," Remo said.

As the two Masters of Sinanju darted down the aisle, Sally scrambled to her feet and tried to bar their way.

"You are lapdogs of the military-industrial complex," she accused, foaming spittle flying from her lips. "America was founded on bigotry and hatred. War is a tool the West employs to distract the masses at home and suppress innocents abroad. There is no just war." She grew increasingly agitated with each shouted bumper sticker slogan, at last throwing her head back and raising her arms in grand rhetorical fervor. "You may kill me. . . ."

"Thank you," Chiun said.

As he darted past her, one deadly hand shot out. Whatever the last cliché Sally McAvoy intended to utter, it was lost in a shocked gasp and a damp thwuck.

"Give pieces a chance," Remo said as he hopped over the body. The head was rolling under a bench as the two men flew out the bus door.

Mustafa ran.

The brush was overgrown. Slapping branches sliced the soft skin of his face. The throbbing pain in his toes stabbed like box cutters with each stumbling footfall. Yet the pain was exhilarating.

He had his book!

The Prophet's wishes would be fulfilled. Mustafa would achieve the greatness that was his destiny.

The devils would be close behind. He would have to remove them, would have to kill them. Them and then millions more.

Mustafa tripped on a rock and fell. The book flew from his hands, disappearing under some scrub brush. Madly, blindly, he dug for it. He found the hard edge, grabbed it, dragged it back to his chest.

On his feet once more. Running.

Small trees grew larger. The underbrush grew thicker. Through the heavy growth, Mustafa saw something glimmering in the bright Texas sunlight.

His heart soared when he broke through the trees. A small, marshy pond glinted enticingly before him, an oasis in the desert delivered to him by the Prophet. Lungs burning, he raced for the water, tearing at the book as he ran.

He would not need the whole book. Half might be enough. He could wipe out the president and the demons who had chased him all around the United States, the two men who had murdered so many of his fellows in the al-Khobar movement.

A handful of pages were clutched in his hand. The pond was closer. Thirty yards . . . fifteen yards . . . ten . . . ten . . . . . . ten . . .

So pumped full of adrenaline was he that Mustafa only vaguely realized that he was no longer moving. His feet continued to charge madly along yet the water remained the same distance away.

Something had snagged his belt. Thinking he had caught a tree branch, he stuffed his Koran up under his arm and grabbed blindly back. His palm brushed warm flesh.

Mustafa wheeled around. No tree branch had snagged him. Mustafa saw a very thick wrist attached to an arm, above which was a very close, very unkind face.

"Take a seat, Ali Baba," Remo said.

Mustafa felt the slightest brush of fingertips at the base of his spine; his body went as rigid as a plank and he pitched forward to the ground.

Remo plucked the book and loose pages from Mustafa's bandaged hands as the terrorist fell. He was noting the blue smears where Mustafa's sweat had touched the pages when the Master of Sinanju slipped up beside him.

"I suppose they'll want to study this," Remo said.

Chiun sensed death clinging to the thing in his pupil's hands. "Do not hold that long, my son," he warned.

For a moment Remo wondered where he could put the book for safekeeping, where it would no longer be lethal. A thought occurred to him and with his toe, he rolled Mustafa over onto his back.

"You cannot stop my great destiny," the terrorist hissed. His sweating face had turned dirt to mud.

"That's what they all say," Remo replied. "Now open your mouth and say Allah."

The loose pages went down easier. The cover was harder. For a few moments as Remo stuffed the Koran down Mustafa Mohammed's mouth, the terrorist's throat expanded like a snake that had swallowed a large rat. Remo found a stick to help tamp the whole mess down. By the time he was done the last pages that were jutting through blubbery lips were turning blue, as was the late Mustafa Mohammed's skin. Remo stuffed the last of the book inside where it would harm not a living soul and clamped Mustafa's dead jaws shut.

"That's one fire out," Remo said, turning to his teacher. "Two more to go."

26

"**After his execution in Trenton State Prison, the** body of convicted killer Remo Williams was sent for tests to a medical research facility in New York," the nice young man with the wide face and the Midwest accent explained.

The three men were all young. One was a policeman, although he did not wear a uniform, and another had said something about being from the state of New Jersey. When she shook hands with the third man, he had said that he worked in a private hospital in New York State. He seemed like such a nice young man, with a pleasant, sympathetic smile and a soothing manner about him.

Mrs. Agnes Whiteman offered the young men tea and some of those fancy packaged swirl cookies with the artificial cherry in the center. In younger years she never would have dreamed of offering a guest store-bought cookies.

"No thank you, ma'am," the detective said.

"The facility was part of something called The Folcroft

Foundation, which was involved in diverse government-funded research," the young man from the hospital said. "This research included medical testing on executed prisoners."

"I don't mean to be impolite, but what does this have to do with my John?" Agnes Whiteman asked.

"Nothing, ma'am," the policeman in the suit jacket and tie said. "Mr. Howard is explaining about the body that was exhumed in Newark a week ago."

This Mrs. Whiteman understood. They were telling her about how John's body had been found in the wrong grave and how after all these years she could give him a proper burial.

Two of her three guests sat on one of the matching stuffed living room chairs. The man who said he represented New Jersey stood. He did not speak much and checked his watch several times as if he were in a hurry to be anywhere but here. Agnes sat on the sofa and for the first time in a long time was not embarrassed by the shabbiness of the old furniture. She was too anxious to be ashamed.

"The Folcroft Foundation disbanded over thirty years ago," Mark Howard explained. "The sanitarium where I'm assistant director was converted long ago to a retirement and convalescent home. But fortunately we inherited some of the foundation's research material."

"I don't understand," Mrs. Whiteman said.

The other two men were growing impatient. "Mr. Howard has helped us determine that the body in that grave is not that of your son," the detective interjected.

Mrs. Whiteman finally realized what these men were trying to tell her. A wrinkled hand raised halfway to her mouth but froze in place. Slowly the age-speckled hand lowered to one bony knee. "Are you sure?" she asked, her quavering voice small and faraway.

"We're sure, Mrs. Whiteman," Mark Howard said, hating himself for the lies, for breaking an old woman's heart. "It took us a while to dig up the research papers. Most of the material was destroyed years ago. Luckily we found some on this Williams person and a few other prisoners. I won't disturb you with the details but DNA testing matched that of the body in the grave. There is not a shred of doubt that the body in that grave is that of Remo Williams."

"But that sample you took from me," she said to the detective who had visited her when the story broke.

"We ran it too," he said. "It didn't match."

"Maybe . . . maybe this criminal and my John had the same DNA," she suggested.

"It doesn't work that way, ma'am. I'm sorry."

The men filed from her house.

Mark Howard was last out the door.

"But an angel told me," Agnes said.

Agnes Whiteman's eyes were moist. A single tear ran down her wrinkled face.

Mark could not tell her the truth. Could not tell her that he had tampered with DNA samples to assure a result that would keep CURE secret. Could not let her know that her son by his death had helped insure the survival of his country and that his reburial in the grave of Remo Williams would see to it that America held on for a little while longer.

The little woman looked so old and frail standing in that doorway. Mark's mother was getting up there as well. He pressed a hand to her forearm.

"I'm sorry," Mark said.

He turned and walked down the driveway.

27

Many hours later, night had descended on the little
whitewashed house in the tidy little neighborhood in Bristol, Connecticut. The camera crews of a week before were
long gone and so none were there to record the two shadowy figures who stole up the driveway in the still hours after midnight when all the world slept.

Remo pressed the wood around the door and the lock
clicked obediently. He and Chiun slipped inside.

"Smith said that he had taken care of this woman," Chiun
complained.

"He did it his way," Remo said. "Breaking an old lady's
heart isn't my way of doing business."

"What about an old man's?" Chiun asked.

But Remo was already slipping away.

Agnes Whiteman was sound asleep in the downstairs
bedroom just off the front parlor.

Remo was heading for her bedside when Chiun took his
arm. The old man shook his head. "If you insist that we do
this thing, let it at least be done with sensitivity."

"Hey, me heap sensitive," Remo said.

But when Agnes stirred, Remo fell back and the aged Master of Sinanju knelt at the sleeping woman's bedside.

Chiun manipulated a cluster of nerves at the base of the old woman's skull. Instantly, decades of grief melted away and Agnes Whiteman's face relaxed. The Master of Sinanju brought his lips to the old woman's ear.

"Accept the fact that your son is gone. Do not search for him. Do not hold out hope to find him for he is forever lost to you in this life."

The old woman's brow furrowed with fresh anguish.

"You have lived many years with your pain," Chiun whispered softly. "You will surrender that now. From this day hence, the memory of your son will no longer cause your heart to ache. Remember as if it were yesterday the joys he brought you in his childhood when the world was young. He made mistakes but he loved you. Hold fast only to these good memories in the time you have left and when your time is over the son you loved with all your heart will be waiting for you fresh and as young as you remember him."

When they left the bedroom a moment later, Remo noted that the anguish that the old woman had carried on her face for decades had melted completely away. Agnes Whiteman looked ten years younger. She had surrendered her pain and could now finally live out her days in peace.

They were back outside and heading down the driveway.

"Would that you thought as much of the feelings of your own father," Chiun said.

"She deserved a happy ending, Little Father," Remo insisted. "Or as close as we could muster. Even though she'll never know it, she helped us out a lot."

"She has never done a thing for me," Chiun insisted. "But then, no one ever has. Your precious Smith, for instance. Has he tracked down my luggage yet?"

"I told you, it's on its way. I want to know what's in there that's so important."

"You will find out when my trunks are returned."

"Not soon enough. One loose end left. By the way, that was nice what you said back there, Little Father."

"Of course it was," Chiun sniffed. "Unlike you I am the height of sensitivity. Now hurry up, retard. As soon as I have my trunks, you have work to do."

Remo was eating a peach when Chiun's fourteen lacquered steamer trunks arrived by special delivery bright and early at nine o'clock. Chiun supervised the transfer of his luggage from truck to living room. Smith telephoned as the last trunk was being placed on the carpet.

"Just a sec, Smitty," Remo said. Sticking the peach in his teeth, Remo fished a fat wad of bills from his pocket and tipped the delivery men generously.

The instant the door shut, Chiun was already moving among the trunks, snapping open lids.

"What was all that noise?" Smith asked.

"Chiun's trunks just got here. Took them long enough."

Remo sat on the raised brick around the fireplace and watched his teacher dig through the trunks.

"They had already made it to South Korea," Smith said. "He is lucky they hadn't yet crossed to the North or I might not have been able to get them back at all. As it is, it cost a small fortune to get them back this quickly. I still do not know why he wanted them returned so desperately."

"Join the club." Remo said.

Smith switched gears. "In any event, the final report came in this morning on Mustafa Mohammed. The CDC have finished examining the book that was removed from his body. The virus was completely destroyed."

"I have my moments," Remo said.

"It is unlikely that the research can be duplicated. Like most of Iraq's WMD programs, this research was shut down just as the invasion of Iraq was starting. Besides, Mohammed's family was crucial to the development of the supervirus. He and his brother were the last survivors. Without any living members remaining, the project cannot be restarted."

"Unless someone figures out a way to use some other family as guinea pigs," Remo said as he took a final bite of his peach.

Remo rarely ate fruit. He'd had half an apple at Christmas and had not expected to have more for months. He savored the last bite of peach and when he was finished he set the stone on the brick beside him. The Master of Sinanju had earlier placed another peach stone there.

"Why?" Smith asked. "Remo, you never did tell me why you and Chiun were going to quit."

Chiun had settled on one trunk in particular. Drawing his kimono sleeves up to the elbows, he thrust his arms down into the deepest recesses of the lacquered trunk.

"Don't sweat it, Smitty," Remo said. "It'll all be taken care of."

"Very well," Smith said after a moment of hesitation. "We are back to regular business. Wildwood Cemetery might actually be a blessing in disguise. It has now officially been determined beyond any doubt that the body there is that of Remo Williams. Whiteman's body was always a loose end but I do not expect we will ever have trouble there again."

"Speaking of that, what was the real story of the poor schmo MacCleary dumped in my grave?"

"Nothing interesting. John Whiteman was a drug addict MacCleary found. He took him under his wing for a time and even used him as the ambulance driver who helped MacCleary bring you back here after the execution. As it happened, Whiteman got into some trouble with a drug dealer and was shot. Right around that time, it appeared as if you were going to work out, so MacCleary arranged the body switch. He was dark-haired, and roughly your build. A perfect fit for your grave."

Remo listened to the cold recitation of facts and when the CURE director was finished, Remo sighed.

"No wonder you and MacCleary were friends, Smitty. Between the two of you cold bastards you maybe could scrape up one heart and one soul."

He was hanging up the phone just as the Master of Sinanju cried out from across the room.

"Aha!" the old Korean announced.

Chiun had pulled an item from the trunk. When Remo saw the battered old object, he shook his head.

"You've got to be kidding me."

28

Remo found his grave in the usual spot but not in
the usual condition.

He had only visited Wildwood Cemetery a few times
over the years, and the first time had been long after the last
shovelful of dirt had fallen over the coffin of John Whiteman. But this time was different. The earth before the headstone of Remo Williams was dark, with a rich loamy smell.

The hole itself was not rectangular, but jagged. Freshly
turned dirt had been scraped back into the grave from
where the Tuesday Peace Brigade had scattered it all
around.

It was strange for Remo to see the grave in this condition.
It had always looked old to him before. The grave must
have looked much like this the first time it was newly dug
after his faked execution. So long ago.

Remo chased the ghosts from his thoughts. He set on a
headstone the little bronze lamp Chiun had retrieved from
his trunks and, creating rapid friction between thumb and
forefinger, he set it alight.

The soft yellow glow in the cold dead of night was a beacon for the lost spirits of Wildwood Cemetery. Remo was only looking for one spirit in particular and he sensed its presence the moment the old lamp glowed to life.

Above a nearby mausoleum, the night sky had grown blacker. Within the patch of all-consuming darkness, a skull-like face frowned down at Remo.

"So you've figured it out," the jinn said.

The figure in black was more of an ambulatory corpse than ever. On the skull-like face, eyes were sunk deep in black hollows, the nose was a brittle chip over slit-like nostrils, and the forehead protruded like a fat knob of white bone. Patchy strings of white hair cascaded over shoulders covered in black gossamer.

"I've figured out you're a fraud," Remo said. He felt the worms stir in winter slumber beneath his feet, drawn to the figure in black. Bats coaxed from hibernation flapped about the figure's head. Nearby, crows cawed in their nests. Despite it all, Remo now understood the truth. "You're not really what you claim to be," he said.

Bony shoulders amid the black robes shrugged. "I am whatever I am called to be. Old Abdullah called for death, so that is what I became. It's all very complicated. I could try to explain it to you, but by the look of you I'd have an easier time teaching quantum physics to a field mouse."

Remo was not in the mood for trading barbs. "Abdullah's the one who called you. That's Mustafa's great-grandfather?"

"Toss in a few more greats, but yes."

"Okay, so what exactly did he ask for?"

"Oh, it was beautiful. Perfect health for himself and his family, and for foreigners to kill one another. You could drive a truck through those loopholes, God love him." The air remained cold around him as the spirit warmed to his subject. "Of course, you can't grant a man perfect health per se, but you can make it so that those afflicted with a cold virus don't come in contact with him. I made sure that only women of healthy stock whose parents had lived to a ripe old age married into that family. Tens of thousands of tiny nudges over the course of a lifetime and a man can live in perfect health until advanced old age claims him, oblivious to the meticulous little interventions of the unseen hand that took place every day of his life. I am good."

"So there was nothing special about them after all."

At this, the jinn scoffed. "I beg to differ. I made them a family of horses. Gave them perfect resistant genes. Never been anything like them. Poetry, that was. And the other wish was even better. Getting foreigners to kill one another was easy. More difficult would have been if Abdullah had wished for them to stop killing each other. This past century has been so wonderfully, spectacularly bloody, in no small part thanks to yours truly. Civil wars, two World Wars, Korea, Vietnam, Communist Russia, China, North Korea, Cambodia. I actually wept for joy at all the corpses, the skulls, the stench. Almost too much beauty for me to take. Give peace a chance indeed. Protesting against wars, pushing them off to some future date, has created so much more death than even I could have imagined. Of course, the Middle East is my masterpiece. They'll never stop because I'll never stop. I'll have that region in my grip long after you go the way of all living things." And Death smiled a rotten-toothed grin.

"You should see your orthodontist," Remo suggested.

"Ah, quipping. Delightful. Well, this has been fun but if we're done here, would you mind . . . ?" He waved a bony hand at the flaring lamp.

"I was in Vietnam," Remo said coldly.

"So you were. Two of those Viet Cong you killed in that farmhouse had children. Would you like to know their names?"

Remo ignored the wickedly grinning skull. "One more question. Are there any more of you left?"

A slight hiss of angry warmth slipped from the enveloping cold. "You mean the old one didn't tell you? I'm the last, thanks to your predecessor, the so-called Great Wang.

You know how he did it? He wound up once in our dimension and won a wish and he simply wished that we would leave forever, never return. Humans are supposed to ask for money and power. Not Wang. He just wanted us out of here. We hadn't planned on that. We weren't prepared at all. But rules are rules. I was the gatekeeper who stayed so that the rest could leave. I am the last. What's that?" A bony brow sunk questioningly over hollowed eye sockets.

The object that Remo had taken from his pocket was small. He bounced it in his palm.

"You were right, Little Father," Remo called. "He's the last of them."

The skull whipped around in time to see the Master of Sinanju slip from the shadows behind a mausoleum. A look of frightened realization dawned when he saw the small object held in Chiun's slender fingers.

He would have fled but the pull of Abdullah Mohammed's lamp was like an anchor around his neck, binding him to this place. A creature unused to the corporeal world, he suddenly realized that he could jump down and try to run away. But even before the thought occurred to him it was already too late.

With a snap of his fingers, the object rocketed from Chiun's hand. Simultaneously, Remo flicked the small round object from the tips of his fingers. Both hard objects struck the creature in the head, one in front, one in back.

Unlike Remo's last confrontation with the insubstantial black mass in Missouri, this time when it was struck there came the normal satisfying crack of solid bone.

An unearthly shriek pierced the night and the jinn slumped into his own robes and toppled off the mausoleum. By the time Remo and Chiun reached it, the jinn was collapsing like an imploding building. For a flashing instant the skull faded and Remo saw what must have been the jinn's true face. It was fleshy and round, vaguely Asian. And then the face and body collapsed to dust and was gone.

Chiun prodded the empty black robes with his toe. Satisfied the thing that had animated them was dead, he gathered the robes up in his arms. The two peach stones that Remo and Chiun had used to kill the jinn rolled out, and Chiun caught them in one leathery palm.

"So Wang got rid of all but one of these jokers," Remo commented. "Is it just me or do we seem to be cleaning up everyone's messes these days?"

"There was a time when these nuisance mischief makers were everywhere. Credit is due Wang for ridding the world of most of them."

"Just as long as credit goes to us for getting rid of the last one, right?"

"Us?" Chiun said. "Was it us or me, Remo, who knew that Wang had learned how to kill these things? Was it your grandfather or mine who purchased that lamp at the fruit stand of crazed Dunzyad at the Khwajah market? Was it us or me, Remo, who had the lamp in his trunk, a trunk which someone has complained about carrying around lo these many years?"

"So I'm not even a footnote, huh?"

"That depends," Chiun sniffed. "Smith has not yet gotten me an autographed picture of Judge Ruth. When he does, perhaps if you get me a nice frame we will talk about your footnote. Your small footnote."

Remo was still staring at the spot where the jinn had vanished for the last time, as if he expected the dust to reform and vanish. But the dust remained dust. Chiun touched his pupil on the arm. "It is dead."

"Rah-rah for the home team," Remo said, sighing. "So you think he was just boasting about making a mess in the Middle East for the past hundred years?"

"Who knows? Before Wang got rid of them, these things were most troublesome, especially in that part of the world."

"So things might get better over there now."

Chiun shrugged. "Directed in their violence Arabs are misdirected. Undirected they are misdirected. Being Arabs they never go in the right direction no matter what, so with these camel-fondling Bedouins who can guess?"

They turned and walked from the mausoleum.

"By the way, just before he disappeared he kind of looked Korean. You want to tell me about that?"

"Oh?" Chiun said vaguely. "I did not notice."

"You know," Remo said, "it's not over."

"No?"

"We got some of them but there's still a gang of them out there. That guy who left us the note back on the roof. Who knows where he is? What he's doing?"

"They are all fools," Chiun said. "Someday they will reveal themselves. When they do, we will deal with them. All hail Emperor Smith and this wonderful kingdom."

"I know," Remo said. "You're just a Yankee Doodle Dandy."

They were walking back past the stone marker on which was carved the name Remo Williams. For the first time, Remo failed to notice his own grave. His eye was drawn to the next grave.

In the excitement of the last few days, Craig McAvoy's last resting place had been trampled. The stick that had marked the boy's grave was snapped and weeds had been uprooted. Footprints in the mud had frozen solid.

"You know, Chiun, this kid deserves better than to be buried next to some anonymous junkie. Smitty doesn't know it yet but he's paying to have him moved to a better plot. And he's getting a real headstone this time. One that tells the world who and what he is. An American hero."

Chiun was holding up his trophy, brushing dust from the last jinn's robes. "Just as long as I do not have to pay for it," the wizened Korean said.

"You go ahead," Remo said. "I'll only be a minute."

As Chiun strolled off, Remo gathered up some broken twigs and used them as a broom to clear the debris from Craig McAvoy's grave. He walked down the path where other well-kept graves were festooned with flowers and from each one, he took only one blossom. When he had an armful, he brought them back and placed them carefully around the final resting place of the young fallen soldier.

He remembered something he had read in a newspaper and although he was not sure of the words, Remo stood at the foot of the grave and softly recited:

"Rest easy, sleep well, my brother.
Know the line has held; your job is done.
Others have taken up where you fell. The line has held.
Rest easy, sleep well.
Peace. Peace and farewell."

When he turned away, Chiun was standing behind him.

For once, the aged Korean said nothing. Instead, he put his arm gently around Remo's shoulders and the two Masters of Sinanju left the cemetery.

Remo Williams and Chiun return in . . .

THE NEW DESTROYER:

KILLER RATINGS

Warren Murphy and James Mullaney

Coming in August from Tor Books

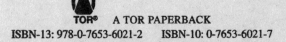

TOR®   A TOR PAPERBACK

ISBN-13: 978-0-7653-6021-2   ISBN-10: 0-7653-6021-7

Remo was whistling the Mexican Hat Dance when he returned to his room at the Miami Grand Hotel early the next morning. Before he slipped his key in the lock he sensed two heartbeats coming from the room beyond. One strong heartbeat he had expected, the other—an irregular gurgle—he had not. Remo stopped whistling. Briefly he considered turning around and making a mad dash for the elevator.

"My son returns, Emperor Smith," a singsong voice said from the other side of the door before calling loudly, "Do not loiter out in the hallway, Remo, lest the hotel staff cart you off with the dirty breakfast dishes. Enter and bid welcome to our most gracious and generous emperor."

"Thanks a lot, Little Father," Remo grunted, sighed loudly and pushed open the door.

Two men were sitting in the living room of the suite.

The first was a wizened Asian in golden morning kimono who sat cross-legged on a sunlit patch of carpet before the suite's balcony doors.

The tiny figure had skin the hue of walnut and speckled with great age. Twin tufts of yellowing white hair clung to the sides of his head above shell-like ears. The hair on his head, as well as a thread of beard at his chin, danced merrily in currents flowing through the room's cool, recirculated air. The skin was stretched thin, like living parchment, over an otherwise bald skull. Slender fingers ended in long, sharp nails which happily tapped away on a flat square object in his lap.

Remo recognized the woman in the framed photograph which the old man held. Chiun, the last full Korean Master of Sinanju, the original and deadliest of all the martial arts and Remo's teacher in lethal techniques that had originated in an ancient North Korean fishing village, brushed invisible dust from his newly acquired prize. He hummed happily as he fussed like a doting parent over a newborn baby.

Perched on the edge of the sofa next to the old Korean was a tall thin man in a gray three-piece suit and starched white shirt. His hair and skin tone matched his attire and, if not for the green-striped Dartmouth tie knotted around his neck, he could have been the subject from a fifty-year-old black-and-white photo album come to life.

A weatherbeaten briefcase was tucked in at his heels. When Remo entered the suite, the gray-faced man stood.

"Remo, what the devil have you been doing down here?" demanded Harold W. Smith.

"I read somewhere, Smitty, that normal people start off with 'hello,'" Remo said. "Besides, what are you so wound up about? Albondigas is dead."

"I know that. I found out after my plane landed."

"So what's the problem? So I took a few extra days. Big deal. As it is Albondigas came in handy. It's not like I could've used some sweet little old lady as bait."

The smile fled Chiun's face and he grunted disapproval.

Smith's brow furrowed as he watched Remo sink to the floor in the lotus position.

"Are you saying you used Albondigas to lure the mugger into a trap?"

"You bet. We can cross both problems off the list, by the way. Two birds with one stone, more or less. I believe in using every part of the buffalo."

Smith understood what CURE's enforcement arm meant. With a sigh, he reclaimed his seat on the couch. "It was clear to us that Albondigas went missing several days ago," he said, "but the information had not made it out to law enforcement agencies. It was not as if the cartel could phone the police. When you did not return any of my calls, I wasn't sure what to make of what was going on down here."

"What do you mean? You called here?"

Sitting in his splash of sunlight, the Master of Sinanju began humming once more, making a deliberate point to remain apart from the conversation taking place around him.

"Several times. But the phone was out of order in your room so the front desk had to come up here with a cell phone. I spoke with Master Chiun. He didn't tell you I called?" Frowning, Smith glanced at the Master of Sinanju.

Remo too turned a bland eye to his teacher.

Chiun hummed more pointedly, seemingly oblivious that he had now become the center of attention.

On the first night when he returned to the hotel Remo had noted the pile of phones that had been harvested from all the suite's rooms and dumped in plastic scraps in the corner of his bedroom. Chiun had already been in a pissy mood before they even came to Miami and Remo had assumed when he saw the phones that Chiun had taken preemptive steps to keep from being interrupted during his meditation. However, given the new prize clutched in the old man's bony hands, Remo began to understand the chain of events that had brought Smith here.

"He must have forgot," Remo said. "They say memory's the first thing to go. Right, Little Father?"

The humming abruptly ceased. Sharp hazel eyes, seeming much younger than the old Korean's advanced years, shot daggers at his pupil.

"Of course I told him you telephoned, emperor," Chiun said. "Before I would forget my joy at hearing your voice, the spring flower would forget the first kiss of rain or the life-sustaining nourishment of the sun. I distinctly remember telling him so if anyone forgot anything, it was Remo who has a long and checkered history of forgetting things. Gratitude for one. He left that somewhere, perhaps at the traveling carnival where he was born. Respect is another thing he misplaced long ago. And kindness. Although, frankly, I suspect he never had that to lose. The thing he has most forgotten is the individual to whom he owes all."

"Not this again," Remo said. "Please. Spare me."

Chiun plowed on as if his pupil had not spoken. "So while it is impossible for the Master to forget a telephone call from you, Emperor Smith, it is well established that Remo would forget his own big feet if they were not attached to his gangly legs. Do not blame me for your sieve-like memory, Remo," the old Asian sniffed.

"Why are you passing this off on me?" Remo snapped in Korean. "You know you never told me he called."

"Because I am not your answering service," Chiun replied in the same language. "No matter what fool's errand brought you to this foul city, this was supposed to be a vacation for me. But scarcely were you out the door when this gray-faced madman began assaulting my ears with that infernal ringing device. I silenced it, of course, as well as the others in each room which were squawking like dying birds. But no sooner had the last one fallen blessedly silent than he was sending runners up to intrude on my peace."

Smith who did not understand Korean could only watch as the world's two deadliest assassins argued until finally he said, "Any time now."

"In a minute, Smitty," Remo said in English. In Korean once more he said to Chiun, "I take it that's when he told you he finally got that for you." He nodded to the photo in Chiun's hands.

The woman in the framed photograph wore a black robe,

her arms folded across her chest. Her lips were turned up in a painful contortion that was as much a wince as it was a smile. Her head was capped in a reddish-brown perm. Across the bottom of the photo was written in big looping script, "Behave yourself. Regards, Judge Ruth."

"Yes, and it was about time," Chiun sniffed. "I was promised this boon months ago. He said that he had finally acquired it and that he would mail it to me. I did not trust that it would get to me in one piece."

"So you flimflammed him onto a plane by making him think I'd gone AWOL just so he'd deliver it personally?"

"It is in one piece, is it not?" Chiun said. He gathered up his autographed Judge Ruth picture and breathed onto the glass, polishing away the moisture with the sleeve of his kimono.

"I've got a riddle for you, Smitty," Remo said in English, eyes fixed on his teacher. "How can you tell when a Master of Sinanju is scamming you?"

Smith shrugged and looked blank.

"His lips are moving. And how can you tell when he's not scamming you? He's dead."

"Ah, more elder abuse," Chiun said.

"Don't start," Remo said. "It's not abuse that I took interest in a bunch of old ladies getting mugged."

"It is when you pay more attention to total strangers than you do to your own father. There. I said it, Remo."

"Big shock. You've said it a hundred times in the past week. I pay plenty of attention to you, Little Father. Did it ever occur to you that maybe I respect the elderly more because of you? Maybe it cheeses me off more because they can't defend themselves like I know you can?"

But the old Korean offered Remo his back.

Obviously grateful for a break in their conversation, Smith quickly chimed in. "Remo, I did not fly all the way down here solely because you were taking too long with the Albondigas matter. Something more urgent has come up. The hijacking of Flight 980 in New York last week."

Remo's brow lowered and he tore his gaze from his teacher's bony shoulders. "I thought we back-burnered that."

"That was only until Mark and I could gather more information." Mark Howard was assistant director of CURE and Smith's righthand man. "The outlook looks grim on a number of fronts, not least of which is the damage this stunt has inflicted on the airlines. Air travel in the wake of this event has dropped by almost fifty percent. My flight down from LaGuardia was half empty."

"Ours was kind of empty the day we flew down here too. But they didn't say anything about it on the TV news so I figured it was just one of those things."

Smith's thin lips pursed. "Television news has become an unreliable source of worthwhile information. The near miss of the Empire State Building was major news for a little while and then it got overshadowed by the mugger story."

"Yeah, the news here has been pretty much wall-to-wall mugger. Since the hijacking wasn't on the news anymore and you weren't calling about it, I figured we weren't getting involved." He shot a glance at the Master of Sinanju.

It was not Chiun with whom Smith was upset. A small harrumph of displeasure made clear Smith's attitude toward a news culture that would elevate the criminal activities of a lone mugger above the hijacking of a plane, the crippling of a major industry and the near loss of thousands of lives in America's greatest city. He quickly reacquainted Remo with the broad details of the hijacking including the near miss of the Empire State Building and ending with the extraordinary escape of the hijackers.

"I must have flipped over to Dragnet when they mentioned the parachutes," Remo said once Smith was through. "I didn't know they got off the plane. From the hype it sounded like they weren't your run-of-the-mill terrorists but who listens to TV news hype these days?"

Smith did not point out that it was TV news hype that had gotten Remo so eager to eliminate the Miami Mugger.

"You're right," the CURE director said. "By definition

they are terrorists, but obviously this event was unusual in the extreme. There is now every indication that the men who hijacked the planes were Americans. While that does not preclude ties to Islamofascism, it does not seem as if these individuals were motivated by religious fanaticism. They were not overheard speaking of religion, they did not act the part of zealots and, most important, they came to the very edge of succeeding yet did not follow through on what could have been a devastatingly effective attack."

"So if they're not the usual suspects who are they?"

"Unknown."

"They bailed out of the airplane, right? Nobody saw them?" Remo asked.

"Everybody was watching the plane. The hijackers got away without even being spotted."

"Well, what about airport security cameras? They must have been seen arriving at the airport. Aren't they broadcasting their pictures all over the place? Somebody must have recognized them by now."

Smith fidgeted on the edge of the sofa. "There was unfortunately a series of security breakdowns in New York, which we assume is how they were able to smuggle their guns and explosives on the plane in the first place. The computerized system was being overhauled that morning and several key cameras were down for maintenance. The hijackers apparently passed through during this lapse, so their images were not recorded. The best we have is the footage filmed by the news crew that was actually on the flight. However, that appears to have been tampered with by BCN. I am hoping that when you and Master Chiun view the unedited footage you will detect something in the mannerisms or speech of the hijackers that others have so far missed."

On the floor Chiun was suddenly interested. His neck craned from the collar of his kimono as he turned to Smith. "Where do you wish us to go?" the old Korean asked.

"BCN in New York has the raw footage. It was taken by

their nightly news anchor's film crew. But, as I said, only heavily edited snippets have been shown on the news so far. I will arrange for you to view the entire footage."

"Gladly do we accept the assignment from our most generous emperor," Chiun said with a bow of his head.

"Why are you so eager to go gallivanting off on an assignment?" Remo asked, eyes narrowing suspiciously.

"Forgive him, Emperor Smith," Chiun confided, "for although he has attained the rank of Reigning Master he is still young in so many ways." As if speaking to a child, he said to Remo, "Because, Remo, while it is our obligation to serve an emperor, it is a joy to serve one as generous as he who has in his great wisdom contracted our House." And in the same instructive tone, he said in Korean, "Because you are finished paying attention to the elderly who are not me and he is giving us free airfare home. I had to pay my own way down here but he may as well pay our way back."

"I paid your airfare."

"And I had to sit next to you all the way down. Believe me, I paid. Let the lunatic pay. I can bring home my prize and store it safely away with my other great valuables."

"You mean that trunk full of stale saltine packets, matchbooks and toothpicks you used to swipe from every restaurant we ever went to twenty years ago?"

"Of course not. This is a special treasure. It will have a place of honor next to my autographed photographs of Cheeta Ching and Rad Rex."

Remo knew both photos well. Both had been attained at great cost, namely the near loss of Remo's sanity. Cheeta Ching had been a network anchorwoman for whom Chiun had developed a great fondness years ago. She had fallen off the national radar a decade before. Rad Rex was an actor on a long-cancelled soap opera called As the Planet Revolves. Chiun locked away the pictures of both celebrities and treated them with a reverence generally reserved for consecrated Hosts in a tabernacle. He took the photos out only once a year to polish the frames and clean the glass.

Remo was just grateful that the images of Cheeta, Rad Rex and now Judge Ruth weren't lined up on the mantel year round and surrounded by curling incense and flickering votive candles.

"That is everything," Smith said. "I will make the New York arrangements. Call Mark at Folcroft in an hour and he will give you your flight details as well as who you will be speaking to at BCN headquarters."

Meeting over, Smith gathered up his briefcase and stood to go. Remo ushered the CURE director to the door where Smith paused.

"Remo, I need not remind you that the nation has a large enough problem dealing with the constant threat from radical Islam. If this is a new terror force we must stop it before it succeeds in whatever is its ultimate plan. I find it particularly troubling that the hijackers were American, if that turns out to be the case."

Remo understood what his employer meant. Smith had spent his youth in the OSS fighting Nazi Germany and had slipped into middle age in the CIA's Cold War struggle against the Soviet Union. Now, as head of CURE, Islamofascism was the latest implacable foe Smith had opposed in his long career. The great enemies Harold W. Smith had faced down in his clandestine life always adhered to ideologies offensive to the American ideals of freedom and decency. That these hijackers might be Americans attempting to foment terror in their own nation, a nation they should instinctively love and fight to their deaths to defend, was unthinkable to the coldly logical and fiercely patriotic CURE director. Rather than comprehend why Americans would be behind the hijacking, Smith would have had an easier time understanding their motivation if they had come from Mars.

"Don't sweat it, Smitty," Remo said, offering a reassuring smile. "We're on the case."

Smith seemed anything but reassured. "Please call me as soon as you have anything to report."

Smith gave a short bow to Chiun and excused himself

from the suite. Remo watched the gaunt old man walk crisply down the long hallway to the elevator, a man who had sacrificed his entire life in service to his country.

"You know, Little Father," Remo pondered as the elevator doors clicked shut on Smith's gray face and pinched, lemony expression, "I know I dump on him a lot, but I'd worry a helluva lot less about this country's future if we could produce just a few more men like Smith."

Chiun cackled at the suggestion but when he saw that his pupil was serious he stopped laughing and shook his head. "The last thing America needs is more lunatics. Madmen you have enough of. What this country needs is more jurists like Judge Ruth to set the rest of you right. Not that I hold out much hope that even she could fix the lot of you for lamentably she is only one woman, after all."

Remo glanced at the unhappily smiling face of Judge Ruth then glanced up at his teacher's wise visage.

"Should I thank God out loud or to myself?" Remo asked.